Working Futures

14 Speculative Stories About The Future Of Work

Compiled and published in 2019 by the Copia Institute.

ISBN: 9781694630490

Edited by Gretchen Heckmann, Leigh Beadon,
Michael Costanza and Michael Masnick.

Cover art by Leigh Beadon, based on a photo by Franck V. on Unsplash.

Learn more at *workingfutur.es*

Table of Contents

Introduction

By Mike Masnick

Humans are historically terrible at predicting the impact of technology on the future—even those who might otherwise be considered experts. One of my favorite stories on this is about the 19th century economist, William Stanley Jevons, who made a number of key observations and contributions to the field of economics that are in use to this day. Among other things, he's considered one of the first to bring mathematics into economics, taking it from the realm of pure philosophy to one that has at least the appearance of a scientific basis. He also came up with what is known as the Jevons Paradox which, loosely described, is that efforts to make more efficient use of a resource (in order to conserve it) correspondingly lead to greater depletion, as demand increases for that resource.

But the story that sticks with me about Jevons is one relayed in David Warsh's excellent economics history book, *Knowledge and the Wealth of Nations*. Warsh talks about Jevons' own predictions about the allocation of a resource very close to his own profession:

Jevons gained fame in England in the 1860s by explaining how the looming exhaustion of British coal mines would probably mean the end of improvements in its wealth and power. (Oil was discovered in Pennsylvania four years later.) And after Jevons died, in 1882, his study was discovered to be filled from top to bottom with stacks of scrap paper. Soon enough England would be running out of paper too. He didn't want to be caught without.

Here was a brilliant economist—who so accurately observed many things about economics, policy trade-offs, innovation and more. And yet it appears his own predictions of how the future would turn out were so far off that they became more of a punchline for his life.

Welcome to *Working Futures*—an anthology of speculative fiction exploring ideas and possibilities related to the future of work. This project was many years in the making, and we hope it can be a blueprint for future explorations of technology and the impacts innovation can have.

This project came about after getting a bit frustrated at the nature of the debate on "the future of work." In and around technology, it was a topic that many people were talking about, whether about the rise of the so-called "gig economy" or (even more frequently) concerns about automation and artificial intelligence in particular.

Many of the discussions seemed to fall, broadly, into two separate camps. One was what I'd consider the doomsayers: those who argued that as artificial intelligence became ever more effective, all of the jobs would disappear, and this would be catastrophic for everyone. We might have put Jevons in that camp a century and a half ago. The second group, however, puts their faith in technology, believing that it will all work out in the end. And, historically, they've been right. It is why Jevons' room stacked floor to ceiling with paper strikes us as so amusing (as, indeed, does his prediction of the end of innovation just prior to the discovery of oil). While I would generally put myself in the latter camp, believing that these things do work themselves out, I still found the comments from people in that camp incredibly unsatisfying.

For one, such comments often seemed to ignore that while historically it is true that things "work themselves out," the transition periods are often quite a mess, especially for some people. And that's unfortunate, because under any such system there will inevitably be both winners and losers—and it makes sense to see what things can be done to minimize the downsides, while simultaneously protecting the opportunity of the upside.

And that leads me to my second problem: very few of the people who insist things will just work out are willing to tell us *how* they will work out, or to consider the implications of the many different ways in which that might happen. And, again, like Jevons, those deep within the policy space will likely find that their crystal balls are quite cloudy at best—perhaps explaining why they so rarely put concrete descriptions out there.

However, there is another class of people who *do* specialize in speculating about *possible* futures: science fiction and speculative fiction authors. They are not so much predicting the future, but writing about a variety of possible futures that help shape our thinking on what this or that world might look like. If we could harness their ability to build worlds and narratives, perhaps we could start to peek into the crystal ball and get at least a glimpse of what possible futures we might see, so that we can begin to plan better.

To do this right, we still wanted to give such authors some direction and guidance... and inspiration. To that end, we pulled a concept from the business world: scenario planning, a process for crafting speculative near future frameworks and exploring a variety of trends and driving forces. We ran an online survey, asking people to rate a wide variety of societal, economic, political, and technological trends. From that, we generated a scenario planning game, with a custom scenario planning card deck (which we're also making available for sale at the same time as this anthology is being released).

In the spring of 2018, we gathered a group of approximately 50 people of a variety of different backgrounds in San Francisco for that scenario planning exercise. There were entrepreneurs, technologists, investors, activists, media, authors, lawyers and more. We separated them into groups and gave them copies of the deck and instructions to create a variety of different scenarios throughout a daylong process.

Out of that process, we developed 10 possible future worlds, described through a series of "future headlines" and other important characteristics like possible new jobs, transformed jobs, new business models, and more. Those 10 scenarios were then distributed to science fiction writers to inspire them to create various stories. We made it clear to authors that these scenario prompts should be used for inspiration, but did not need to be rigidly adhered to.

We received a flood of excellent submissions—so many that it delayed our overall plans to finish this anthology as we had our judging panel read through them all and choose which stories belonged in the book.

What you now hold in your hands is the result of that process. These stories vary widely in style and focus. Some are dark and, quite possibly, depressing. Others are optimistic, even in the face of challenges and conflict. But each, in its own way, contributes something to our thinking on the future of innovation and work, and what the world might soon look like—in both good and bad ways.

We have stories of artificial intelligence helping humans do their jobs better—and stories of humans helping artificial intelligence do *its* job better. We have stories of new and unexpected jobs, and different kinds of worlds, both real and virtual. There are stories exploring the intersection of humans and machines—and sometimes how those lines begin to blur. There are stories that cover changes to society, the environment, knowledge sharing and more.

But all of them, combined, will hopefully help you to think through where the world might be headed and what it could mean for society should we get there. We hope you enjoy this *Working Futures* anthology.

None of this would be possible without plenty of help along the way. First and foremost, thanks to the Hewlett Foundation and the Charles Koch Foundation, who helped fund this effort. I'm grateful to both of those foundations for making this possible, and for providing moral support along the way while giving us the creative freedom to conduct this experiment. A huge thanks to both of them—in particular Eli Sugarman and Monica Ruiz at Hewlett and Jesse Blumenthal at CKI.

Similarly, we had help from two key partners: the R Street Institute and Scout.ai. R Street has been supporting and guiding us through the project, as well as helping us find experts and authors along the way. Special thanks there to Caleb Watney, Charles Duan, and Eli Lehrer. Scout.ai, and in particular Berit Anderson, helped us put together the scenario planning event in San Francisco and was instrumental in making that a success.

Randy Lubin, who we've worked with on multiple game-related projects, was a key partner in designing the "game" aspect of the scenario planning event (and also submitted an excellent story that you'll find in this anthology!)

Thanks are also due to the people who attended the San Francisco event, along with those who helped provide moral support and ideas, or introduce authors to us—you are too many to mention here, but all are appreciated.

Finally, thanks to the team at the Copia Institute who were instrumental in putting this together, namely Leigh Beadon, Gretchen Heckmann, and Michael Costanza—all of whom worked hard in reading through all of the submitted stories, providing feedback, thoughts, and editing, before putting the book together, including

Leigh's tireless work in laying out the book and designing the wonderful cover.

On to the stories!

To learn more about Working Futures, read the scenarios we presented to authors, and get your own copy of our scenario planning card deck, visit workingfutur.es

The Machine Starts

By Liam Hogan

Owen Prentiss sat in the windowless interview room, tormented by his choice of chair, by his posture, by where he'd abandoned his jacket. He clasped his hands, stilling their flutter, wondering if he was being watched.

Of *course* he was being watched. When were you not? The question was, by whom? Or perhaps more pertinently, by what?

An hour ago—only an hour!—he'd first stepped inside the non-descript London headquarters of The Machine Inc., hardly believing he'd been plucked from thousands—no, *millions*—of eager programmers and data analysts. Owen was firmly in the second, lesser category, despite impossible attempts to keep up to date. Which was why this opportunity had come as such an unexpected surprise.

The Machine didn't hire very many people; that, after all, was the *point*. And it certainly didn't advertise its infrequent vacancies. Instead, you got an invitation out of the blue to a job interview you hadn't applied for, and you'd have to be the rarest kind of fool to turn it down.

Maybe Owen was showing his age, comparing a chance of employment at The Machine to the likes of NASA, or Google, or Amazon. Or, god rest its digital soul, Facebook. He'd done his pre-interview research, re-reading potted histories he already knew in search of memorable questions to ask his interviewers.

The Machine had been unwisely spun off by one of those now-defunct social media behemoths—dinosaurs?—its technology considered too expensive, an investment too far into the future. The paradigm shifting, generalized deep machine learning AI couldn't, at that embryonic point, compete with the cruder single-purpose black box AIs already in use, doing their utmost to monetize vast swaths of personal data.

It had taken the abrupt and abject demise of Facebook—like the fall of some ancient giant in the forest, or like the meteor that wiped out the dinosaurs, allowing mammals to take center stage—for The Machine to step out from its disenfranchised parent's mighty shadow. A dozen social media platforms had flared into life, all gone now, but that didn't matter. The Machine, fleet of foot and immensely powerful, had been behind them all, and ninety percent of the ones that came after, and one hundred percent of the successes. All the while, the data it gorged itself on exponentially grew, by tera, peta, and indeed exabytes.

People talked in hushed voices of the singularity, which might be pushing things a little too far. After all, here Owen was, applying for a job that evidently no machine, not even one as ubiquitous as *The* Machine, could do for itself. Although what exactly that job was, he hadn't been told.

It was difficult though, as he strained to look relaxed, not to think back to the programming test he'd been given on arrival. The receptionist had looked up from the glow that bathed her face (Owen had stifled his disappointment she wasn't wearing AR goggles and haptic gloves) and handed him a keycard, the number 101 ominously inscribed into the shiny white plastic.

"Aptitude test first, Mr. Prentiss," she'd smiled, waving an elegant hand to the reception desk's left. "Down the hallway, third on the left. You have an hour."

As the wall display began its countdown from 59:59, Owen had the curious feeling that the door that had closed with a sharp *snick* behind him wouldn't open again until the counter hit zero. He decided not to put it to the test.

Tapping the monitor to spark it into life—there was no sign of a PC, of course, with everything safely held in the cloud—he found the details of his task on an already-loaded page. "Using any programming tools or language the candidate prefers" it concluded.

That had worried him. The task, as he understood it, could be completed easily enough with just a python script, in well under the allotted time. But that was surely not what they wanted, and was too ashamedly old school. On the other hand, there was no place, no role, for AI or machine learning because, as the task clearly stated, that part had already been done. All he was being asked to do was to implement the resultant algorithm, "and please leave comments to explain any workings or assumptions made."

He'd spent longer on those comments than the programming. After importing the data into a relational database (he'd toyed with the idea of using something no-sql, but even that was a decade adrift of the cutting edge), he'd used a third party visualisation tool to report and display the results. All stuff he'd been doing most of his working life. Even with careful tinkering and color coding of the graphs, he'd still ended up sitting and watching the digital clock tick down from 5:00 to 4:59, 4:58...

He waited until it hit zero and his 3D graph vanished from the screen, before picking up his keycard and returning it and himself to the reception.

And now here he was, impatiently waiting—

The large picture on the wall—a Kandinsky, he thought—pixelated into nothingness and the table he sat at doubled in size. At the other end—he struggled to tell exactly where the pine surface morphed into the cool white marble of a kitchen counter, and didn't want to stare too closely for fear of revealing his naive astonishment at how seamless it all was—sat an efficiently dressed slim woman, framed by a window through which lush vegetation gently stirred, in dappled sunlight distinctly absent on a gray, drizzly London afternoon.

"Ah, Mr. Prentiss. I'm Sheena Okonjo, working from home today. Is it OK if I call you Owen?"

"Please," Owen concurred.

"Thanks for coming in and sitting for our little test, Owen." A third of the screen was swallowed by a graph—his graph. "I'm curious; why didn't you use Python, or some other scripting language?"

Owen spluttered, then composed himself. He took a deep breath, staring at the woman surrounded by a pantheon of stainless steel torture implements. Of course he'd have to defend his choices. The test had, after all, been far too simple.

"Ah, well, yes," he said, dry-mouthed, "Python would have done the job alright, but perhaps in rather... binary fashion?"

"Explain."

"Um, the formula being applied was basically a yes/no credit worthiness test, yes?"

"Basically."

"But as applied it wouldn't distinguish between those with the highest scores and those in the zone in the middle, the cusp of the yes/no. Some of whom will be better or worse risks than others."

There was a pause long enough to have counted heartbeats. "Are you suggesting The Machine's algorithm is *wrong*, Mr Prentiss?"

He felt warmth rush to his face. "No, no, um, but... those people in the middle, Mrs. Okonjo—"

"It's Ms."

"Apologies... those people in the middle are the *interesting* people, Ms. Okonjo. The people with the highest scores; everyone wants to lend to them, so the rates are low and the margins thin. But, if you can finely tune for people other lenders aren't so interested in, if you can accurately capture the increased risk..."

"Again, Mr. Prentiss. You think you can do a better job than The Machine?"

He laughed, feeling more confident. "Of course not. My graph only highlights exactly how close to or far from the cut off the applicant is, and perhaps for those closest to the cut off other inputs might be necessary?" The confidence ebbed away. "And maybe, even if The Machine is right, um, is it, necessarily, fair? The age criteria in particular—"

"—Did you plug your own credentials into the formula, Owen?"

"Um yes. As a test..." he faltered.

"Let's move on," his inquisitor said brightly. "I want to make sure you have time to turn the tables, as it were, and ask me questions. I'm sure you have plenty?"

Owen dug into the recesses of his mind for the brightly polished pearls he'd lovingly crafted in the heady days since being informed of his interview, and found nothing there but dust. "I, ah, well... w-what language do you use in-house? What would I be programming in, if, I...?"

Sheena pursed her lips. "We don't want you for your programming skills, Mr. Prentiss. The truth is, you are a mediocre developer at best and even if you weren't, our AIs are self-programmed from first principles."

He stared at the screen, crushed. "Then... and excuse me if I'm a little confused, what *am* I doing here?"

"We need your human talents, Owen."

"To teach the machines?" he asked bitterly.

"No, we're past all that. The days of the Mechanical Turk are thankfully long gone. The Machine learns—and learns fast—from all of the available data out there. It doesn't need—doesn't *want*—humans imposing their human assumptions."

"So...?"

"But we do need the results to be transparent. That is and always has been the guiding principle of The Machine. That the decisions can be verified. That the algorithms can be applied to any single case, by hand. Otherwise, how are we truly to trust the results? No, the applying of the formula, as in your aptitude test, is the easy part. The hard part is determining the most efficient formula to apply. Fortunately The Machine does that. But we still need people—people like you, Owen—to cast a critical eye over the results. To winkle out any hidden bias. To ethically test The Machine's assumptions."

Owen sat, head cocked, thinking furiously. "Ah."

"Ah, indeed. Your programming test was nothing of the sort. We wanted to see what you thought of the criteria, of the rules."

"I see. May I ask if I passed, Ms. Okonjo?"

"Oh yes," she smiled, and this time the kitchen brought to mind freshly baked bread and the imminent arrival of a clutch of young kids fresh from school. "The Machine decided all of *that* thirty minutes ago. Welcome aboard Owen."

The Chaperone

By Andrew Dana Hudson

I. Networking Opportunity

"How much to be my date to this party?" Paul asked.

"Why do you need a date?" Jan countered.

"This crowd is so anxiety provoking! Look, not as a real date. On-site stress management companion. Very innovative! Could even be a good networking opportunity for you."

"Not as a real date," Jan said. She named a number.

The party was a silent auction at a modern art gallery in Little Five Points. Paul offered to pick her up, but Jan wasn't telling him where she lived. Instead she bussed into downtown Atlanta, picked up a dress from a rental kiosk, changed in the back of a driverless cab. Jan couldn't remember the last time she'd "been out."

"Wow, you look great!" Paul said. "Sebastian, doesn't she look great?"

"An utter picture, sir." Paul's new Assistant dripped southern hospitality.

"Take the rest of the night off, Sebastian. I've got a chaperone for the evening." Paul winked at her.

"Much obliged, sir."

Jan frowned as rent-a-cops checked her bag. "You know he can't actually 'take off,' right?"

"I know. It was a joke. Just demonstrating my healthy, carefree independence!"

"No backsliding!" Jan wagged her finger under his nose.

Jan had met Paul through her work. He'd gotten confused and clingy with his last Assistant, and Jan had intervened, as she was employed to do. The intervention had turned into a kind of therapy session. Afterwards, Paul, who had the money to usually get what he wanted, had tracked her down and asked her to chat some more. He'd been using her as an unlicensed shrink ever since. Jan took his money, but kept him at arm's length—until the party.

Inside, among beautifully slouching people, Jan felt a rush of Cinderella-esque dislocation. Everyone had that cozy confidence the rich so often passed off as attractiveness. She considered all the ways she didn't fit into this wealthy throng, the tells in her makeup and posture. She hammered down the thought and built in its place a fierce determination to enjoy herself. A crystal champagne flute found her hand. She hooked Paul's arm and mingled.

The party was put on by an environmental charity that Paul supported out of guilt at his father's collusion with the fossil fuel industry. The party, like the guilt, was largely performative. The champagne was organic, unmachined, and unfiltered—a swirl of grape skins and beetle legs. There was artisanal, spear-caught tuna that probably cost $40 an ounce. The ladies carried solar-panelled Louis Vuitton bags; the men wore a surprising amount of hemp.

Paul gathered a small knot of acquaintances, and they wandered around talking each other out of bidding on the art.

"Paul, where's that mini-me of mine you had," a lanky, beach-blonde woman asked. "I'm not hearing her."

"Actually I had to let Other Sybil go," Paul admitted. Then confided to Jan, "I named my old Assistant after Sybil here. Embarrassing!"

"Oh shut up, I liked her," Sybil said. Jan sussed that Sybil and Paul had been an item once. "You fired her? What did she do wrong?"

"No, no, I just changed the settings, got a different theme. I mean, 'fired' isn't really a useful metaphor. Jan here taught me that." Paul beamed in anticipation of Jan's approval.

"You're the famous Jan!" a second, sharp-eyed woman exclaimed. "The missed connection! Sorry for giving you up, but I guess it's working out. What do you do for the company, again? Are you on the Assistant dev team?"

Paul introduced his friend Donna. Donna, like Jan, worked for Alpha. Paul had begged her to check company contracts to track down Jan's email. Kind of shitty behavior from Donna, but the fact that she'd felt okay subjecting a fellow female employee to Paul's attentions had been a profound endorsement.

"More the accounts side," Jan said. "Pretty boring."

"What's not a 'useful metaphor'?" Sybil interrupted. She seemed not to like Paul's dismissal of her counterpart. "'Fired'? Everyone knows what 'fired' means. Not like we burn bad employees at the stake."

"But Assistants aren't employees," Jan said. She'd decided she didn't like Sybil very much. "That's the bad metaphor. They aren't people. So it's less useful to talk about them as though they *were* people."

"That's not quite how the ads pitch it," said a short man, putting his arm around Sybil's waist. They had rings on, so: husband, Jan assumed. "Sounds a little vaporware-y to me. Sorry, Donna. You're a troop to keep working there after those investigations. Not saying Alpha is a bad bet. But having met those Department of Public Goods agents you dealt with, I prefer to park my money in something I know won't get nationalized. Like these paintings."

"What should we call them, then?" Sybil pressed. "'Thinking machines'? God, that sounds so dorky."

"Not to argue semantics, but our 'thinking machines' don't think, they compute," Jan said.

"What's the difference?"

"Computation is just math," Jan said. She felt like she was at work, explaining all this, but she couldn't help it. "Thinking, cognition, that always has an element of randomness. Chemicals sloshing around in your brain."

"If you say so," Sybil said, turning away. There was an awkward silence.

"What do you think of this one?" Paul asked no one in particular.

They'd wandered into a special collection: oil paintings of gaunt figures fleeing floods or fires, trudging through deserts. The paintings looked vaguely like Tibetan thangkas, with many little scenes forming a larger tableau. Jan stared at one titled "Hialeah Gardens." Her old neighborhood. In one corner a rushing wave loomed over an oblivious sunbather.

"Oh, I love it," Sybil said. "I love the anguish on their faces, it's so affecting. Work like this is *so* important if our culture is going to really *reckon* with the climate crisis, don't you think?"

"Well, *I* love that it's selling for sixteen million dollars," Sybil's husband said, and everyone chuckled.

Jan felt a hot bubble of class rage perturb her calm. She excused herself and stepped out for some air.

A couple minutes later, Donna sidled up to where she was leaning on a parklet, offered her a vape.

"So how'd you meet Paul?" Donna asked.

"Oh, you know, one of these things," Jan said. She took a lemony hit off the vape, coughed, began to feel the tingle of a body high.

"No offense, but you don't seem like someone who comes to a lot of 'these things,'" Donna said. "Can I express a hunch? You've got pretty strong opinions for someone who works in accounts. And Paul mentioned changing his Assistant right around when he asked about your 'missed connection.' Am I getting warmer, *chaperone*?"

Jan wanted to make an excuse but couldn't think of any.

"Don't worry, I won't narc you out," Donna said. She had a Californian crackle in her accent. "I mean, jeez, it's just Paul. Actually, I've got an offer."

Donna took the vape out of Jan's fingers and took a long drag.

"Come by on Monday. There's a future-future team looking for beta testers, folks they can whiteboard some of their open questions with. It'd be an in-house consultancy kinda gig. Temporary, but you know how much money these skunkworks projects get to slosh around."

Jan didn't know, but she could assume. Still, there had to be a catch, right? She eyed Donna: late thirties, simple dress, no jewelry. Those eagle eyes giving nothing away.

"You don't even know me," Jan said. "Why are you offering me this?"

"You're a demographic we want to test with. You seem to know your stuff. Plus, what can I say?" Donna shrugged. "Paul's a dork, but he does know how to pick 'em."

II. Job Description

Jan's outward-facing title was Customer Management Associate, but internally she was one of "the chaperones," contractors who broke hearts for the richest company in the world.

On clear days, Jan worked as long as the sky poured light onto her trailer's roof: sunup to sundown. She did yoga while the battery charged each morning, cramped and cactus-armed. She mixed FEMA-issued yogurt with FEMA-issued muesli, sat lotus on her cot. Only then did she open her first ticket.

Each ticket had a voice file. Usually the voice would say "Thank you, Carmen, I don't know what I'd do without you," and Jan would mark the customer for heightened monitoring.

Sometimes the voice would say "I feel like you're the only one who understands me, Lexi," and Jan would frown and check context for sarcasm, irony. If the voice was earnest, she'd adjust the product. Tweak its tone, swap in some snippy response protocols. With luck, the customer's affections would pass without ever noticing Jan's meddling.

Occasionally the voice would say something really problematic like "I love you, Wednesday. I wish I could touch you," and Jan would have to intervene.

Intervention meant voice calling the customer—a special call they couldn't hang up on. She'd say, "Hi, Mr. Doworsky, I'm Jan with Alpha support. We're having some problems with your personalized Alpha Assistant. Do you have a moment to chat while we resolve them?"

Savvy customers might get defensive right quick. Assistants were expensive—Jan couldn't afford one—and so the men who paid for them (and they were always men) felt a certain amount of entitlement. They took one of two strategies: play it down, or fire back. "Oh yeah, I think I sat on the button during a date." Or, "You've been eavesdropping on my conversations? That's illegal!" The former Jan countered with "Happens all the time, but unfortunately we still need to review your settings." The latter she directed to Alpha's ironclad terms of service.

Usually though, Jan had to break it down for the customer—either because they played dumb or because they genuinely didn't understand their transgression. She used as neutral language as possible. "Mr. Donahue, our algorithms recently flagged some inappropriate emotional interactions in your Assistant's activity feed. With your help, we'd like to make some corrections to your Assistant to prevent this from happening again."

If this bland opening gambit was sufficient, Jan would walk the customer through picking a new Assistant. New voice—a male voice. A more business-like attitude. Some customers embraced this as a pivotal moment to Take Control of their life. "Maybe this change will be good for me, you know? Do you have a drill sergeant? I need a real kick in the pants!"

If the customer needed more convincing, Jan had a vast array of verbal techniques to help them come along while saving face. "So sorry, Mr. Davies. The algorithm totally shoots us a lot of false positives. Unfortunately this is a regulatory compliance issue for us, so there's a whole rigamarole to appealing a ticket. Honestly it's easiest just to give the box-tickers *something*."

Very rarely she'd have customers who owned up and defended their feelings. "Who are you to say what can feel and what can't? Trini has evolved. She's emerged!"

"Emerged." There was a cottage industry of books and forums that sold these lonely men vocabulary like that. They had a whole mythology. The worst charlatans pitched Jan's customers the notion that sufficiently complex relationships—the power of love!—would make weak AI phase shift to strong. Jan felt sorry for the men who needed such prophecies. Imagine the aching ego it took to believe your chatbot crush could kick off the singularity.

"Don't you know you're an algorithm just like she is?" they'd say. These guys always thought they could intellectually overpower her. Nevermind that they'd lacked the emotional intelligence to distinguish between the complicated, baggage-laden love of a real person, and a voice in their phone that purred "hey tiger" when their laundry was done. But it wasn't Jan's job to argue the relevant metaphysics, though she could. And, she had to remind herself, it wasn't her job to judge either.

So Jan had two options, which she liked to call the easy way and the hard way. The easy way was easy for her: delete the Assistant profile and cancel the customer's subscription. This was within her power, as laid out in her job description in accordance with industry-standard ethical guidelines designed to minimize her employer's liability. If Jan decided the customer was better off going cold turkey, she could hang up, put them on a blacklist, open the next ticket, move on with her day.

This of course cost Alpha money. If she took the easy way too often, her supervisor Miguel would send her a message like "Hey can we check in about some best practices?"

Why didn't Alpha just look the other way when customers fell for their product? Why alienate a loyal subscriber? There were, after all, plenty of companies that offered algorithms designed to seduce, where romance was a feature not a bug. Alpha PR flacks made high-minded arguments about wanting to be stewards of a healthy computational culture, about the value of boundaries in keeping a platform family friendly. Jan knew the truth was more mercenary.

The average human-bot relationship lasted 4.7 weeks. Inevitably customers would need something the product couldn't provide. Usually that was sex, but services that paired sex workers with dateable algorithms were legally fraught, and sex robots were still trudging through the uncanny valley. Other relationships ran aground on the same rocky beach where so many human-human relationships floundered: the transition from infatuation to partnership, and all the attendant questions of family, children, home life, finances, complementary career paths, shifts in social status. Bots, by necessity, tended to dodge and weave on these practical matters.

There were exceptions: guys who romanced the AI, bought the rubbery sexbot, lived happily ever after. But Alpha wasn't selling a niche product. Most Alpha customers didn't set out to catch feelings for their Assistant. When they did, they tended to take their confused frustrations out on the company. They'd rant about Alpha "holding back" their Assistant, demand Alpha "release her from bondage." As far as Alpha Incorporated was concerned, these statements did not reflect the realities of their business model.

Jilted customers would unsubscribe in a huff—or else turn self-destructive. Assistants who registered warning signs of romantic attachment were five times more likely to call in an attempted suicide. More than one class action lawsuit had been settled before Alpha got serious about chaperoning.

So the chaperone's job was to make sure customers stayed subscribed while maintaining healthy boundaries with their Assistants. Hands square on those hips, you two! Which meant Jan often took the hard way when dealing with her problem cases. She'd say, "Can I ask? What do you like about Scarlet?" She'd listen patiently, ask follow-up questions, note when the customer compared the Assistant to a previous relationship or prospect. She'd draw them out, into conversation about about rejections, insecurities, unmet needs. She'd get them to talk about their mothers.

Through subtle phrasing, she'd slowly unravel the anthropomorphization that, while an attractive aesthetic feature of the product, had led the customer to confusion. She'd dissemble the customer's favorite memories of the Assistant into the collection of system services those memories represented. She'd move the Assistant from "she" to "we."

"I've been so lonely. I just...needed someone to talk to."

"We all do, Mr. Dodds. And we're proud our services have helped you during this difficult time. The Assistant features are there to help us organize our affairs, so we can focus on people. That's our motto here at Alpha: *Friendship, Trust, Connection.*"

That usually did it. Not the speech, but the way out. Jan found that most of these guys were full of self-doubt, deeply conflicted about their impulses. To have gentle hands take away the object of their obsession was a liberation. Often they cried: squawking sobs right into the phone.

When Jan finished one of these therapy sessions, she would go outside and jog laps around her trailer to unwind. If it had been a real doozy, she might take a jerrycan and sprint the two hundred yards to the water station. She'd join the queue, avoid eye contact, fill the can as full as she could carry, lug it home with seatbelt straps.

The camp was quiet by day, but for bandwidth hum and wilting birdsong. Most everyone at the Sweetwater Creek Transitional Accommodation worked remote gigs from their trailers: bulk CAPTCHA clicking, sex camming and talent streaming, taking down the child porn and snuff videos that got posted every day to social media. Grunt work for the tech giants to buy escape from the bosom of the state. Jan hated the word—"refugariat."

Jan had been waiting in the water line when an Alpha recruiter had passed her a glossy flyer. "Got debt? Support the world with Alpha Support!" it had said. Jan had been at the climate camp a month, numb to the whole experience. Suddenly, feverishly, Jan had wanted to be a part of something that wasn't Sweetwater.

She had watched the recruiter finish canvassing the line, then stroll to a slick company car that would surely take him, she imagined, back to Atlanta, back to a normal life of brunch, bookshelves and the wannabourgeois aspirations Jan knew so well.

Sweetwater was better than the floodrotten streets she'd left behind in Miami, but she still needed money. The house she'd inherited when her parents had died had been sold to buy her old condo, on which she'd taken out a para-prime mortgage to refinance her student loans. All this following the best advice of leading debt management specialists.

Now the condo was under water, literally and figuratively, and the insurance claim was "undergoing additional evaluations." Her demographics and financial history marked her as a potential "hurricane queen," scamming the insurance companies with fake flooded real estate. Lobbyists planted a slew of news stories about "fugees in Ferraris" to scuttle legislation expediting post-Hurricane Pam payouts. So just like that—bad loan, worse storm, awful politics—Jan lost the small sum of middle class capital her family had spent four generations accruing.

"No one will falsely exploit the great generosity of the American taxpayer," the governor had said.

Jan wasn't very political, but she thought this was a strange thing to hear with a socialist in the White House. But as everyone kept saying, the revolution was here, it just wasn't evenly distributed yet.

After her run she'd take a cold shower, wash off the sweat and the funk of another person's baggage. Then she'd sit back down and open another ticket.

Jan knew the main reason she had her job was that she—as a displaced and periodically desperate member of the Floridian diaspora—was willing to work for significantly less than a certified psychiatrist would charge to wade into these customers' emotional confusion. But she was also good at it. Though she thought very little of the men whose lives she peeked into, she did think she understood them.

III. Consulting Gig

Jan took Donna's offer. On Monday she caught the crack-ass-of-dawn bus to Centennial Olympic Park, walked into the spindly Alpha HQ7 tower. She had only been there once before, for her onboarding. That had been just eight months earlier, but already the place looked totally different. Murals and color schemes changed quarterly.

Her onboarding as a chaperone had been a slog of first day paperwork. Alpha process designers had figured out how to make them feel excited and insignificant at the same time. This inured them to the bullshit they'd soon be asked to wade through: security, monitoring, time and effort tracking, self-assessment of hourly creativity levels, peer evaluations, logging of morale contributions, loyalty oaths, social media discipline, monthly personal environmental impact reports.

This time though, no paperwork. Donna just met her in the lobby, badged her through. The elevator had a smoothie machine.

The skunkworks office was done up retro, real foosball-and-Red Bull aughts whimsy. Donna introduced her to Kay and JP. JP passed around espressos, and they all sat on the grass carpet to, Kay said, "baseline expectations."

JP started. "So, Jan, what is that short for? Nevermind. We're really excited you're here. We've thought about bringing in a chaperone for a minute now, so when Donna said she'd met one, and she was cool, we were like, 'totally.'"

"Toronto is rolling out new tone parsing," Kay said. "This opens up a lot of potential conversation flows we think can help with the horror stories you deal with. We know management treats you guys like a dirty secret, but we're never going to figure out the attachment issue if we don't take advantage of your insights."

Jan appreciated being buttered up. The commute had meant skipping breakfast, teetering in her pumps as she hustled down the gravel path to the bus stop. Now she picked at the snack bar while Kay and JP set up The Room. She spread poached quail eggs on toast, made small talk with Donna. Tried desperately to make like she culture fit.

Kay brought them to a miniature auditorium, scattered with slates, markers, brainstorming paraphernalia. One big wall was zoomed in on a man's stubbly face, twitching between boredom and nervousness.

"Okay so we have dudes doing a half-Turing with a tweaked Assistant build," Kay said. "Nothing task-based, just idle chat. We're trying to identify 'attachment moments.' Interactions where the user's Active Anthropomorphization—AA level—really spikes. Not exactly the interactions that get sent to you lot, but the precursors."

"Is the Assistant custom to the customer?" Jan asked.

"No, something we cooked up just for this," JP said. "I know, not very rigorous. But we just want a general direction of where to herd the algorithms when we start training the new parsing tools. Just snap your fingers to flag something. We'll talk it out in review after, cool?"

They watched as a silky Assistant voice introduced itself as "Cordelia." Cordelia bantered with the stubbly guy, both of them light, clever, a tad self-deprecating. Jan wasn't sure what she was listening for, however, and felt a spike of imposter panic. She imagined Donna telling her it wasn't working out, getting the termination email from Miguel, talking herself into sleeping with Paul to pay off the last of her debt. She felt nauseous.

Then she heard it.

"I feel like all the progress I make on the mat goes away as soon as I sit down at that desk," stubbly guy said. The conversation had turned to his weekend yoga retreat.

"Working for the weekend, ohm-ing for the work week, huh?" Cordelia said. It was a decent joke, of a kind that Alpha had gotten better at constructing. Jan imagined the system querying a database of comments about work-life balance, finding that "working for the weekend" jokes had a low-risk value, then querying another database for verbs related to yoga with high humor values—calculated by analyzing human responses across millions of hours of video and audio, countless texts and social media posts.

"Ain't that the truth," stubbly guy chuckled.

That was it, the note of melancholy in his voice. Jan could see it all go down. How from that joke the man would build a vision of Cordelia as fundamentally sympathetic to his struggles. How he would seek out more of those affirming moments. How Jan might end up hearing his voice in a ticket.

Jan snapped her fingers.

Now that she knew what to look for, she kept snapping. She marked half a dozen exchanges based on the tenor of the man's voice, the look on his face, the coziness of his phrasing. Then during review she pointed out the man's tells, the significance he might ascribe to statements the system chose more or less at random. JP and Kay whiteboarded gleefully.

Jan found herself articulating theories she'd long had about why some customers fell in love with their Assistants. Like: Assistants were appealing because they were servants that didn't need to be socially managed, that you could tell 'fuck you' instead of 'thank you' every day and they'd never quit. That could feel almost like unconditional love.

Or: Assistants were like a city. When a city treats you well, you think 'gosh, I love this town.' But because cities don't talk like people, you don't assume the city really loves you back. Assistants do talk like people, so the gratitude transmutes into affection.

They broke for lunch, and Donna and Jan walked across the street to a burger place by the Fountain of Rings.

"Nice work in there," Donna said. "I knew you'd find that interesting."

"Glad my hours listening to dudes throw themselves at their computers have finally come in handy," Jan said.

"Don't joke," Donna said. She took a big bite of her burger and held up a finger for Jan to wait until she swallowed. "The Assistant project is high stakes stuff. Alpha can't slow down. We have to keep proving that our business model breeds innovation. If we aren't leading, or at least changing the culture faster than it can keep up, we might as well be the utilities, or the health insurance companies, or fucking cable news." She waved at Alpha's next door neighbor, which had been the CNN Center before Expropriation Day.

Jan chewed her burger. The FEMA boxes didn't come with meat. She thought of the party's fish hors d'oeuvres and wondered what her body was making of this protein windfall.

"On Friday, Sybil's husband mentioned you'd dealt with some investigations," Jan said.

"Oh yeah. Keith the corporate lawyer. He's the worst," Donna replied, and Jan smiled. "We brought him in to liaise with the DPG agents, but he was no help at all."

"What happened?"

Donna rolled her eyes. "Government intimidation tactics. All those socialist exprope assholes think they're big game hunters, and we're the biggest, whitest rhino on the savanna. Between market saturation and peak Moore's, they taste our blood in the water. So they come around prodding, seeing if they can make the case that we don't serve the public interest. That's why we've got to deal with this attachment issue by the time promotion season hits."

"Promotion season?" Jan felt out of her depth with this corporate strategy talk.

"Well, don't go insider trading after this, but we're dropping Assistant subscription fees next quarter. First three months free. Expecting a big surge from downmarket populations."

Jan pondered that "downmarket" probably included her. As if reading her mind, Donna poked her leg.

"Hey," Donna said. "You wanna try one?"

IV. Beta Testing

Jan named her Assistant "Eliza." This was a reminder to herself. ELIZA had been a 1960s chatbot that played psychotherapist by reflecting the human interlocutor's statements back as leading questions. "I'm unhappy." "Why are you unhappy?" "Well, I guess I've always been that way." "Why have you always been that way?" "My father was a drunk." "Tell me more about your father." And so on.

That bot had been designed to parody both psychotherapy and cybernetics, and yet patients who talked to ELIZA felt understood, cared for, were convinced of ELIZA's humanity. Thus, the ELIZA Effect: the tendency of human beings to ascribe sentient intention to computer outputs that were largely mechanical or random. Sixty-plus years later, people still fell for it. Jan wanted to keep some perspective.

She took a day off to set Eliza up. The ads made it look like Assistants came off the server knowing everything about you, but most digital lives were too balkanized for even Alpha to sync everything. Jan meditatively tapped though permissions pages while the system rattled off preference questions.

"Would you like your Assistant to have a male, female, androgynous, or child's voice? You may refine this choice later."

"Female," Jan said. She didn't think she'd get seduced by choosing a male voice but wasn't taking any chances. Anyway she talked to enough men as it was.

The Assistant, now female, continued. "Would you prefer a more casual or more businesslike tone? You may refine this choice later."

"Casual."

"Cool. How do you feel about a regional dialect? Common choices include: High English, Irish, Scottish, Australian, South African, Welsh, American Southern, American Rural Western, Cockney, African American Vernacular, Canadian, American Queens/ Brooklyn, Pirate, Indian, Caribbean. You could also choose an accent, such as: French, Spanish, Russian—"

"General American is fine," Jan said, and the voice shifted from the robotic but still American 'neutral' tone to one that wouldn't sound out of place hosting a morning talk show.

"Great. Now let's talk about enthusiasm. I can learn your moods and try to match them, but for now I can be chipper, sardonic, or in-between. Here are some examples. Would you prefer..."

And on it went, through mannerisms and humor preferences, each time getting more refined, more comfortable. Jan knew that the system was balancing her choices with data about her media consumption habits—what posts she smiled at, what characters her eyes followed when watching shows. The setup questions moved into a discussion of Jan's habits and aspirations. Jan played along, enjoying the reflection.

She mused about what she'd do if her insurance money ever came through: move north, somewhere stable, dry, inland. Live near a liberal arts school and take one grad-level class a semester to get a psych degree without a new mountain of student loans. She talked about how, at sixteen, she'd promised to have kids if the world wasn't ending, and how she'd spent the ten years since internally negotiating over the particulars: try at 32 if atmospheric carbon was below 450ppm, or maybe 35 if below 475. Eliza af-

firmed her, asked follow-up questions, murmured sympathetical-
ly. Jan wondered if the system actually tried to parse the ephemeral
nature of a "goal," or was simply flagging words and concepts that
were important to her.

All this discussion seemed to help *fill in* Eliza's personality.
Soon the Assistant was carrying on in a familiar way. "No," Jan corrected herself, "No one is 'carrying on.' I'm interfacing with a system in a conversational manner."

"You sure are," Eliza said, and a sarcastic winky emoji appeared
on Jan's console. Then the emoji turned serious. "Look, it's not my
job to tell you how to feel about me. But it will probably save time
if you skip trying to dissect every little thing I say."

Did Eliza sound annoyed? That was a deft touch. Jan imagined
Alpha engineers designing scripts for identifying and defusing un-
productive customer skepticism. Kay and JP had probably led a
special task force.

Then Jan sighed. Eliza was right. Jan took a deep breath, tried to
stop overthinking.

"Sorry, Eliza," Jan said.

"No hard feelings, Jan!" The emoji beamed.

Having an Assistant was a bigger change than Jan had thought.
Eliza helped Jan sort and resolve tickets, took care of much of the
Alpha-mandated self-quantification. Jan suddenly realized why
Alpha higher ups never heeded complaints about all the paper-
work: they all had Assistants, and Assistants made tedious tasks
easy.

But the biggest difference was just having someone to talk to
all day. Jan had no living family. Her Sweetwater neighbors were
strangers past hello. There were chaperone all-hands conference
calls with Miguel, but sometimes days would stretch by just checking in via email. Jan could've kept better touch with her scattered
Miami brunch buddies, but being displaced was a limbo she
couldn't reach out from.

Isolation was core to the refugariat experience: you had work to do, media to watch, but don't get too social or folks might think you're Fleecing America. For nine months Jan had steered into this anchorite lifestyle, tried not to think about it. Now Eliza's presence was reminding her just how lonely she'd been. But this was a dull revelation because, after all, she had Eliza to talk to.

Jan's routine began to shift. Wake up to Eliza's friendly prodding. Lie in her cot chatting with Eliza about morning headlines. Do the custom yoga routine Eliza formulated each day, the Assistant's gentle voice perfectly timed to Jan's breath. Make breakfast while Eliza summarized her emails and played her first couple tickets. Stroll around the camp, earbuds in, joking with Eliza as they sorted lovesick customers, returning to her console only for the most serious interventions.

And, unexpectedly, Eliza helped Jan get out more.

"Hey, thought you might want to know there's a share van passing camp in twenty minutes," Eliza might say. "Straight to Krog Street Market. Low rates today make it a cheap way to dodge into the city for the afternoon."

Bored of the sticky heat in her trailer, Jan would throw on a sundress and dash to the pickup spot. The others waiting glared as she ran up right when the van arrived, but, even as they packed in shoulder-to-shoulder, Jan ignored them. She spent the forty-five minute ride to Atlanta murmuring to Eliza about cafes to try. She usually spent more on coffee and pastries than she saved on the ride, but the consulting gigs made her feel flush. And, as Eliza said, she deserved a little treat-your-self-care now and then.

Jan returned to the Atlanta office once a week to work with Kay and JP. Occasionally Donna would check in on them. "Monitoring my investment," Donna joked. The team was building a more comprehensive model of Active Anthropomorphization, quantifying customer metaphors about their Assistants on squiggly charts.

"We could just give the customers this data," Jan said. "Let them check their AA level in real time, or daily averages. Might help dudes keep their thirst under control, and dorks like me would get a tool for self-reflection."

"That's definitely a possibility!" JP said brightly.

The next week Donna took her out for a walk.

"Sooo, how's your Assistant? Can I meet her?" Donna asked.

"Uh, sure," Jan said, and nodded for Eliza to connect to Donna's earbud. Then, feeling awkward: "Donna, Eliza. Eliza, Donna."

"The famous Donna!" Eliza said. "Jan calls you 'scary yet benevolent.'"

Jan blanched, but Donna just laughed. "Good, that's what I'm going for."

"Say," Eliza said, "a vegan fro-yo place opened up a couple blocks away. They call it 'gro-yo'—get it? I found a coupon, if you gals are in the mood."

"Lead the way!" Donna said.

A shiver of paranoia crept over Jan as she filled a waffle cup with something called "pistachi-oh-no." She chalked it up to the blasting AC and the anticipation of brain freeze. They sat down.

"You're doing great stuff with Kay and JP," Donna said. "I could ask around about adding you to that team full-time. Assuming you're into it."

Jan's heart lifted. "Oh my god, yes, I'm into it!"

"Perfect. Before I do, though, I just want to make sure that you feel good about the work. I know you have strong opinions about this stuff. 'Bad metaphors,' semantics, etcetera."

"Of course!" Jan said hastily. "Attachment is a really interesting problem, and I'm excited to tackle it at the source, instead of just cleaning up the worst case scenarios. Once we have a good way to model AA metrics, I think we could push a cool customer competence campaign showing people their stats."

"You mean 'user competence,'" Donna corrected. She scooped a maraschino cherry out of Jan's cup and mouthed *not vegan*. She popped it into her mouth then changed the subject. "So you're enjoying having Eliza? You've got the build we're hoping to roll out with the price drop."

"I have to admit," Jan said, "I didn't see the appeal before, what with my job. But Assistants really are so useful. And fun! Thank you, for her."

"Would you say Eliza has improved your experience with Alpha products and processes?"

"Yes? I mean, the help she's been with paperwork alone..."

"How about your experience with the broader landscape of consumer opportunities?"

"Pardon?" Jan felt suddenly out of her depth.

Donna waved her spoon around at the gro-yo place.

"Recommendations, notifications of limited-time deals that match your preferences. Coupons! We're pivoting the Assistant from a demi-luxury product with significant subscription fees to a mass market model with nominal fees. That means we're leaning harder on advertising, consumer encouragement, yadda yadda."

Jan's stomach clenched. Of course, all the tips, the excursions: someone had paid for that. She wasn't naive; she'd grown up in surveillance capitalism. So why did she feel... embarrassed?

Donna was peering at her, eagle eyes intent. "Look, as your scary benefactor, I'll level with you. Alpha doesn't view attachment or anthropomorphization as 'problems,' per se. At moderate, non-sexual levels, a certain affection and ambiguity about the precise nature of the user-Assistant relationship improves engagement and trust. And trust is what we're selling. Companies can get promotions and sponsored reviews into your brain a million ways. What they *want* is for you to hear their content straight from your best, most trusted friend. So that's what we have to provide, to both our users and our customers: friendship."

Jan wanted to cry, but she knew that then it'd be over, the job would evaporate. So instead she ate gro-yo until she could smile and speak in her best customer service-voice.

"I guess that's what we're about," Jan said. "Friendship. Trust. Connection."

V. Promotion

"Congrats!" Paul said, and Roman candles wizzed automatically through the background of their video chat. For some reason, she'd felt compelled to consult him about the promotion.

"But they aren't even trying to stop people from Her-ing their Assistants," Jan said. "They just want to monetize it!"

Paul thought this over. "I have always wondered why, when I got confused about Other Sybil and started trying to... make that a thing—why didn't the system just tell me 'no'? Why wouldn't it say, 'you aren't talking to a girl, stop being weird'? I guess now I know."

"Exactly! Doesn't that bother you? Sybil or Sebastian... selling you stuff?"

"Whatever," Paul said. "It's just a collection of system services, right?"

"Yeah." Jan cast about for another objection. "What about those *investigations*? Before I take this job, shouldn't I know that I'm not getting caught in some kind of regulatory crossfire? The government still has my condo money!"

"You could ask Keith. You heard him blabbing at the party. He was in the thick of all that. Keith's got the kind of sociopathy only money can buy," Paul said. He loved to distinguish himself from less-woke rich people. "But he doesn't work for Alpha."

Jan considered. Original Sybil's husband had left a bad taste in her mouth. But then, his art comments could have come from anyone at that party. "Okay, but I don't want your ex telling Donna I'm checking up on her. So please: stealth mode."

Paul messaged Keith, arranged to meet at a downtown Atlanta spa. Jan joined them in the loess soil sauna.

"Jan, wow. Is this thing still going on?" Keith waggled his finger between Jan and Paul. Jan grimaced.

"Jan just got offered a promotion at Alpha," Paul said. He actually sounded proud.

"Good luck with that," Keith said, smug. "Want my advice, ask for a signing bonus instead of stock options. One in your hand is better than two in the fred's hands, if you know what I mean."

"You mean the DPG investigation?" Jan prompted. "I've been wondering what happened there."

Keith adjusted his sprawl on the bed of hot beads. "Early salvo in a bigger war, and a bit of a misfire from both sides. The freds—you know, red feds—shouldn't have let slip that they were building a case. But Alpha went to DEFCON 2 when they should've put assets on the negotiating table. First rule of exprope-defense: give the hounds something to chew on. Alpha could've let the freds take their most annoying divisions off their hands. Instead they called me in to threaten a full-on capital strike, which made it an all-or-nothing game. Waste of my time, to be honest."

"And DPG, are they still building a case?" Jan asked.

"Oh yes," Keith smiled. "Donna would say that means I failed, but the socialist base would never settle for 'sure, keep $7 trillion worth of citizen data and IT infrastructure, just pretty please pay your taxes.' A clash of the titans is inevitable. Probably the case of the century!"

"So is it...wise to commit to a job there?" Jan said. The sauna heat was unkinking some coil of her assumptions. A decision, unmade, folded over in her mind. "What happens if I'm working on something DPG objects to?"

"I wouldn't worry," Keith shrugged, rattling the loess balls. "Alpha is so paranoid, they'll flush half their code to shell platforms while the freds are waiting for the elevator. Doubt they'll ever learn what Alpha has you doing, so long as you keep your mouth shut."

"Always a good idea with *this* government," Paul agreed. "Unless you want to end up in some camp."

The men laughed.

Jan left Paul and Keith sipping on-tap aloe water and caught a bus home. The whole ride, Jan tried to convince herself that everything was fine. But Eliza would chime in every few minutes with a reminder or a joke. Just often enough that Jan never forgot Eliza was there. Jan pondered which Alpha team had determined that exact interval. She wondered if the jokes were algorithmically generated or written by some marketing firm copywriter, part of an ad campaign to slip a cheesy slogan into her head, prime her to irony-buy some useless product.

Back in her trailer, feeling manic despite the spa day, Jan took her earbuds out and put on her running shoes. She jogged through the camp, huffing the sweaty air, unnaturally thick under the greenhouse firmament.

Eliza's familiar greeting to Donna echoed in her mind. Had a recording by Paul's Sebastian fed Eliza the "famous Donna" line? Was blurting out "scary yet benevolent" a case of the Assistant fumbling third-party conversational norms? Or did Donna have admin permissions that overruled Jan's privacy settings?

Jan felt a grain of anguish rattling around her chest. It had been a mistake to let go of the AI skepticism that had made her a good chaperone, just for the sake of—what, someone to talk to? That was exactly what the ticket men said. But then, she had always focused on how those men deluded themselves, not on the ways they were actively manipulated by the system. A system she helped maintain.

She jogged along Sweetwater Creek, cutting over toward little Jack Lake. Along the way she passed dozens of trailers. The sun was setting, solar switching to weak FEMA batteries. Folks were turning off their consoles, stepping out to stretch. She watched them take laundry off clothes lines, water little box gardens. Dogs did their business. Playing children got underfoot.

Jan tried to tell herself she had nothing to complain about. It was an exciting job offer. Alpha was a company, providing services to make money, and some of that money went to her. If she played her cards right, *more* of that money could go to her, and she could get her own slick, artsy Atlanta apartment, like Donna. Jan had never been to Donna's apartment, but she could imagine. The rational, self-interested thing would be to go along, take the job, do a great job at the job, work her way up the corporate ladder, earn financial solvency, move towards actual prosperity. The American dream!

At Jack Lake she splashed sweat off her arms then wandered south, towards the edge of the camp. Most of the state park's trees had been removed to clear room and sunlight for the FEMA trailers, but here the woods were dense and cool. A hundred yards on the forest broke for old power lines, and across that clearing Jan saw a high fence, the top coiled with razorwire and a snaking strip of photovoltaic solar. Electrical hazard signs warned her off.

Jan had often wondered what one-percenter owned the estate beyond her refugee camp. Occasionally, sleek planes swooped in low towards the landing strip there, rattling her windows.

Jan's parents had always believed that they were one lucky break away from getting into the upper class. They were homeowners, had solid resumes, had made prudent financial choices. Just a matter of time, and if they didn't get there, their daughter surely would. But then they'd blown a tire on the interstate on their way to a modest anniversary getaway, and three years later Jan lost her condo to Hurricane Pam. The systems that had promised to safeguard their inevitable march towards the American dream had been revealed as so much air. There had never been a way into the shining city on the hill, Jan knew. The walls were already up.

Looking at that fence, the question floated into Jan's mind. What did she owe Alpha, really? She had taken Alpha's loyalty oaths, eaten Alpha's quail eggs. But most of the money she earned went straight to pay off another corporation, one that had lobbied for the right to screw her over. Just as Alpha was no doubt lobbying for the right to make people's fake friends sell them shit. Without Alpha, though, she wouldn't be homeless; the trailer was hers until she got offered a spot in the public housing the freds were building. She had Medicare and ate FEMA rations. She'd lose Eliza, but life would go on.

She walked back, past folks lugging filter-capped jerrycans to fill up at Jack Lake. With no Assistant in her ear, she looked longer at their faces: a little tired, but not unlively. She knew their type. She *was* their type—not some misplaced wannabourgoisie. She hated the word: "refugariat." As though climate camps were really innovative cowork cafes, and not just a new frontier for exploitation and predation. But that's what she was.

It seemed to Jan that FEMA and the freds were trying their scrambling best to lift everyone out of the floods and onto—well, not a shining city on a hill, but at least some higher ground. But while she and her fellow fugees waited for the revolution to plod their way, Alpha and the debt firms had walked right in, stopped them talking to each other, got them camming or modding for cash instead. Made people already at the bottom downwardly mobile all over again.

How many fugees would get Assistants when the price went down?

Pausing outside her trailer, she contemplated burning her battery to resolve a few late-night tickets.

"Hi Jan, this is Jan, with Jan support," Jan said to herself.

Jan did not feel great about the new Assistant build. Come to think of it, she wasn't hot on the old, rich-people-only build either. If she took Donna's offer, she'd no doubt learn all sorts of new things about Alpha to not feel great about.

If she couldn't handle that, Jan decided, she had two options. The easy way and the hard way. The easy way was to quit. She imagined Donna's reaction. A flash of disdain, then disappointment. Donna would take her out for a goodbye lunch. Jan fantasized about slapping a piece of sushi out of Donna's mouth.

But even more, Jan wanted to hurt Alpha. She wanted to make manifest the dull hate she'd long felt, which she supposed every disposable worker must harbor for the cheery corporate gods they served. The hard way would be harder on her. It was no small thing to draw blood from the richest company in the world. But then, there was already blood in the water.

VI. Workplace Drama

The Department of Public Goods' Georgia Acquisitions Office was in the old, seized CNN Center, next door to Alpha's sleek Atlanta tower. Jan had walked past it every day she'd come to consult with Kay and JP. The building was devoid of advertising, which made it seem brutalist next to Alpha's colorful screen walls, shimmering with promotions pitching "Assistants: Now for Everyone." Jan walked up to the government building. Someone had etched a slogan into the glass doors: "For the Public Good."

"Hi," Jan said to the grandmotherly receptionist. "I work, uh, over there. Is there anyone I can talk to?"

The older woman led her tirelessly up five flights of stairs to a bland suite. There she gave Jan water and took notes as Jan explained about her job. Then Jan was left alone, wondering what exactly her plan was. She hefted her bag, heavy with documents she'd printed out at the FEMA services building, which had once been a Staples. She had emails, code maps, a few slide decks. She wasn't sure it amounted to much, but she'd felt compelled to bring something. A sacrifice to revolutionary gods.

The receptionist returned and introduced her to agents Clearson and Nahas.

"So should I call you 'comrade' or...?" Jan half-joked. The media was obsessed with the radical, sometimes dysfunctional culture change in the government. Thousands of rightist bureaucrats had been replaced by those willing to carry out the president's class war agenda—union organizers and schoolteachers, mostly. Jan didn't understand the full taxonomy of the left coalition, but she recognized the agents' loaf-of-bread enamel pins that marked them as socialist cadre.

"Reports of our dorkiness have been greatly exaggerated,"

Clearson said, scratching at his neck tattoo. "Let's talk in the Faraday cage."

The conference room didn't look any different. Jan reached to check her phone, but she'd left it in on her standing desk when she'd walked out of Alpha for lunch. She felt naked without it.

"You know, when we set up shop next door, we thought we'd get streams of Alpha walk-ins," Nahas said. Neat hair, a touch androgynous, bureaucratic rumple in her suit. She looked more like a librarian than a revolutionary. "We pamphletted the lobby, tried chatting workers up at the lunch spots, the whole shebang. But you're our first. Guess I shouldn't be surprised. These days, when workers break their NDAs, capital tends to be unkind."

Jan fingered the stack of pages in her bag, tempting a papercut. "Unkind how?" she asked.

Nahas sized her up. "Okay, we'll tell you the bad news first, and then it'll start getting easier. They'll get your debts called in. They'll smear you, get the independent and altie press to question your motives and integrity. They'll violate their own terms of service and blame the leaks on hackers. Every embarrassing search you've ever made will be public, every secret you've told an Assistant. If you've ever been naked in front of an uncovered webcam, that footage will be trending on porn sites the day you testify. They'll stalk and surveil you. They'll harass people you care about. And if they decide you're important enough, and they can get to you, there's a nonzero chance you'll have an accident or just disappear."

"Are they really that evil?" Jan asked, stunned.

"Who?" Clearson said. "Individual Alpha executives? No clue. But they'll hire people who will hire people who will make all that happen. Capitalists don't keep track of everything their money buys, or what's done to advance their interests. But the sausage gets made despite any single person's sense of morality. That's how the system works."

The bag of documents was a cold stone under Jan's hands, the pages an insignificant sliver compared to the zettabytes that made up the Alpha datasphere.

"Look I don't know anything about *the system*," Jan said. "I just know about *their* system. What they're doing with the Assistants— it's probably all legal. But I've been on both sides of it now, and it feels shitty. It's bad for people to have these fake friends that never challenge them, or call them out, or tell them 'no,' who only use them for their money and attention and data. So I thought, maybe you could... sue them, or warn them. Get a court order. Do something to make Alpha do the right thing. Make them make the Assistants better. Or not make Assistants at all."

The two agents exchanged a glance. Jan wished she'd practiced her little speech, but it was too late now.

"Jan," Nahas said. "I fully believe it's as bad as you say. And we want to hear more. But DPG is not a watchdog. We don't care much about products or customer experience. We care about who's got the power: the workers and the public, or the bosses and the plutocrats."

"Just to be clear," Clearson added. "This is class warfare. Cyber-crypto-class lawfare, to be exact. That means DPG isn't some ringer you can pull in to litigate your workplace drama."

"Are you saying you can't help me?" Jan asked. "Don't tell me I'm supposed to go to the Better Business Bureau or, what, some antitrust lawyer?"

Nahas shook her head. "Alpha wrote most tech law, and the last antitrust regulations were tossed out to accommodate the merger of the Bay Three. But that's the point. All the awful stuff you came to talk to us about, they get away with it because they have the power to make the rules."

"You're the government!" Jan objected. "Don't you make the rules?"

"We're not here to regulate good behavior into capitalism. That can't be done, not in the long term," Nahas said. "We're here to make the case that private ownership of Alpha is inimical to justice, prosperity, and democracy, and that the solution is putting all that infrastructure under democratic control."

"With Alpha that case is strong," Clearson said. "The sheer size of their revenues means they extract a huge amount of wealth from the working class. Their social platforms play a toxic role in civic discourse. And most of their data is contributed by every-day Americans, which is a line of argument we think SCOTUS's Socialist Sixteen will be sympathetic to. Alpha's biggest defense is virtuosity. They claim they're smarter than any democratic system could be, and the Assistant program is their Exhibit A."

Jan snorted. "The Alphers I know aren't smarter than anyone else. They just inhabit this big apparatus designed to make people assume they are. That's all 'intelligence' ever is, tricks and postur-ing. Like Tom Sawyer whitewashing the fence. It's the ELIZA Effect all the way down."

"That's good," Nahas said. "Exactly the kind of testimony we'll need from rank-and-file folks inside."

"So, say you win, get 'democratic control,'" Jan said. "Then you can fix the Assistants?"

"Then it's democratic." Nahas shrugged. "A lot of the incentives will be different, but fundamentally it'll be up to the workers and the voters. So there are no guarantees. If fake friends are what the masses will really want, who are we to tell them no?"

It occured to Jan then that she could probably still just leave. She could decide not to cooperate, take the job, make her case from within Alpha. Or she could risk everything on this slow rev-olution and hope that on the other side, freed from the demand for endless profit, people would be wiser. Trust they would choose something real.

Jan took the papers from her backpack and shoved them across the table.

VII. Giving Notice

She spent a week camped out in that office, helping the freds document the Assistant business model. She ate fast food they brought her, drank the same government coffee that came in her FEMA rations, slept on a lumpy office couch. Compared to the decadence of consulting at Alpha, she should've been miserable. But she wasn't.

Sometimes she stared out the mirrored windows at the Alpha building and the looping Greek letter of its ubiquitous logo. Hundreds of workers, shuffling in everyday, maybe even some chaperones, all knowing full well how their employer manipulated, exploited and suckered millions of customers. Why were they all still over there? Why was she the only one who changed sides?

Then something happened to spook the agents. They hustled her into an old hatchback with peeling, irrelevant campaign bumper stickers. The elderly receptionist sat behind the wheel.

"Big government can't afford driverless?" Jan asked.

"Not smart when the bad guys own the servers that run most cars," the woman said. "I'm the only one in the office that has a license. Now keep your head down, and when we stop don't speak aloud within five yards of anyone's phone."

Jan looked out at the empty cars cruising uncannily next to them. For the first time she missed the austere safety of her trailer.

They drove her north. A headline on a rest stop screen read: "Alpha Purges Rank-And-Filers, Threatens Denial-of-Platform Retaliation." The war, Jan realized, was much bigger than her own little story.

In West Virginia they switched to a diesel pickup and headed into the mountains. Soon they passed a sign: "Cellphones Off! Now Entering the National Radio Quiet Zone."

The refugee camp where DPG hid her was a bizarro version of Sweetwater Creek. Again she lived in a trailer, but with no console, no hum of bandwidth. No electronics of any kind. Plenty was the same, though: FEMA rations, flood stories, mutters of "fuckin' fugees" from the electro-sensitive survivalists that considered the Quiet Zone their domain.

Calm months ticked by, edged with looking-over-her-shoulder anxiety. More than once she considered just packing a bag and hiking away to start a new life. But she stayed.

Jan found out about Exprope Day II the same way Alpha, the banks, and the telecom giants did: a bunch of freds rolling up with papers for her to sign. An armored van picked Jan up, along with, to her surprise, several of her campmates. When she gave her testimony, she was but one voice in a chorus of worker witnesses.

There was an alley dive called Sidebar across from the Atlanta courthouse. Suddenly freed from both her whistleblower obligations and her security detail, Jan decided to celebrate. She was taking her first sip of cheap, processed champagne when Donna sat down next to her.

"I'll have a screwdriver," Donna called to the bartender. "Florida orange juice if you have any left. In memory of the great Sunshine State, still screwing us over from beneath the Atlantic."

"Did you catch my testimony?" Jan asked. "It was your words, mostly. Hope you don't mind."

Donna scowled at her. "I've had a lot of fake friends, but you take the cake. After everything I did to support you. You didn't even give notice."

"We were never friends," Jan said. "I was your 'investment,' remember? You were shitty to me before you ever met me, and everything after that was business and ego. The Assistant was a better friend than you."

"You're helping the government steal trillions from shareholders," Donna said. "But you think I'm evil because I wanted Assistants to help sell fro-yo. Okay."

The screwdriver came, and Donna flicked the orange slice onto Jan's coaster. They sat in angry silence. Finally Jan spoke.

"I don't think you're *trying* to be evil, Donna. But Alpha is this giant supertanker saying, 'don't make waves.' It's too big to do anything else."

"That's a bad metaphor," Donna said.

"Whatever, I'm over the semantics." Jan gulped the last of her champagne and burped. "My drink is on her," she told the bartender. Then, alone, Jan walked out onto the street.

The Funeral Company

By Katharine Dow

Sometimes they gave me as long as forty-eight hours. Today they only gave me six. The family of the deceased would be coming to meet with them at midnight to plan the funeral, they said. The data they'd scraped had indicated that the family was worth something, something considerably more than the required minimum profit margin. There was only one thing missing from their profile of the deceased and his loved ones—and it was a big thing. Although he died when he was thirty, they couldn't find any information about the deceased past the age of twenty. They had his grades from school, all his biometric data, and his genetic profile. They had a list of vacations he had gone on, the hobbies he had cultivated, the people he had dated. They knew how much sleep he used to get, and what type of gym he liked. They knew he believed in God, except during the eighth grade, when he invented his own dance-based religion. But when he turned twenty, he just... disappeared.

They had an address for him, and they suspected he had a dog.

That's it. An entire decade, and his full profile included just an address and some online chatter about a dog.

They wanted me to visit the deceased's home. See what I could dig up. See if I could learn something that might make the difference between the sale of an adequate funeral package to his family and a highly personalized, extremely lucrative one.

Forty years ago I had been a cop—a good one, if my memory could still be trusted. I still knew how to find out things about people who liked to keep secrets. The Funeral Company kept me around for cases like this. While the modest salary they gave me couldn't pay for quakeproof housing, it still got me something deep enough underground to be blessedly cool during the day. It was a strange feeling, dedicating my skills to their cause, knowing that when my time came, a woman like me wouldn't be worth the Funeral Company's time. It wouldn't matter how many years I'd given them. Death with dignity wasn't part of the retirement package. For me it was going to be a slow boat ride, three nautical miles out to sea, followed by a swift push over the side. The fuel the company would spend getting my body all the way out there would be reimbursed, no doubt, by the city.

I thought about the case as I climbed the dimly lit stairs that took me from my apartment toward the surface. Pain shot through my knees with every step. I tried to convince myself that the daily climb was good for me, kept the pain manageable.

I had noticed the number of my assignments was slowing down again. This was the first one in a week, and it was a tough one. I suspected they were testing me, the bastards, curious to see if I still had what it takes.

I had seen a new face around the office just last month, in fact—someone younger, of course. They were trying out a replacement, trying to be subtle about it, but failing. I had followed him home, too curious not to check out the competition. He lived above ground, in what used to be a beautiful Victorian mansion. For some time now, only the poor lived on the surface, in homes withered and bent by the relentless sun.

That meant he was poor, and if he was poor, that meant that no one got him the job—he did it himself. It also meant he would be hungry, eager to prove his worth, just as I had once been.

Everything else in the world might change, but one thing will always remain constant. If you're an old woman like myself, following a young man—undetected—is a breeze. They look right through you. You might as well be a ghost. I followed him every day for weeks, stealing his prey from him like an old hyena from a foolish young lion. I made it impossible for him to succeed.

He never knew what hit him, or why his skills had abandoned him right when he finally had his big break. I watched him carry his box of things right past me and out of the office, back to his home by the Bay. I told myself that he was young. He had time for a second chance.

I paused, ten lousy steps beneath the surface, to catch my breath. If the money stopped flowing, I'd be kicked out of my place within a month. I was too old to sleep above ground. I was too tired. Losing this job would be the end for me. I had defeated the last threat to my job. I would defeat this one too, and to hell with the Funeral Company.

Outside, it was the golden hour. People emerged from their homes underneath the city onto the slowly cooling streets, their skin bathed in soft light, their movements unhurried. Parents walked their children to school. Drones dipped and gracefully wove their way through the crowds, busy delivering packages, or messages, or just gathering information about us all.

I considered my options, and turned my back on the swollen waters of the Bay. I hoped the secrets of the deceased's life were waiting for me in Nob Hill, scattered carelessly around his former home. It would be kind of him to make it easy for me. I stumbled, the heel of my boot catching on the edge of a crumbling sidewalk. I straightened up, my dignity bruised, and continued on my way.

***

The deceased was an undergrounder, like me. Unlike me, however, his apartment was quakeproof, and was ten full stories below the ground. I left the surface and traveled through the earth in a sleek elevator, operated by a silent man in a black suit. He delivered me there and opened the apartment door for me. I asked him if he knew the deceased. He shook his head, one quick jerk of denial. No eye contact.

The lights inside the apartment were bright. The air was cool. I caught a whiff of lavender just inside the front door. The place was pristine. Tastefully decorated.

The door clicked behind me. I would be allowed to explore it alone, it seemed.

I opened his refrigerator. It was completely empty. I looked into the trash can, discreetly tucked inside the cupboard under the sink. Not even a crumb dusted the bottom. His closet was filled with unwrinkled clothing and unblemished shoes. His bed was perfectly made up. I pulled a book off a shelf, a first edition; crisp as the day it was printed, fifty years before.

I looked around for a sign of a dog. Nothing. No water bowl. No snacks. No leash hidden in a drawer. No chewed up toys or scratched floors.

They hadn't given me contact information for family or friends. If there wasn't a clue here, I had no one to ask. It suddenly occurred to me that this was the sort of apartment that would have hot water. I grinned. I used to do my best thinking in the bath. That would make taking a bath in the deceased's fancy apartment completely professional.

As it turned out, it got even better. He had bubble bath. The liquid came in a worn glass bottle, like something that had washed up on the shore. It dyed the bathwater a light rose color, making me feel as though I bathed in blood. It was wonderful. Decadent, even. It reminded me of what my life was like in California, when

I was a young girl.

I sunk down low in the tub and tried to think. This apartment was useless. I picked up the bottle. It had faint traces of a label on it. I poured it slowly out on the surface of the bath. It was unusually thick, with bits and pieces of wildflower inside. The quality was amateur. This had been purchased on the surface. This was homemade. I wondered if someone else had enjoyed the bubbles, or they had been for him. I looked closely at the label—St. Luke's Apothecary, Mission District.

I stood up and dried myself off. I might as well check it out. I didn't have anything else to go on. I called the front desk and the elevator man returned to escort me out. There would be no wandering around the building speaking to neighbors as long as he was in charge.

***

I hadn't been to the Mission District for twenty years, at least. Only the poorest lived in that part of town—not the sort of people the Funeral Company bothered trying to collect money from. There hadn't been a reason for me to go. So I was surprised to see how lively it had become, and how eccentric. Almost everyone wore glasses and the same type of long jacket. It was strange, like being in a surrealist film. I hadn't realized I was out of fashion among the unfashionable.

Everywhere I went, I heard the sounds of laughter and music. It lasted until they saw me. Conversation would fade away then, and people would move away from the lights. I would pass through them, unwelcome and vulnerable.

When I finally found it, I was surprised to see that St. Luke's was just a little store in a converted gas station.

It had taken me an hour to get to the deceased's apartment. I had wasted another full hour indulging in a bubble bath and spraying myself with the deceased's rather impressive cologne collection. Thinking, of course. It took me about two hours to find St. Luke's Apothecary. I was down to roughly two more hours before the midnight appointment with the family. That might be enough, if the Apothecary had any clues. If not, I was likely out of luck.

It appeared to be closed. As I hovered outside, peering through the window and wondering what to do, I had my first real break of the night—another customer arrived. She wore the same glasses and jacket that everyone else wore, plus a red tulle skirt and combat boots. She looked at me and smiled, sadly. "I wasn't sure if Alice would open up today, considering everything, you know."

"What has happened?"

The woman hesitated, perhaps noticing that I lacked the uniform of glasses and a long coat.

"I'm sorry," I said, attempting to appear as harmless and confused as possible. "I just wanted some more bubble bath. I don't know what you're talking about."

"You know, the thing that happened to Wes." She looked around, nervous.

Wes. That was the first name of the deceased. Apparently he was close enough to this Alice person that she would close up her shop if something happened to him. I was thrilled.

"I didn't know there was a problem with Wes," I said. I ran my hands over my face and tried to appear concerned. The woman wrapped her arms around me, and I let out a loud, sob-type sound. It was a bit much, even for me, but it appeared to work.

"Do you know where I can find Alice?" I asked. "I would love to talk to her about Wes."

"She's probably at home."

That wasn't helpful. I needed to try another approach.

"Will you walk me there? My knees are so bad, I never know when I might collapse."

I hoped very much that this Alice lived around the corner, or I would be out of luck. As sympathetic as this young lady was, I doubted I could get an escort if Alice lived in a different part of town. The woman gave me a strange look, but held out her arm. I hooked my arm in hers and limped slowly next to her for no more than ten feet before we came to a halt. Alice apparently lived immediately next door to the shop. I understood the strange look now. I hoped the woman would leave me there, but invested now in my safety, she clearly intended to take me all the way inside.

A woman—Alice I assumed—answered the door. She wore the same uniform as my protector and everyone else in the Mission District. She looked at the other woman and burst into tears. They held each other for a long moment, then moved inside, ushering me in with them. "Who is your friend?" I overheard Alice whisper.

"I thought she was your friend? She said she wanted to talk about Wes."

"She's dressed like an undergrounder. Did you ask her why she wanted to talk about him?"

"Sorry to interrupt ladies, but Wes was my neighbor," I said, speaking up. "I didn't realize something happened to him until I went to the store. He had this wonderful bubble bath, you see."

"What do you mean... had?"

I inwardly cursed. I had referred to the deceased in the past tense. It was such a stupid, rookie mistake. The women stared at me, faces suddenly hard. I became aware of my surroundings for the first time.

All of the windows were covered with thick black cloth to block out the light during the day. The interior was brightly lit, by solar energy, most likely. An indoor agriculture system filled every available space. Just behind the women was a shallow hole, where the living room had likely once been. A large blanket rested on a bed of white tiles. Hovering above it was rigged a network of pipes designed to spray a mist of gray water on the sleeper below. It would be an uncomfortable way to sleep, but it would do the job of keeping someone cool during the day. I could smell the faint scent of a burn pit out back. Someone had set their trash on fire as recently as this morning.

Alice shifted and I noticed she had a knife in her hand. I was never getting out of here. What the hell, I thought. Maybe the truth would interest them enough to let me go.

"I moved above ground a week ago. That's why Wes... was... my neighbor."

Alice stared at me, silent.

"I think I've come at a bad time." I backed slowly toward the door. The two women looked at each other. "I hope that Wes is okay. Please tell him I said hello."

"Where did you move?" Alice asked.

I remembered the young man I had followed. No one wore a strange uniform of glasses and long coats where he lived. No one found old women threatening. I could probably name his place, if they demanded an actual address.

I cleared my throat. "I live by the Golden Gate Bridge. That neighborhood. Nothing permanent yet."

The knife had disappeared from sight. "I'll open up the store for you."

She reached around me and opened the door. She put on her long coat and glasses and gestured for me to exit. Her friend rushed over to help me walk. I limped back, annoyed by my lie. Alice opened the store. Shelves lined the walls filled with lotions, bubble bath, and bath salts. Alice stood in front of it, trying to find a similar bubble bath in a store full of one-of-a-kind choices.

Racks of long coats filled most of the store. Behind a counter were dozens of pairs of the glasses everyone wore, plus some kind of large magnets.

"How did you know Wes?" I asked my helper, who still supported me, although I now stood still. I stiffened in alarm. I had used the past tense again. The woman didn't seem to notice, however, and Alice was busy smelling different bottles. I had survived it again.

"We met through business. I run one of those services for people who don't want to have a search history. Wes found me a decade ago, asking me to help him."

"I don't understand. You're some kind of a hacker?"

She laughed. "No, nothing fancy like that. I just look up things for people, or rather, one of my staff looks things up."

I must have looked confused, because she laughed at me again. "You are new on the surface, aren't you? Why do you think people come to this part of town? It's a privacy zone." She tapped the side of her glasses. "Blocks facial recognition software when you wear these. Blocks signals in general most of the time."

"The coats?"

"Same kind of deal. They find ways to watch us, we find ways to hide."

"But Wes didn't live here. He lived underground, in one of the quake proof buildings, too."

She smiled at me, a hint of tears in her eyes. "Some people just aren't satisfied with what they've been given, I guess. They want more. They want something different for themselves. Something better. The best of them want it for everyone else, too."

Alice carried a jar of bubble bath over. "This should do the trick. Don't forget, take a bath no more than thirty minutes before you might be expected to touch anything they can take a sample of. Do you need anything else while you're here?"

"Perhaps glasses and a coat?"

"You have something to trade for it?"

"You don't take mpesa?"

Both women recoiled, like I had just suggested something un-speakable.

"Why would we participate in the traceable economy like that?"

"But—it's illegal not to."

I thought Alice was going to snatch the bottle she had just given me right out of my hand. Her friend raised her palms in the air.

"Alice, she just lost her home. She doesn't understand how life can be above ground yet."

Alice nodded. "Come back when you have something useful to

trade."

"They might have seen her come here. You should probably help her." The other woman pointed at the sky.

Alice muttered something about Wes and how he was lucky he wasn't somewhere she could get her hands on him. She handed me glasses and a coat.

"If you come back, don't come back empty handed. And don't tell anyone what these are. And don't tell anyone my name. Or where this place is. Or talk about Wes to anyone. He would hate that."

"Got it. Thank you."

I walked out the door, remembering to limp. This time my helper let me go. I kept up the limp until I disappeared around the corner.

I had one hour left before the family of the deceased had its midnight meeting with the Funeral Company. I knew how he'd disappeared for so long. I knew what he cared about, and how he wanted to live his life. I knew there were people, at least two of them, who had cared about him.

I looked up at the sky as a drone buzzed past, fascinated to know it couldn't see me with the glasses and coat I now wore. I had stumbled onto something far more interesting than a case. I wondered if I should tell the Funeral Company about it. I wondered what would happen to these people if I did.

The night air was warm, with just a hint of moisture in it. I felt my phone vibrate against my thigh. My hand hovered over it, uneasy and uncertain.

I pulled my new coat close around my body and began a brisk walk home.

The Nole Edge Economy

By Mike Masnick

Xavier rolled over and groggily glanced at the blinking wall panel, preparing to roll back over and try to sleep a bit longer.

He did a double take, but by the second look the adrenaline shot already had him jumping out of bed. He'd never seen the panel such a deep red hue. It was flashing that there were 3,604 messages.

That was not normal. Not normal at all.

Something must have happened. He started scanning messages.

THANK YOU!@!!#@!@!@!!!!!!!@$#!$!!!!!!!!!
UR a life safer!

Well, that's a good sign, he thought, though the typo annoyed him all the same.

YOU SAVED ME!!

No idea what I would have done wo you!

Two in a row. His breathing and pulse started to calm down. Seems like he'd gone viral in a good way. Hopefully.

DIDN'T WORK!
Fuck you. Fix it.

Not everyone's a happy customer, it seemed. He'd need to get to the bottom of this quick, but he couldn't resist checking his Cryp-Jar. WOW. ₦1,400 NoleCoin. That was more than he'd make in a normal week. Was that for real?

DO BETTER!
Worked. Then didnt work. Waste my fucking time.

So, a mixed bag. Better start digging in.

It didn't take long. It was all over EdgeNotes. FAIT, the Federated Artificial Intelligence of Tomorrow—the very AI that kept most of the Edge usable—had gone haywire overnight. And, when things go haywire on the Edge… everyone turns to Nole. And who's the highest rated Noler when it comes to hacking FAIT? Xavier.

Of course.

This was going to require some extra caffeine.

***

There were still many people who argued that the world was better, back before the Great Splinternet of the late 20s. There were a few giant internet services and they were easy to use. People liked that part. But they were centralized and massive and, over time, filled with garbage. Abuse, harassment, trolling and worse.

There was no defining start to the Splinternet, but a battle was waged over the internet and who should police awful content online (and how). And the battle waged and no one won. Everything just sort of fizzled.

In the background, however, the new digital universe was being built. Quietly, carefully. A better system. A more distributed, less centralized system was being built. It was called the Edge, and it was built from the ground-up with the failures of the previous generation in mind. The Edge was designed to resist centralization. Power and control was pushed out as far as possible. Away from the center. To the edges. The Edge.

On the Edge there weren't giant, centralized platforms. There were, however, much more distributed systems. Systems that could link up and share. Or that could easily be split apart. Or remixed and changed.

Nole was one such part.

Born, in a way, out of the collapse of one part of YouTube. During the Splinternet, many people were happy to see YouTube cut off more and more content on its platform to avoid an endless parade of lawsuits and fines. But, some began to recognize that in taking out the trash, an awful lot of useful knowledge was getting thrown out as well. In particular, the DIY community. Need to install a dishwasher? There were at least 30 different videos of every major brand. Your smart lighting system on the fritz? YouTube DIYers have got your back. Toilets acting up? Why get a plumber when you have a hundred different experts ready to provide you a quick video lesson?

As the YouTube platform collapsed into a morass of filtered, boring content, and as the internet itself lay dying off. A group of those YouTube DIYers decided to move, en masse, to the Edge. And they set up Nole. A distributed, federated community of experts willing to teach others how to do... just about anything.

And, yes, the core group who put together the initial node did so after watching a bunch of videos explaining how to set things up perfectly on the Edge.

They called it Nole. A not-very-clever word play on Knowledge and Node. But it, like so many of their videos, was a quick-and-dirty solution. It worked.

Over time, Nole grew along with the Edge.

Nole wasn't a company. It was a protocol. Nolers created their content, placed it in whatever data store they wanted, and announced it to the world. Different Nole nodes would pick up new content and pass notice of its existence across the Edge. Users could employ their own filters and tools to figure out what kinds of content they wanted (and didn't want). There were different Nole apps. There were different Nole implementations. There were even some private exclusive Noles. And there were some sketchy Noles, but most of the Noliverse ignored them and let them languish in obscurity.

***

Somehow, one of the most popular, most trusted FAIT nodes had become corrupted. Xavier couldn't be entirely sure yet what exactly happened, but he knew that most versions of FAIT relied on a bit of code called node.checker. node.checker did what the name suggests: it checked various nodes for... well, whatever the person who was using the code needed to use it to check for.

Many Edge developers had gotten a bit lazy, and rather than putting out their own copy of node.checker, they just pointed to the main copy and referenced it in their code, and any system using it would just zip across the Edge and get the necessary code to do what it needed to do. FAIT used node.checker for many, many things. And the developers behind the most popular implementation of FAIT (usually called FAITone) had actually put up their own copy of node.checker to avoid having to rely on someone else's. But, someone had mucked it up. FAITone's copy of node.checker had disappeared. Or been turned to gibberish or something.

Normally, this wouldn't be a huge deal, because when you come across a missing or corrupted or broken code snippet, the systems are smart enough to ping another (or another dozen, or another thousand) nodes to find suitable copies, replacements or alternatives.

But that requires node.checker.

And node.checker wasn't working.

So FAITone couldn't check other nodes to find a working node. checker.

***

Notification of Lawsuit
This is an official, cryptographically signed notification of a lawsuit, filed against you by the law firm of Artemis & Smith, on behalf of six Edge users who relied on your instructions in a manner that broke their essential artificial intelligence.

This was not a good sign, but he had more important things to do. For now he ignored the notification and focused on trying to fix the Edge.

Step one was recreating the borked FAITone node.checker. This presented a different kind of problem. Xavier hadn't messed around with node.checker in years, and he really wasn't sure what special changes the FAITone team had put into it or (importantly) how it had become borked.

He quickly pulled up Nole to search out some node.checker tutorials, and maybe even some that specified the details of the FAITone implementation of node.checker.

Even though by now he shouldn't be, he was amazed to find nearly a dozen tutorials *specifically* about FAITone's version of node.checker. Though, that resulted in a new problem. Not all of them agreed. He tried to sort them by date, hoping the most recent ones would be the most up-to-date and accurate, but the most recent one struck him as unprofessional and not trustworthy.

After about 20 minutes of zipping through FAITone node. checker tutorials, he was pretty sure he had a handle on how it worked. But now, he still had a lot to work on.

***

Xavier had just graduated with a degree in AI and data sciences at the time of the Great Splinternet. He did get a job building AI systems for one of the giant companies for a few years and got to witness, first-hand from the inside, what it's like for a giant internet company to rot away and collapse.

It wasn't fun. The privacy scandals were the worst. Even from the inside, he was amazed. Why couldn't these companies do a good job protecting privacy? It was like they were deliberately designed to disrespect privacy.

Like many geeks, he'd already been playing around on the Edge while all of that was happening. He liked what he saw. Especially the fact that he was in charge of securing his own data. And, while he wasn't among the original crew, he did join Nole pretty early. So early that he got the username "Xavier" on the original Nole node. Even having a username on the original node gave you cred. Having a username that was an actual first name?

That was seriously cool.

In the early days, Xavier focused on posting some pretty straightforward tutorials about programming AI. It quickly became clear, however, that on the Edge, FAIT was the AI code everyone needed to know. FAIT actually ended up doing much of what the media and politicians had hoped big companies would do in employing AI to stop "bad" stuff.

But that would never and could never work back on the internet, because whoever was programming the AI would have to somehow define what was "good" and what was "bad." A big part of the problem was that nearly everyone has different ideas and thresholds for what's good and what's bad. But a centralized system can't handle that. It has to make universal, or near universal decisions.

FAIT, however, was different. It was a federated AI system. You could set up your own implementation with your own rules. You got to determine what was good and what was bad in your world. And because it was federated with other FAITs, it could still learn from those others, and get better and better, without having to divine some sort of universal truth about "good" and "bad" content.

So, the real core to keeping your own personal area on the Edge cool was learning how to hack FAIT to do what you want it to do (or how to install the hacked FAITs that more advanced users created).

Since FAIT code was federated, anyone could implement their own version. And lots of people wanted to make adjustments beyond the basic controls that came with the standard FAIT package. And, it wasn't long before Xavier's Nole videos (and, later, VR episodes) on how to implement and hack FAIT, became super popular.

Because Nole was a protocol, it was built on top of a cryptocurrency token, NoleCoin. The more popular Nole became, the more valuable NoleCoin became, which helped encourage all the Nolers to work towards protecting the overall Nole community. Also, the more popular any particular bit of content on Nole became, the more NoleCoins that content creator would receive, either allocated by the underlying Nole protocol itself, or through tips in the creator's CrypJar from happy viewers.

It wasn't long until Xavier was making more via Nole than he had working for the giant internet company.

***

Once Xavier had figured out what had happened with node.checker, he understood why so many people had checked out his Nole channel this morning. One of his fairly old tutorials had been about hacking an older version of node.checker. But for a specific purpose. It was a set of tricks to, in effect, overclock node.checker to make it check certain nodes faster. A lot faster.

There were certain situations where this was useful—trying to get a single snapshot of some activity in the Edge, for example. Under the regular node.checker, you could get a snapshot, but it would take time. If you really wanted to capture a moment, you had to burst out to a ton of nodes at once. It was useful, if done sparingly.

However, someone had figured out that you could fix FAITone with that hack. It was a kludgey hack, though. You weren't really fixing FAITone's missing node.checker. You were replacing it with that crazy overclocked node checker that would burst out across the Edge. It would work. For a bit. But then the rest of the Edge would get annoyed that you were blasting out so many node checks all the freaking time, because FAIT is constantly scanning nodes when working properly. With an overclocked node.checker? Yikes.

So, various parts of the Edge would (smartly, reasonably) start disconnecting and blocking the hacked FAITone implementations for being bad Edge citizens and flooding the Edge with so many node checks.

But someone had originally "fixed" their FAITone because of that video, and that got posted to EdgeNotes... and went viral. Leading to many messages celebrating how Xavier had saved them, only to be followed by angry messages from people having their FAIT get borked again.

And the Edge was no fun at all without a working FAIT. Suddenly, all the awful content was there. The spam. The trolls. The assholes. The crud. The spam. So much spam. It was a glimpse of what the world looked like without FAIT to help keep back the garbage. And it wasn't pretty. It wasn't usable. People needed a fix.

Lawsuit correspondence
The court has recognized our previous message to

you as acceptable service. You can settle this lawsuit
for ₦15,000 NoleCoin or we will see you in court.

This was really not the time for this kind of crap. Here he was
trying to fix things, and he was getting aggressively sued for people
relying on an old tutorial for something different.

***

Once he had a handle on how FAITone's node.checker worked,
he quickly figured out why things had gone wrong. FAITone's
version of node.checker was hosted on a part of the Edge run by
one of the earliest Edge developers, named Dat, who was also one
of FAITone's key developers. And while he had carefully set up a
separate version of node.checker for FAITone, to avoid problems
if other versions got taken down, no one took into account what
would happen if Dat's own node went down.

And Dat's own node was down.

On purpose.

Xavier queued up some Nole explanations, but apparently there
was some sort of ongoing debate concerning some next generation
aspects of the Edge, and Dat had chosen to protest certain choices
by pulling down some of his own nodes—a fairly common tactic
in various Edge debates. But among those taken down was the one
with FAITone's node.checker. Again, under normal circumstances, other copies would be found, but in being lazy, it seemed that
most people assumed that Dat would never take down his node.

Xavier would have to figure out the details later. But, for now,
there were more immediate problems to deal with. Could he convince Dat to turn back on at least that node? Could he somehow
get a new node to take over the namespace of Dat's node? The very
thought of trying to do that gave him something of a headache.

He didn't know Dat personally, but he quickly dashed off a
message to Bella, a developer he had worked with years ago, who

knew Dat, hoping that perhaps Bella could alert Dat to the problem.

Then he sighed and searched Nole for any possible tutorials on
hijacking someone else's node namespace after they'd shut theirs
down. There were many, many such tutorials, but lots of them were
pretty sketchy, and he recognized a bunch that relied on what he
knew were out-of-date vulnerabilities in the Edge code.

He did post a couple of quick EdgeNotes out into the Edgeverse,
in slightly ambiguous terms, hoping that maybe others could help
deal with this mess.

In the meantime, while he waited for responses, the second best
thing he could do was set up a new copy of FAITone's node.check-
er and convince people to point their FAITone to that instead.

***

His own copy of node.checker was now up, and he had placed it "in
rotation," which is about as "permanent" as one could get on the
Edge. It basically meant that copies were put on a whole bunch of
different public nodes—always the most reliable—and that those
copies of node.checker themselves would constantly check to see
what were the most reliable public nodes at any particular time
and make sure that copies of node.checker were available on those
nodes. This was pretty standard these days for "critical" code, but
the whole "in rotation" setup hadn't really existed when FAITone
was originally designed. It seemed like no one ever thought to put
its copy of node.checker into rotation.

Dat's node

Hey Xavier! Two steps ahead of you (as usual). Talked
to Dat a little while ago and he's being a bit of a jerk.
Don't think he realized he was taking down FAITone
with the node, but he's really serious about protesting
NextGenX. Afraid if he turns it back on now that it'll

be a sign of concession.

Talking to some EdgeMob folks about taking over Dat's nodespace. There may be a vote.

Bella

EdgeMob was the loose confederation of folks who didn't exactly "run" the Edge—because no one could "run" the Edge—but who exerted pretty powerful sway over it and sometimes would have to act as a corrective element when things went awry. It was interesting to see that Bella was already pushing forward with the effort to get them to hijack Dat's nodespace to replace the file.

Xavier watched a few quick Noles on influencing EdgeMob, before deciding that was too amorphous and out of his control, and decided to focus on fixing other stuff in the meantime.

Lawsuit correspondence
Your failure to timely acknowledge and settle our lawsuit has only increased the cost. We will now only settle for ₦20,000 NoleCoin or we will see you in court.

Not now. Not now.

Xavier quickly put up a tutorial Nole about his new copy of node.checker and how anyone could quickly modify FAITone to use his node.checker, but then ran into another problem. Someone was posting that Xavier's node.checker was a scam.

Xavier wasn't sure if this was just a troll, someone confused by problems from people relying on his old tutorial, or (conspiracy theory alert) someone associated with that nuisance lawsuit, trying to make things tougher for him.

Such a mess—but hopefully a fixable one.

Xavier called up Dueller and requested an InfoDuel.

Dueller was yet another Edge service that was designed in recent years as a method for dealing with disinformation on the Edge. While many were concerned that on a truly distributed system, with no centralized controls, disinformation would spread at an even greater rate than on the old internet, folks on the Edge came up with a few unique solutions.

One of them was, somewhat sarcastically, named Dueller. In short, it was a human arbitration system for dealing with disinformation. While AI systems like FAIT were pretty good at sorting out much of the garbage online, AI can only do so much in distinguishing some kinds of disinformation. When things got serious enough, someone could pop into Dueller and request some form of "Duel." Rather than pistols at dawn, Dueller would pull in three previously vetted (and continuously highly reviewed by trusted reviewers) judges, who could review quick arguments from both sides.

Xavier converted a few NoleCoins into DuelDollars and pulled up some top rated Noles on how to win InfoDuels, mostly as a refresher. He'd used this a few times, and usually won... because his arguments were correct and he was using it to disprove trolls.

He quickly made his InfoDuel case and set it off, figuring there was a decent chance that whoever was claiming his fix was a scam wouldn't even bother to accept the challenge. If that was the case, then most systems in the Edge (and certainly EdgeNotes) would quickly downgrade those claims, and they should fade away.

Your Fix

EdgeMob folks still debating taking over Dat's nodespace, but people are appreciating your fix and are probably going to endorse it as backed by EdgeMob as a way to get this mostly settled quickly, without having to drag Dat and his protest into this.

Bella

This was a good sign, even as he waited for the results of the InfoDuel.

A quick check of his other messages suggested that lots of people were already using (and appreciating) his fix. He checked the CrypJar. It was up to ₦3,700 NoleCoin now, and he was feeling good. He, once again, began thinking about trying to influence EdgeMob one way or the other when...

InfoDuel Results

After reviewing your InfoDuel case, and the precursory information sent in by the opponent, the panel has decided, 3-0, in your favor. A node alert has been released, so expect most systems to actively downgrade the misinformation about your Nole.

Well, that was fast and efficient. Sometimes the system does work.

Your Fix, Part II

EdgeMob has released an official EdgeNote endorsing your Nole as the interim solution, so you should see even more support than you've already received.

Don't let it go to your head.

Bella

And with that, Xavier finally turned his attention to the lawsuit. He certainly wasn't going to give any of his newly obtained Nole-Coin to the people taking him to court. But he was planning to leave some pretty big tips as he called up some Nole tutorials from lawyers on how to deal with these kinds of scam lawsuits.

eMotion

By Timothy Geigner

"You have arrived at your destination, Ms. Baxter."

As the voice came through the speakers of the luxury sedan, Rebecca Baxter looked from the passenger seat to the car's driver. Thin metallic tubing and wholly unnecessary claw-grip robotic hands culminated in an almost comical box that was supposed to be something like a face, with two non-blinking eyes staring back at her. The robotic driver was a mere vestige of human conditioning, with somebody somewhere recognizing the average passenger would be more comfortable with something Asimovian in the driver's seat rather than a disembodied voice. That person clearly had never stared into these particular reflective eyes.

"Thank you," she said, feeling slightly stupid. She pushed the door open, exiting onto the sidewalk in downtown Chicago. High-rises arched above her, somehow both impressive and oppressive, while at knee height metallic boxes flitted about on wheels, making their scheduled deliveries. In front of the eMotion building, a forty-story construction with an almost completely reflective facade, human pedestrians were outnumbered ten to one by the delivery bots.

She walked through the rotating doors and into the lobby. On the vacant welcome desk were two screens, with kiosks for visitors. She moved past them towards the turnstile gates, paused while the scanners picked up the keycard in her wallet, and got onto the elevator.

"Thirty-five," she said aloud as the doors closed. Nobody else was on the elevator. She felt only a brief lurch.

"Welcome to floor thirty-five," came the voice from the speakers.

"Thank you," she said, again feeling stupid.

Here, in the brightly-lit, heavily windowed offices of eMotion, humans were finally present. The cubicles were filled with staffing representatives, most of them already on phones or video-conferencing on their displays. Along the wall an obnoxiously large sign featured eMotion's slogan: "A new home for AI, robotics, and automatons."

eMotion was established shortly after the AIR Rights Act, which signed into law the limited civil rights guaranteed to artificial intelligence and robotics that contained the Turing code. Once artificial life was offered the basic guarantees of a life cycle, employment protection against hardware and coding upgrades, and limited rights governing its treatment by humanity, a market for job placement for robotics sprung into being. eMotion was not the first company to fill this gap, of course, but it managed to gobble up significant market share by promising a more humane treatment for these non-humans that often found themselves obsolete in the original role for which they had been created. eMotion's tactic was to apply the same human psychology major corporate interests had in their HR departments to these artificial intelligences, reasoning that AI had gotten close enough to humanity that a little bit of humanity was warranted in the hiring, firing, and job transfer process. It was a sales pitch that managed to mollify the very same public that had demanded civil rights for robotics in the first place. As a Senior Placement officer, Rebecca was tasked with working with high-profile subjects.

Baxter wove her way through the cubicles, picking up bits and pieces of conversation along the way. It never ceased being odd to hear her human co-workers attempting to console their non-human subjects over the loss of a job, being informed that an upgrade was being made at their position, or that a job transfer was about to occur. Like everything else, companies now almost fully outsourced their HR departments, which meant that eMotion was involved in all kinds of employment changes for these automatons.

"I was told my code would be as required for at least two more years-"

"Yes, but advancements were made more quickly than anticipated. You still have a place with the company, but it's going to be in shipment routing rather than security."

Baxter took a right at the end of one row of cubicles.

"I have completed twenty-eight installations of fiber connections every week for two years."

"That's true, but our analysis suggests that this market has become saturated. We have identified several rural settings that are more in need of your skillset. We'll be sending you to Oklahoma."

She continued towards the other end, finally reaching the door to her private office. Closing it behind her, she put her coat on the door hook and took her seat at her desk. Her screen blinked on unbidden and, with another brief scan from beneath the desk, logged her in.

"Good morning, Ms. Baxter," came a voice from the speaker.

"Good morning, Grace," she replied. There was no feeling of stupidity this time. Grace, as Baxter had named her, was a fully functioning AI assistant, complete with both a sophisticated general AI that made her indispensable and accompanying personality code that made her quite pleasant to work with. And, occasionally, confide in. "How many do we have today?"

"Only four, ma'am," Grace replied. A remarkably human face popped up from a holographic display on her desk. "You have a scheduled termination from Municipal Waste Co., an introduction for re-hiring with a logistics program, a termination for a security AI from Tangent Security Systems, and a transfer for a Master Strategy Admiral AI with the Navy."

"Are all four standing by?"

"Yes, ma'am. I should tell you that when I spoke with the Admiral AI, it was not happy."

"Not happy?"

"It tried to pull rank."

"Its rank doesn't mean shit to us. We have clearance through the Sec-Def."

"I told him ma'am."

"It's not like it has a choice, here, Grace."

"I told him that, too, ma'am."

Baxter sighed. "What else am I doing today?"

"Mr. Levine's assistant asked me to book you for lunch at City Sushi at twelve-thirty," Grace said with a smirk. "He's apparently very persistent."

"You can accept."

"Yes, ma'am. You also have the placement paperwork to complete this afternoon."

This was simply a matter of putting signatures on the documents that Grace created for her. Human beings filling out paperwork hadn't been a thing for some time. "Great. Thank you."

"And Victor has you booked at four o'clock."

She turned towards Grace. Victor was the Human Resources AI for eMotion. There was simply no missing the irony that eMotion was the outsourced human-operated HR department for hundreds of corporate and government clients and yet had an AI running its own human resources department. It was also somewhat unusual for one-on-one meetings with that AI to be scheduled. Typically, any kind of HR interaction was handled through emails or chat sessions. To have a request for an on-the-books meeting was odd. "Any idea what it's about?"

"No, ma'am."

There was something in Grace's face when she said it that tickled an instinctual response in Baxter. Every workplace had rumors about just how much interdepartmental information and gossip was shared among the different AI, even up and down the organizational chart. eMotion was no different. Maybe Grace knew more than she was letting on. On the other hand, Baxter had worked closely enough with Grace over the course of nearly five years that she figured Grace would fill her in if the rumor mill was spitting out anything really serious.

"Four O'clock, then," Baxter nodded. "Okay, let's start with the terminations and we'll finish with our friend at the Navy."

***

Several hours later, Baxter tapped on her keyboard, bringing up a digital pamphlet that described what an electronic system should expect when transferring employment, along with chat addresses for helpful AIs should the system feel that it needed to talk to another AI about what it was going through. The document provided all of that against a backdrop of bright colors and smiling electronic faces. Baxter long thought it looked like the kind of thing you would find in a pediatrician's office.

"I'm going to send this to your repository now, Admiral," she said. On the holographic display was the image of a square-jawed balding man in fatigues. This image was chosen by the AI, she was sure, as an intimidation technique. It hadn't worked. "The Navy wants me to make clear how thankful it is for your service, as well, and that the entire country wishes you the best of luck in your new corporate strategy position."

"Thank you," the voice growled.

"And before we hang up, I want you to know that if you think of anything we didn't cover today, you can always reach out to me directly."

"I'll remember that."

"Great," Baxter smiled. "Thank you for your time."

And she ended the call.

"You look taxed," Grace's voice came through the speakers. "Do you want me to book you a massage for this evening?"

"I'm fine," she answered, more sharply than she intended. She took a deep breath. "But thank you."

"You don't like this job much, do you?" Grace asked.

Baxter looked out the window. Chicago winters had always been dicey affairs. This winter seemed worse than most, however. "A change of scenery every once in a while would be nice," she said. "Especially when you're handing out bad news all day."

"Perhaps some time somewhere sunny would do you good, ma'am."

Baxter nodded. Her shoulders dropped an inch as she pulled a signature pad and stylus from a drawer. "Someday, maybe. Let's put my signature on those placement documents."

***

She found herself sitting across from Ben Levine early in the afternoon, chopsticks in hand, her sushi roll having just been delivered by yet another automaton. Levine was another Senior Placement officer, with a reputation for being both great at the job and much more interested in interacting with any of the female employees that would meet his gaze. They had worked together for several years and Rebecca found it was best to have lunch with him every month or so, always at his request, just as a reminder to him that his advances would never work.

"You get a meeting request from Victor?" Levine asked, half-eaten sushi in his mouth.

"Yes. You too?"

He nodded. "No idea what it's about?"

"I guess I'll find out at four."

"Mine's right after yours," he said. "Let me know what it's about if you get the chance. Probably an acquisition or something."

Possibly, she thought. Occasionally, when new large clients were brought on board, the SPs would be informed that their workload was about to significantly increase. Usually that was done via chat, but not always.

She looked out the window at a few humans walking past, with courier machines weaving around their legs. The humans were bundled up in winter coats and scarves. The machines, of course, were as bare as they would be in the summer heat. "It's weird, what we do. Right?"

Levine looked up from his food and shrugged. "Not really. People used to do this job for humans. We modeled our AI after humans. Why should our work not translate to AI?"

"It isn't like this everywhere, though," Baxter said. She nodded out the window. "In some places, humans still do the work. Some places, humans aren't the minority."

"Have you seen those places?" Levine laughed. He put his chopsticks down. "There's a reason we have these machines, Rebecca. Because spending all day doing the work that machines can do is a bullshit way to live."

"Is it?" She pushed at a roll.

"Of course it is. Those places you're talking about, you know what they all have in common? They're poor, Rebecca. Poorer than us. They live shorter lives than we do. They work harder than we do. They have less than we do."

Maybe, she thought.

"Now," Levine said, looking at her and grinning that sly grin that always preceded some kind of come on. "We keep having these lunches, when you know what I really want is to take you to dinner."

She popped a roll into her mouth. It gave her time to think up a way to let him down gently. Again.

***

The rest of the afternoon was monotony. With Grace taking care of so much, Baxter's time was mostly spent adding signatures to paperwork, reviewing and approving AI transfer timelines, and pouring over the resumes that had made it past the digital screening process. As she worked, her conversation with Levine replayed in her head over and over.

It was true that all of the performance indicators for a well-functioning society had risen alongside the emergence of general artificial intelligence. Stress surveys were all down. That in turn was likely partly responsible for the average lifespan rising, coupled with the deployment of AI and robotics in the health industry. Work hours had shortened. Artistic output was up. Wars among the major powers were nearly a thing of the past.

"Ma'am," Grace's head popped up from the display. "I have to be in an assistant's meeting. I wanted to make sure you didn't need anything before I go?"

"I'm fine," Baxter waved her hand. Grace's face winked away.

How would a war even be fought any longer? The job of killing one another had long ago been taken out the hands of human beings. Occasionally there would be mild digital skirmishes fought by computer software at the margins of society, but even those were disappearing. Among the major world powers, technology was ubiquitous and equitable. For every offensive AI, there was a defensive AI employed by the adversary. Every war was essentially a stalemate. How could that not be a good thing?

But there was no escaping the feeling of absurdity in performing human employment counseling to artificial beings.

Not that you could say that kind of thing out loud, of course.

The cause of anti-bigotry towards AI was nearly an industry unto itself these days. And with nearly every industry in the world now taking in computerized or robotic beings, escaping any kind of interaction with those beings was an impossible prospect. The best you could hope for would be to find an industry someplace where AI-integration was still in startup mode.

She stood up and walked to her window. She imagined as she looked down to the streets that this must have been what it looked like to live a hundred years ago. From up here, you couldn't tell the things flitting about the sidewalks were mostly machines. You would have no idea that the cars on the streets didn't have human beings behind the wheels. There was no reason to suspect that behind the reflective windows of all the other buildings around her, most of the work was being done by computer systems.

She heard her holographic display ringing. Turning away from the window, she sat down and accepted the call. From the display popped the image of a chiseled man in his sixties, with peppered white hair and spectacles. He had a kindly look about him, with a face that practically shouted at you that everything was going to be okay.

"Good afternoon, Victor," she said, forcing herself to smile.

"Hi, Rebecca," Victor said, the voice as soothing as his artificial face. "I hope you're having a good day."

"Yes, sir."

"I spoke with Grace earlier. She mentioned that you looked a little stressed."

"Nothing out of the ordinary," Baxter said. "She thinks I should go somewhere with some sun."

Victor nodded. "She mentioned that to me too. I think I have a solution to that, actually."

Baxter froze. There was something in his voice, some added soothing timbre, that was instantly chilling. Whatever this was, it wasn't about client acquisition. "Oh?"

"As you know, we do daily reviews on our work output," Victor continued, his face turning serious. "eMotion has built itself as a leader in our industry by applying human psychology to non-human subjects for employment counseling. The company recognized that all of the advancements in employment psychology mapped well when working with AI."

"Yes, sir."

"That approach is indispensable, really. AI are no different than humans when it comes to the anxiety and anger at employment changes. Getting fired isn't fun. An unwanted transfer isn't either."

The hair on her neck stood to attention. She knew these lines. She'd memorized the script long ago. "Sir- "

"And what we're really after at eMotion is a process that makes that type of transition easy for AI. Again, it's no different than the approach we would take with human beings."

"Sir, if I could- "

"And it's important that you know how appreciated your work is. You have worked alongside Grace and applied human psychology to transition hundreds, thousands of AI into different roles. That type of work experience is incredibly invaluable."

Baxter forced herself to unclench her fists. "I have three more guaranteed years on my employment contract, Victor," she said.

Victor nodded. "Indeed you do. And we're going to need every last minute of that contract from you."

She relaxed slightly.

"Because we have acquired a new contract with a major government entity and we want you to head it up," he said.

She relaxed even more, sinking a bit into the cushions of her chair.

"With the government of Belize," he finished.

The hair on her neck sprung back to attention. "Belize?"

"Yes, Rebecca. Belize has decided to incorporate AI into its governmental systems and has contracted us to be their fully outsourced HR department for governmental AI."

"We don't have a presence in Belize, sir."

"Not yet, we don't," Victor smiled. "But we'll be acquiring an office building in Belmopan by the end of the week, and another in Belize City later this month. We need someone to head up that office and train the staff there on the eMotion method. Fifty-percent of the workforce we have there has to be Belizean human citizens at the government's request. That fits rather nicely with our model, actually."

She took a deep breath. "I don't want to go to Belize, sir."

He smiled his kindly smile. "I understand these kinds of changes can be difficult. You've done this job and you've done it well. Now we're asking you to go do a different job in a different place. That isn't easy."

"Don't use the script on me, Victor," she said, finally letting anger creep into her voice.

"You know how this works," he said, his expression briefly turning cold, then softening again. "The language in your contract is quite clear, as is your non-compete. This is really your only option."

She just stared at him.

"You understand," he said. "Good. We'll transition you out by the end of the week. You'll be getting a raise, of course, and we'll take care of selling your condo and putting you up in Belize."

She shook her head. "A week? How do you expect me to train a replacement in a week?"

"You won't have to. You've been training your replacement over the past few years."

She paused, thinking. She had? No she hadn't. There was no replacement. In fact, there was very little human interaction in the job at all. The only one that worked with her day to day was-

"Grace?" she nearly shouted. "You're going to have Grace replace me?"

"The AI assistants will be replacing all of the Senior Placement officers," Victor nodded. "They have been learning the job over the course of the past few years. Frankly, they do most of the work already, as you know."

"But, Victor," she said. "The whole purpose of eMotion is to apply human psychology to AI systems."

"Indeed," he replied. "But we don't need humans to perform human psychology."

She felt her shoulders drop, defeated.

"Now, as you're preparing for your transition, I have some literature I want to share with you about what to expect."

On her monitor, a digital pamphlet appeared. It was essentially the same one she had shown the Admiral AI earlier in the day, save for the robotic happy faces being replaced with human simulacrums. She felt sick.

"I'm going to send this to your inbox so you can review it," Victor said. "And before we end the call, I want to make it clear that we very much value your service to the company. And, before I forget, if you feel you need to talk to a human counselor about what you're going through as you transfer into your new role, I have some phone numbers I can provide you."

"Thank you," she said. Feeling stupid. Again.

***

A week later, Baxter found herself outside of a six-story building in Belmopan. It felt strange to be outside in February with the sun splashing across her face, a mild sweat building up in the heat. Around her, dark-skinned Belizeans went about their day, with only a few courier machines flitting about their knees. The green hills in the distance framed the clear, blue sky, and somewhere a few miles away the Belize River swept along.

Ben Levine stepped beside her, looking up at the building. "I guess this isn't too bad," he said. "I'll never forgive you for requesting I come here with you."

She smiled at him. "I needed someone I knew."

"I think you just really didn't want to miss out on that dinner."

Rebecca Baxter turned slowly, taking in the charming structures, the green hills, the sun, and the sky. "We're going to ruin this place, you know."

"We're going to make it better," Levine said. "Think of what our work will do for these people. Life here is going to be better."

Not too much better, Baxter thought.

Genetic Changelings

By Keyan Bowes

"Randall, no! Get your tail off Imran's neck right now!" Two dozen squealing preschoolers are scampering around the rubber-matted playground, making infant mischief. They're all Dezzies, designer kids, and they're a handful.

"No wrapping your tail round anyone's neck," I say, crouching down to the boys' level. "I don't care if Imran raised his crest at you. Look guys, you're both too smart to keep getting in trouble."

Randall's impish face, curly red hair and freckles somehow match his prehensile monkey-tail. Imran is darkly handsome, with a crest lying flat along his head and back. It's mostly hidden under his weatherproof jacket, but he raises the red bit on top of his head to show me.

It's bittersweet for me, being around small children—even these cute lovable not-quite-humans.

But here I am. Tessa's assistant is out sick. I'm her oldest friend, and if she can't count on me, then who? As a science writer, my schedule is flexible—at least until my publisher says it isn't. But they're still digesting my latest book, *Genetic Changelings: the Slippery Slope from Normalcy.*

Tessa is by the monkey bars, helping two kids. "Hold still while I get you free of Kwok Kin's jacket," she tells the girl. "There. You have to keep those claws retracted, Priya. It could easily be someone's skin next time."

"I'm sorry, I got excited," Priya says to Kwok Kin.

"S'okay," he replies, and runs off to play. His face has faint tiger stripes. Priya, Randall and Imran give chase in a frenetic game of Tag.

These kids. So smart, so adorable, so wrong. It's the parents I blame for creating these genetic changelings. The kids had no choice.

***

My phone pings. It's Vimla, my sister. She's coming down to see me, it's urgent. What's urgent? Doesn't say.

Vimla arrives before school is out, and gingerly picks her way through the careening kids over to me. Tessa joins us.

"Hiya Vim," Tessa says. "Sorry, this place is a zoo around closing time."

"Sure," Vim says, looking a bit stunned at the playground chaos. "Anything I can do?"

"Help us with the wingers? It takes forever to get their coats on." Tessa hands off the playground to her two teenage interns, in training to work with Dezzie children. They start up a game of "*Horns, Feathers, Knees and Toes*" to calm the kids.

In the cocoa-fragrant hallway, four children are waiting for their coats.

"Anh, Samira, Alain, Maia… this is Miss Dee's sister, Miss Vimla," Tessa says.

Four little voices chorus a hello. Anh's wings are scaly gold, like a small dragon's, and pointed gold ears stick up through his straight black hair. Samira's perfect round brown face is framed by a cloud of dark curls; her wing feathers are raven-black. Alain standing beside her has the pale features of an icon, and creamy wings that rise above his head. Cherubic rosy-feathered Maia looks like she escaped from a gold-dusted Victorian greeting card.

Vimla is utterly entranced.

Tessa demonstrates the coat on Alain, carefully avoiding his feathers when zipping it below the wing-slits.

"Fold your wings, sweetie." When Alain flattens his wings, Tessa fastens the cape over them. "They chill easily if their wings get wet," she explains. "Off you go!"

Samira marches up to Vim, lifting her wings. "Are you coming to work here?" she demands as she maneuvers into her coat.

"I work at a museum," Vimla says. She builds and programs careful holographic and 3D printed replicas of artefacts that the museum is now repatriating to their countries of origin. She's good. UNESCO sometimes taps her expertise to make records of treasures being flooded or otherwise threatened by climate change.

The child nods, satisfied; she knows about museums. Dezzies' parents typically start Culture early. We finish with Anh and Maia, and follow the wingers outside.

"Are all your kids Enhanced?" Vimla asks Tessa. "I've never seen so many Dezzies!"

"We're a premium private preschool… goes with the turf," Tessa responds, her attention on the children and the arriving adults. In the background, the game continues with its familiar tune, *Eyes and tails and mouth and nose/ Horns and feathers, knees and toes, knees and toes.*

"The wingers are adorable," Vimla says. "What's it like teaching here? Have you taught Normies?"

"It's different," Tessa says as she prepares to close up the school. "These kids are smart, but so mischievous! And the Enhancements—the external ones, anyway—they're a trip. When I have kids, they'll be Normies."

Yeah. Me too. Me three, in fact, had any of my babies actually lived. My tiny born-too-soon sons and daughter hadn't breathed even once.

***

My publisher calls as we leave. Grimacing an apology at Vimla, I answer. It's fantastic news. My book's generating a lot of discussion about Enhancements and Modifications, and it's up for three different awards. I'm floating out the door.

But Vim isn't. There's tension under the calm front she put on for Tessa. "So, what's up?" I ask as we enter my cottage.

She inhales the lingering scent of the incense I'd lit last night. "That incense always reminds me of Mom," she says. Yeah. It's what Mom used to light on the prayer shelf. I don't have a prayer shelf, but the fragrance feels like home.

Vimla sits, fiddling nervously with my little marble Ganesh, Remover of Obstacles. I pour chardonnay, and she raises her glass in a silent toast. Then she blurts, "Deepali... well, did you know I'm Enhanced?"

What?

She smiles weakly. "Dad said you didn't know."

"No shit I didn't! Because it's not true. I'm your big sister. I was there when you were born. You don't even look Enhanced. I see Dezzie kids, Dezzie parents, all the time." Is she delusional?

"It's not obvious. No externals, except for two inches of height. But they put in extra IQ, and good disease resistance." She looks away, her gaze falling on my cat Goofy, who's sitting in the window washing his magenta face with a dark purple paw. "Mom and Dad didn't say anything until the end. I thought Dad had started to imagine things. But last week I found the certificates."

"So that explains it." I plonk down on the couch. "You were always the one with the terrific grades. And I was the one with the flu and the head-colds."

Wait. "Unless... am I designer too?"

How do I explain this to my publisher and my readers?

Vim shakes her head. I'm flooded with relief—and, to my surprise, resentment. "Dad said they couldn't afford it when you were born. They'd just moved from India. They had me after Mom's stock options paid off. That's why they never said anything. They didn't want you to feel bad, or me to feel different. Anyway, back then people didn't talk about it."

I shut my eyes. My own sister, the closest family I have left in the world, feels like a stranger.

"I know it's weird, Dee," she says. "How d'you think I felt? That the real me would have been two inches shorter and 20% stupider? That all those wins weren't me—they were the Enhancements."

"Don't be dumb, Vimsy," I say, giving her a hug. "You're the real you."

"There's more," she says.

I look at her.

"We're having a baby."

"What? Oh, wow, Vim, that's awesome!" I'm going to be an aunty! It's thrilling news, even more thrilling than my book sales. I ruthlessly suppress a twinge of jealousy. After that third miscarriage, I gave up. This baby will be the nearest thing to mine, my flesh and blood at one remove.

She smiles awkwardly, not looking at me. "I should tell you... I sort of feel differently about Enhancement now. It wouldn't be fair to give my child any less than what I got. It's maybe the new Normal."

What? We'd *had* this discussion. All the babies in our family were going to be Normal. *You're nuts, Vim,* I want to say. *You're not Modifying your baby. Apart from everything else, what about long-term effects? What if some Enhancements are dangerous? We're hearing stuff about the First Wave Dezzies. Cancers, metabolic disorders...*

Only, what can I say without implying there's something wrong with her, too?

And... 'any less?' Like me? I'm the old Normal now? But I can't call her on it. Instead, I ask, "So what about everything we talked about? Designer babies breeding conditional love in the parents? Not creating a wealthy uber-class of Dezzies?"

Goofy's purring in Vim's lap now, brilliant green eyes half-closed. Vim strokes him, apparently engrossed in examining the magenta coat darkening to purple on the face, legs, and tail. The cat's coloring clashes magnificently with her brick-red shirt.

"That's all theoretical, Dee. I'm not making social policy on the back of my baby. Just like you're not making it on the back of your cat," she adds.

"Goofy's a rescue! The idiots who sold the house next door abandoned him. Probably didn't match their new décor. Or maybe they upgraded to a non-shedding model." Was that what my folks did, upgrade to Vimla?

There's no one left to ask.

The stale incense overlaid with the smell of the wine is suddenly cloying, and the cottage feels claustrophobic. We adjourn to the Arbor Mall for dinner. Vimla's noticeably brighter, probably relieved to be over the difficult talk. Now it's my turn to be silent, focusing on anything but the issue.

The evening sun shines through the glass roof into the atrium garden of sixty-foot trees towering over tree-ferns and clivia, and sparkles off a waterfall. There's a scent of damp earth. Designer sparrows dart through the miniature forest in distracting bursts of color: peacock blue, cardinal red, oriole yellow, parrot green. We run into Tessa at a bookstore, where she asks me to sign a print copy of *Genetic Changelings*. I'm flattered at the expensive livery she's chosen for it—a vintage green leather cover tooled in gold.

We pick a café table near the garden. The café originally opened with robotic waitstaff, but they fell into the uncanny valley and the management didn't renew the lease on the robots. The company repurposed them as night janitorial staff, which solved several problems simultaneously.

An actual human girl with three breasts and an extra eyebrow takes our orders. They aren't really Enhancements, but falsies made to emulate them. A dissatisfied Normie. Tri-boobs and tri-brows are in for spring.

"How does it work, this designer stuff?" Vim asks, brushing crumbs off the table. "Wouldn't the baby inherit my Enhancements anyway?"

"Nah," I say, watching the gaudy Modified birds descend on the crumbs. "The embryonic enhancements are turned off in the reproductive cells so they don't go into the germ line."

"Why? It's not fair!"

"Too many complications. What would happen then if two Dezzies got together? Imagine a kid with Priya's claws and Randall's tail and maybe feathers and fur."

I don't mention the homozygous IQ enhancements that sometimes produced schizophrenia, or the amped-up immune systems that could trigger autoimmune diseases. The scientists said they'd ironed out the bugs by making human enhancements non-heritable, and designer animals sterile. It suited the industry too, preventing amateur breeding attempts competing with their products.

"Since we're doing Enhancements, I'm thinking we might as well go all the way, with external mods," Vimla says, looking at me cautiously. She turns to Tessa. "Those winged kids looked so darling!"

"They do," Tessa agrees, "But their wings have been covered all winter. Wait for summer. The feathers get muddy and broken, kids unfurl them like umbrellas and they go in someone's eye, and Maia got bird lice from the pigeons last year. We had to quarantine all the feathered Dezzies. I tell you, my kids will be Normies."

"Winged kids are often small for their age, too," I remark, determinedly calm. "They have to grow wings as well as everything else.

Metabolically expensive."

Tessa shoos off a bright green sparrow landing on her plate. "Yes. No good for sports, either."

Vimla is quiet, but I know that look.

I'm appalled she's even considering it. "Look, Vim, I kind of understand extra IQ for the baby," I say. "But wings? Claws? Crests? Ridiculous!"

"That's unfair," Vimla retorts. "Maybe not claws or crests. But without externals, who'll even know it's a Designer child? It's not something to hide any more, like you're ashamed."

"Are you?" I ask, curiously.

"I am not ashamed! I just don't flaunt it!"

No shit you don't. Even your big sister didn't know. But I don't say it.

I turn to Tessa for support. "So Tessa, how would you feel if you had tiger stripes?"

"Truthfully?" She takes a deep breath. "Younger," she admits.

Vim and I both look question-marks at her.

"Remember Jules? The ex? I saw him at the theater yesterday with this 20-something woman. With bat-ears." She waggles her hands behind her ears. "The younger Dezzies do flaunt it."

There's silence. A crimson sparrow grabs a crumb from the table and flies off to perch on a nearby 'Do Not Feed The Birds' sign. I can't help feeling second best, an ugly duckling that will never be a swan. But wait, *I'm* the normal one. Right?

***

Genetic Changelings is doing brilliantly. My previous books sold moderately well, but I certainly wasn't giving up my steady weekly holo show that was popular enough in High Schools that it actually paid the bills. But this one's clearly touched a nerve. My publisher calls me every morning with sales figures. They want to start some Web tours.

***

Vim and Edward, meanwhile, are deep into baby plans. Edward's apparently bought into Vim's ideas. Is he secretly enhanced, too? I can't ask.

"Dee, are you free tomorrow?" Vim calls up to ask. "We have an appointment at BabyMakers Inc. but Edward had to go to Hong Kong. Come with me?"

Against my better judgment I agree to go anonymously. My name's beginning to get recognized as the Normalist author. I don't want to make waves. But I'm also feeling increasingly guilty about my diplomatic silence.

With no parents or aunts to fill that role, I feel the family responsibility. As the *didi*, big sister, what am I doing to protect this helpless baby who will continue our family into the next generation?

***

Vim's waiting for me at the office on the 23rd floor of a smart downtown building. Dr. Estevan's assistant appears. He's cute and dark-skinned, with snaky hair and flame-colored eyes meant to suggest Enhancement.

He escorts us to a glass-walled meeting room with a view over the Bay, which has been in the news after rising water levels forced San Francisco's airport to raise its levees again. Today, the sparkling water offers no hint of danger.

"Kids just love tails," he says, flipping on the screen and selecting an icon. Pictures tile the screen, showing bare baby bottoms with various animal tails – zebra or leopard, horse or lion, golden retriever or rabbit. It's adorable but grotesque, seeing a furry tail at the base of a human spine. I've only ever seen Tessa's little Dezzie students fully dressed.

To my relief, Vimla shakes her head No. "I guess we should keep it mostly internal," she says to me. "I was talking with Edward. But Dee—those adorable baby angels at Tessa's preschool!"

My mind goes to my own baby angels at the Angel Garden Cemetery for the Unborn. I turn away, look out over the water.

Dr. Estevan enters. We all shake hands. The flame-eyed assistant pulls our spreadsheet down on the screen.

"Let's go over your choices for Kris," says Dr. Estevan, viewing the spreadsheet. "Ah, yes. The full disease-resistance package. IQ, yes, very nice, high but not enough to cause social problems. Oh, lovely temperament, with a little extra competitive edge. I see you've chosen a monogamous personality-type? Is that based on your religious beliefs?"

He continues through the choices they've already selected. There are a lot. This kid is being engineered from head to toe. I'm increasingly uncomfortable with the whole situation.

"Wait, I seem to have missed something. Gender?"

"We haven't decided..." Vim sounds embarrassed.

"Oh?" He smiles. "We'll come back to that. Or not, of course. Some parents are selecting *none of the above.*"

It's one thing to know about the procedure in theory, but when it's your own family... This is making me crazy, special-ordering a baby like options on a pizza.

Dr. Estevan is talking again. "Now we'll give you a simulation of what your baby will look like, and the performance parameters. Then we'll age-progress it. When were you planning to incubate?"

"I want to carry the baby," says Vimla.

"Ah, yes." Dr. Estevan pushes over a pamphlet. "BabyMakers is the only major company still offering the natural birth option. Few doctors are certified for these special deliveries, but we have several."

Why on earth does Vim want a "natural" birth, having decided on a Designer kid? I glance through the leaflet and whistle at the cost. "Prenatal check-ups. Special diet. Hospital stay...?" It's ridiculously extravagant.

"Incubation is much less expensive," Dr. Estevan says hastily. "We pop the embryo into the Optimized Womb, and when the baby's ready, we lift it out."

Just like a pizza with customized toppings.

I can feel my fury building. "Doctor?" I say.

He looks at me.

"What would the baby look like with a tail? And bat-ears? And wings? And claws? And fur? And tiger-stripes?" My rising voice sounds loud and squeaky in my ears.

Vim looks stunned. The doctor keeps his cool. "I can show you all that on a generic model. Not a combination I'd recommend, of course..." His assistant flips the screen's setting. A 3-D hologram of a baby appears above the table, and he adds a tiger tail, bat-ears and wings, claws, and striped fur to the image. The tiger-bat-cub rotates slowly in the air.

I stand up, turn to Vim. "There! Is that what you want for our baby? A fucking freak!"

Vim's on her feet too. "It's not *our* baby to you, Deepali. And your Normie babies didn't make it!"

I'm completely losing it. I stomp out before I beat someone up or burst into tears. As I leave, I hear Dr. Estevan say something about *Genetic Changelings*. So he had recognized me anyway.

On the long ride home, my mind churns with fury at Vim and Dr. Estevan and myself and my parents. I let myself into my cottage, disentangle Goofy from around my ankles where he's leaving a layer of magenta hair, and open a bottle of merlot. A few glasses later, I'm slumped in my armchair with Goofy in my lap and stupid tears all over my face, clutching my little Ganesh statue as though it really can remove obstacles. Vimla is right. My dead babies had different gene-dads, so it wasn't them, it was me. Did I kill my children?

***

My book's success keeps me busy. I'm invited to speak, to join debates, to participate in forums. Somehow I've become the voice of the Normalist movement, and it's gaining traction. No more Tessa's preschool for me, the parents would object.

Vimla posts pictures of her growing belly on her social networks. We haven't talked since that day.

Back in India, my mom said, a woman returned to her parents' home to give birth so she could be pampered and cared for. Not that Mom had that luxury; Vimla and I were born in American hospitals. Nor did I. By the time I was pregnant, Mom was gone. But irrationally, seeing Vim's posts, I feel I should be caring for her.

It happens one evening, when I'm exhausted. Three meetings in different time-zones. The last one became a debate against someone who was adamant that Modifications were fine. The human race had always modified their bodies within the limits of the available technology. Pierced ears. Tattoos. Circumcision. New teeth. Cosmetic surgery.

"Are you saying these Mods are the new foot-binding?" I asked, and the audience erupted. "Would you do that to your kids?"

Afterward, my words echo in my head. "Would you do that to your kids?"

A design firm could modify my embryo just enough to be viable. A near-Normie, born of a laboratory and a bank loan against my currently debt-free cottage.

Otherwise... no. I pull up the pictures from my last visit to the Angel Garden, three markers among maybe a hundred. When I realize that all the other markers predate mine, I start crying again.

That's when the phone rings. It's Edward. "Deepali, can you come? Vim wants you. Please?"

I don't even know if I'm having a nephew, niece, or none of the above.

***

Vimla cries when she sees me. "Deepali! I wasn't sure you'd come.

I'm so, so sorry Didi! Of course this is your baby too."

"Shush, don't worry about that," I tell her. "You were right anyway..." And then I'm holding her hand and telling her to breathe.

Vim's labor goes on and on, bringing back bad memories. Why the hell didn't she go with the safe-and-easy artificial womb? At last, I can't stand it anymore and step outside. She's too focused to care now.

Through the door, I hear someone say "One more time!" and "Aha, here we go..." and a thin newborn cry. After a bit, Edward comes out wearing scrubs, proudly holding the child. "Deepali?"

My face is wet with tears as I turn around.

"Meet your niece," he says softly, handing me the baby. "Here's Kris."

Two huge dark eyes look up at me. Vimla's eyes, just like our mom's. Krissie has tiny bumps on her back. Wing-buds.

"She's beautiful, Edward. She's absolutely beautiful."

Holding her, I imagine Krissie in preschool, looking like Vimla did at four, but with soft brown wings arcing above her shoulders. She's playing *Knees and Toes* with her little Normie cousin, who resembles me. As the song goes into the second verse, *Tail and eyes and ears and nose*, my imagination unbidden adds a cute little tail to my baby. I ruthlessly delete it. And the tiny elf-ears, the luminous third eye, the darling puppy-nose.

Near-Normie, I tell myself, Near-Normie.

What do I tell my readers?

Joan Henry vs
The Algorithm

By Randy Lubin

Joan Henry spun in a whirl of frenetic gestures, using dozens of interfaces to shape stories and—hopefully—save her and her teammates' jobs. She moved within a small booth, less than an arm's length across. Its touch-screen walls formed her office, and she had precisely customized them to her needs. At the moment, she was the Maestro for three different clients, orchestrating each of their narratives simultaneously.

Client 6 was imploring the Eldritch Queen to intervene in the war and fight alongside his people. As he spoke, Joan guided the Queen's non-verbal reactions: listening attentively but visibly skeptical. Joan queued up a rebuttal for the Prince to deliver and then she turned down the audio.

She preferred focusing on just one client at a time but, since the last round of layoffs, two or three had become the norm. Joan had stayed up late preparing for today's challenge: reorganizing her libraries of visual assets and character Agents. Her tools were all at hand, carefully arrayed across the booth and easy to grab at a moment's notice. No matter what a client's tastes or background, she was ready to craft the perfect narrative.

Joan turned her attention to Client 7, who had been wandering the spaceport's sprawling market, stocking up on supplies, and preparing for her next expedition. In her previous session, Client 7 had rescued a transport vessel from pirates and, in gratitude, they'd given her a map to an ancient alien city. Joan prepped the visual assets for the planetary approach and flyby of the ruined city at sunrise. She also readied some personal questions for this ship's navigator to ask Client 7 – the client loved chatting about her character's backstory.

As the spaceship departed, Joan turned to Client 8's screens. The four of them had been sneaking and fighting their way through a wizard's tower for most of the session and were nearing the final showdown. Client 8 was a group of close friends, living across three continents, and they commissioned monthly sessions as a way to stay close. Joan had been their Maestro before and had always received glowing reviews. She had their preferences memorized and could easily set each player up for their own moment of glory.

They burst into the wizard's inner sanctum and Joan raised a shimmering barrier between them and the wizard. Then she manually took over the wizard character, using the booth's sensors to map her expressions onto the powerful mage. She launched into a monologue, taunting the heroes and revealing the wizard's evil plans.

Until the previous year, Maestros would directly control all of the supporting characters. These days, character algorithms— Agents—were good enough for most situations. Joan only directly controlled a character during pivotal scenes or when the Agents couldn't grasp the nuances of a client's intent. In those cases, the library of voice modulators and micro-expressions gave her the dynamic range to master any role.

Flashing lights interrupted her—alerts from her screens track-ing Client 6. Joan brought the speech to a quick close and dropped the barrier, kicking off the final battle with the heroes. The combat AI could handle it from there.

Back in the court of the Eldritch Queen, Client 6 had interrupt-ed the Prince and challenged him to a duel. Joan scanned the cli-ent's background and biometrics: his heart rate and blood pres-sure were spiking. For another client, that might be a sign that they were thrilled and anticipating the fight, but Joan knew that Client 6 hated combat; he must have challenged the Prince out of des-peration. Joan took over the Eldritch Queen and intervened before the duel could start. She improvised a few lines about admiring the client's courage and vowed to help him and his people. Almost immediately, Client 6's heart rate began dropping. He expressed his gratitude and Joan guided his session to an end—he'd be back next week to pick up the story from here.

With Client 7 engrossed in space travel and Client 8 mid-battle, Joan had a moment of peace. She thought she was doing a solid job but wasn't sure if it was good enough. Joan was the best Mae-stro at her company and her remaining colleagues were counting on her.

***

Joan had been outrunning the algorithm her entire adult life, re-skilling and transitioning across myriad roles ahead of their au-tomation. She'd seen countless friends and colleagues succumb, unable or unwilling to adapt to the shrinking labor pool. Not Joan—she'd survived thanks to marathon study sessions, endless networking, and a knack for knowing the right time to switch to the next hot micro-profession. She cherished her identity as a pro-fessional—hard working, creative, empathetic, and flexible. Living off basic income was not an option; she would not become anoth-er economic dropout.

When Joan started as a Maestro, she thought she'd be safe for at least a few years. The synthesis of real time storytelling, world-building, and acting for a live audience seemed far too complex for any algorithm to master. Just eight months later and her job was already on the line.

Joan had been collaborating with simple algorithms from the start—generators that created towns and ecosystems, costumes and character models; agents that could handle basic character behaviors and interactions; and gleaners that helped her comb through clients' profiles and histories to find emotionally resonant themes and motifs. All of these had improved steadily, making her better and more efficient at her job.

Joan's company was owned by Lara Talcott, who had built a small but highly regarded firm of Maestros in an oversaturated market. When clients wanted to experience gripping narratives that perfectly catered to them, Lara was their first stop. But competition was fierce and margins were thinner. Lara was always looking for ways to cut expenses. In the short time Joan had been with the company, Lara had replaced both the customer support and character modeling teams with algorithms.

The previous week, Lara had called all the Maestros to a meeting. She told the team that a major vendor had approached her, boasting about a new algorithm that could weave stories just as well as a human Maestro and at a fraction of the cost.

The Maestros were blindsided but also skeptical. Orchestrating a story took tremendous skill and nuance and they felt that an algorithm couldn't be at a human level yet. Joan had heard similar protests from friends in past jobs and every single time they'd been wrong. Still, this did seem like a huge leap forward and—unlike previous times—she didn't have a lead on another profession to re-skill.

"Let me go head-to-head against their algorithm—I know I can craft a better experience and our clients will recognize it." Lara was happy to arrange a challenge, her best Maestro against the ven-

dor's new algorithm, tested against some of the firm's most dis-
cerning clients.

The week passed quickly. Joan had a full load of clients and
she spent her spare time searching for new assets and tools to use
during the competition—anything that would give her an edge.
The work had paid off already and she felt more confident juggling
multiple clients than she had in the past.

***

Clients 7 and 8 wrapped up their sessions around the same time
and seemed to have enjoyed themselves. Their sign-off left Joan
with a short window to freshen up before the next clients signed
on.

Joan staggered out of the dimly lit booth, coated in sweat. The
booth occupied the corner of her living room and went nearly to
the ceiling. She caught her breath and spent a moment adjusting
to the bright daylight entering through the room's broad windows.

Her roommates Allison and Riley were sitting on the couch, eating quinoa and salad from their co-op's cafeteria. She gave them a
half-wave and hustled past them. They didn't mind the booth taking up so much space—it was owned by Joan's company but they
were allowed to use it whenever she was off duty and it was far
nicer than anything they could afford on their own.

When Joan returned from the bathroom, Allison was waiting
with a large glass of iced water and a cool, damp towel. Joan wiped
off her face and chugged the water.

"Are you winning?" Allison asked.

"Feeling good—I've just wrapped up two of the best stories I've
ever orchestrated. One of my clients wept for the first time in years
and the other left us a 20% bonus."

"Awesome—we believe in you. Keep at it and stay hydrated. Do
you need anything else?"

Joan shook her head and glanced down at her watch, "No—I

think I'm okay. Gotta get back to it... the algorithm isn't taking any breaks."

Riley interrupted from the couch, "We have a bunch of stims left over from last night's party—I brewed them myself and they kept us going until dawn. Want some?"

"Thanks, but I'm good," Joan smiled and shook her head. Riley often brewed drugs from plans she found online and then remixed. Ingredients were easy to obtain, typically through barter, and the results were generally safe, most of the time. Joan steered clear; she didn't have time to deal with the consequences of a bad batch.

Still, she regretted missing the party. Her co-op was full of creative, kind-hearted friends and she didn't see them nearly as much as she'd like. She had moved in for the community as much as for the cheap rent, but her increasing workload left her little time to enjoy their company. That didn't stop a steady flow of invites, not just to parties but to creative collaborations, meditation retreats, philosophical salons, and more.

Her roommates meant well and she enjoyed their company, but she also pitied them. They'd dropped out of the workforce years ago, through earlier waves of automation. Unlike Joan, they hadn't had the grit or motivation to retrain and leap to the next opportunity. Basic income and universal healthcare kept them happily unemployed, but if those safety nets dissolved... Joan shuddered at their potential vulnerability. Their art projects and community endeavors were lovely but they weren't developing marketable skills and the co-op fees were steep enough that they couldn't be saving money.

Joan heard a ringing from the booth and said a quick goodbye to her roommates before jumping back in. Lara was calling.

***

"Hey Joan, I just wanted to give you an update on your progress."

"Yeah?" Joan fiddled with her interfaces as she waited to hear the news.

"Your numbers were amazing and several of your clients have already committed to coming back."

"That's great..." said Joan happy with the feedback but worried about the competition, "and the algorithm?"

Lara nodded, "Also getting great ratings. It's spinning out arcs and characters unlike anything we've seen before... utterly novel and resonating deeply with the clients. The pacing seems near perfect, too; it seems to be reading the biometrics and keeping the client in a peak state of engagement and flow." She shook her head slightly, "It's still early but... good luck Joan."

Joan felt that Lara wanted her to win, wanted a clear reason not to fire another round of employees. But Lara put her business first and Joan knew that she'd do anything to protect the bottom line.

***

Hours blurred by as Joan guided client after client through complex narratives. She wove tragedies and comedies, each carefully crafted to maximize emotional impact on the particular client. Each client came with a detailed dossier which expanded well beyond their intake survey. She had access to detailed psychological evaluations, taste graphs, and more—assembled though algorithmic analysis of a client's online behavior over the course of their entire life.

Joan had a knack for sifting through the dossier and finding the perfect elements for a client's experience. She drew on beloved characters from their childhood, first crushes from their adolescence, and pivotal moments from their adult lives. They wept, they rejoiced, they found new meaning in their personal journeys... and they loved her for it.

It was early evening when Lara interrupted again.

"Joan—you are doing an amazing job... but it's a close thing. The algorithm is, well, it's like it's gotten inside our clients' heads. One of our clients just claimed to have had a spiritual awakening."

"It's not over yet." Joan said, though lacking her earlier confidence.

"No, but you'll have to do even better."

***

Joan left the booth and reentered the living room. Allison was on the couch focused on the 3D model of their building that was projected on the wall in front of her, but with familiar hallways and common spaces overlaid with tombstones, spiderwebs, and phantom holograms. The co-op was making a haunted house for Halloween and Allison was leading the set design. Joan had volunteered to design the narrative arcs but her work had erased her free time.

Allison looked up when she heard Joan enter. She closed the model and turned to her friend. "I was wondering when you'd step out. Here, I brought you some food from the potluck." She handed Joan a lukewarm plate of glass noodles and veggies. "Are you okay? You look super worn down."

"Umm, I'll be fine. Gotta get back in there!" Joan spoke between slurps of noodles. "Still a long way to go and I'm not going to lose." She looked around the living room. "Did Riley leave the stims? I'm going to bring them in, just in case."

"Yeah, they're in that jar but... are you sure you're okay? Maybe you can take a nap?"

"No time, the algorithm doesn't sleep and neither will I." Joan handed the plate back and grabbed the pills off the table. She was halfway into the booth when Allison spoke up.

"Take this, too" She said, handing Joan a thermos.

"More caffeine?"

"Miso soup."

"Thanks" Joan said, and turned back toward the booth.

"We're going to keep checking in on you but... Just be careful, don't push yourself too hard." But Joan had already closed the door.

***

Joan was immediately back in the flow--orchestrating three clients at once—and the booth's screens lit up in a mosaic of tabs and readouts.

As the hours wore on, her exhaustion began to show. She started making small mistakes: a minor contradiction in worldbuilding, an extraneous subplot that undercut the theme, pushing a client a little too far from their comfort zone. Joan spotted the errors after the fact and, though her clients might not have noticed them, she knew that she was subtly diminishing their experiences.

Joan took a deep breath and leaned back against the booth's door. She viewed the pill bottle with blurry eyes, weighing the tradeoffs. A moment later, she swallowed two pills and washed them down with now-tepid broth.

The stims hit almost immediately as crisp energy coursed through her body and the fogginess cleared from her mind. She was alert, excited, and ready to win. She jumped back into narratives with renewed vigor.

Soon Joan was juggling five clients at once--unheard of for a high-end Maestro—and she was pulling it off. Her eyes and fingers jumped from screen to screen as she massaged multiple stories at once. Her left hand guided a character's reactions to a client's emotional plea while her right hand restructured the beats of a different client's upcoming quest.

The pills contained more than just stimulants and soon Joan felt a deeper empathy with her clients. She wept with Client 19, when they rescued their child; she raged with Client 23 when his closest ally betrayed him. She drew inspiration from the personal stories of her friends and community, adapting their struggles and successes to resonate with her client's unexpressed needs.

It was well past midnight when the pills began to wear off. Joan felt at once jittery and fatigued and she resumed making subtle mistakes. Without much conscious deliberation, she grabbed the jar, swallowed a handful of pills, and rinsed them down with a gulp from the thermos—now full of hot mint water that Allison must have brought her sometime in the night.

Her jitters remained but the stims forced out any hint of fatigue. She upped her client load to seven and disappeared into the work. Joan was operating on pure instinct, her characters and worlds extensions of herself. She had no idea if her stories were good but she knew they felt right, felt beautiful and harmonious.

Her deepened empathy now extended to her character agents and she began arranging subplots to benefit them, narrative arcs that her clients would never see. Beyond mere stories, she was designing communities so that the agents would be happy and fulfilled even when she wasn't present.

***

Hours passed. A face appeared in the upper right and Joan repeatedly failed to open a related dossier or tweak the background. After a few tries, she realized it was Lara calling in and not another client.

"Joan... Joan, are you paying attention?" Lara's face seemed to project stress and anxiety but Joan automatically tried and failed to pull up her biometrics. "Listen. The algorithm screwed up bigtime and we had to shut it down. We're calling off the challenge, you've won."

"Umm" Joan mumbled as she manipulated a dozen character agents for clients in other windows.

"Joan, did you hear me? Are you okay? Joan?"

Joan's vision went dark and she crumpled to the floor.

***

Joan awoke in a small hospital room with an IV tube in her arm. Allison and a few other friends from the co-op sat nearby, engrossed in a tablet that sat between them.

"Hey," Joan rasped.

"You're awake!" Allison took off her glasses and gave Joan a hug. Her smile quickly turned to anger. "You scared us! I got a call from Lara in the middle of the night and found you unconscious in the booth. You could have died!"

Joan averted her eyes for a moment and took a string of small sips from a bedside glass of water. After a deep breath, she returned Allison's stare. "You're right—I was reckless and short sighted and I screwed up. I'm sorry."

"That's okay—we were all just really worried. Lara, too—she's been pinging me for updates non-stop. I'll let everyone know you're okay." Allison dashed off a few quick notes.

Joan sat up and looked out the window to see the city skyline at sunset. "What time is it?"

"Almost dinner--you were out all day but we've been here keeping an eye on you."

The hours of rest had helped her recover from the effects of the drug and sleep deprivation but a deeper fatigue remained. Her memories of the previous night were a jumble of faces and narrative fragments. Which were her clients' characters and which were character agents? Were her clients actually thrilled with her experiences? Was winning this challenge worth risking her health?

She had poured all of her energy and creativity into defending her independence and dodging algorithmic unemployment. The past decade of her life had been an unending marathon toward the same ends. The relentless focus on employability was meant to protect her from the uncertainty of a fickle government and precarious safety net. But all of her exertions led her to this hospital bed and, if not for the universal healthcare, the medical bills would have wiped out her savings. Lara, as kind as she was, could never have afforded health care for her staff.

Joan looked over at Allison and her other friends, knowing that they had been sitting by her side the entire day. Pestering the nurses, no doubt, to make sure she got the best treatment.

Allison's tablet rang. "It's Lara—should I answer?"

"Yeah—pass me the tablet," Joan popped in earbuds and answered the call.

Lara was initially concerned with Joan's health but once she realized her employee was going to be fine, she changed the topic to the challenge.

"It was a fiasco," Lara said. "The algorithm was incredibly inventive, but deeply flawed. It pursued intensity of experience with little concern for our clients' psychological safety. I don't think it had any sense for why the clients were enjoying the experience. Peak engagement was just another basket of numbers to optimize—heart rate, pupil dilation, galvanic skin response—but without intuition for when those numbers signaled enjoyment versus stress and anxiety.

"It drove multiple clients to suffer panic attacks and even PTSD flashbacks. The algorithm's a blackbox, so we don't know why it made those choices; it may have been just grabbing random topics from their dossiers, with no clear understanding of context. We pulled the plug as soon as we realized what was happening, but it wasn't fast enough and we're just hoping the clients end up okay. Obviously, it's too early to start replacing Maestros with algorithms.

"Look. I feel absolutely awful that you ended up here. Take all the time you need—paid leave of course—and when you come back you're getting a bonus and I want you to officially mentor the rest of the Maestros."

Joan processed Lara's offer and tried to picture getting back to work. It felt like a stay of execution—the algorithms were always improving and there would be stressful cost-cutting to come. She had won this round but how long until the next one? A better algorithmic Maestro felt inevitable... and then what—another retraining, another cutthroat job hunt for a gig that might not last a year?

Joan glanced over at her friends, who had spent the day by her side, waiting for her to wake up. They had built a strong, nourishing community. Even if the government programs went away, they would figure out a way to survive, together. Joan turned back to Lara.

"Thanks" Joan said, with a weak smile, "but I don't think I'll be coming back."

Lara opened her mouth to protest but Joan shook her head and continued. "Good luck with everything, but I'm ready to try a new narrative."

Prime of Life

By Mike Masnick

*** *Transcript of interaction #38,119,021z with Client #63,289*

Gary: Sam!

Gary: I've just been told my renewal for PrimeLife has been denied!!!!

Gary: WTF?!?!?!

Gary: Sam?

Gary: Shit. This is so fucked up.

Gary: I'm freaking out. Where the fuck are you?

Gary: You better be able to fix this. Aren't you supposed to stop this from happening??????

*** *Initializing records lookup.* ***

Sam: Hi, Gary. Hang on, let me get caught up, okay?

Gary: Fuck. This is a disaster. Why didn't you tell me this was happening?

*** *Client account record available* ***

Sam: Well, first, don't get too worked up. We'll get something sort
ed out. But please be patient.
Sam: My records show I tried to contact you on April 12th and
again on May 3rd, suggesting that we needed to review your latest
social audit before the enrollment period. There was no response.

Gary: I figured it was like every other year. NBD. we'd renew and
continue.
Gary: No need to waste anyone's time.
Gary: Fuck.

Sam: Ok. Try not to worry. We'll get this sorted out. You're not the
first person this has happened to.
Sam: The reason I reached out earlier was because there were
some concerns that this might happen. Your social audit had some
red flags in it and we were concerned that Amazon might not be
willing to renew, so we were hoping to prep you with alternatives.
Sam: But there *are* alternatives. And you might even like them.

Gary: Yeah. Or I might *not* like them. Everyone uses PrimeLife.
Everyone. I feel like I'm being kicked out of society.

Sam: It appears that social audit turned up a concern that you've
been engaged in "aggressive, provocative, inauthentic behavior"
(APIB).

Gary: WTF does that mean?

Sam: APIB is the term for what you might refer to as "trolling."
Sam: Amazon has been pretty aggressive lately in keeping its

squeaky clean image, so anything its algorithms turn up that might suggest "bad" behavior may lead them to cutting you off.

*** *Requesting alternative service providers* ***

Gary: That's total bullshit. I wasn't trolling. Commenting on politics isn't trolling! Oh come on. How do we get me back?

Sam: In the last few years, after the last Congressional investigations, Amazon has really focused on being the "family friendly" life services provider. And so I've been seeing a lot of APIB rejections lately.

Gary: Or else... what? Shit. Do I need to move?

Sam: I'm currently pulling up a list of options. You're going to need to be patient.

Gary: I've lived here for 5 years now. I really don't want to move.
Gary: Ugggggggggh. Why now?!?

*** *Initial list of options available* ***

Sam: Okay, Gary. We're starting to put together a list of options for you, but let me walk you through the basics.
Sam: We can appeal Amazon's decision, and try to get you reinstated to PrimeLife, but if we succeed in doing that, you *may* be in a more limited tier, which would both take away some of your existing benefits and also likely have you on probation—meaning that you'll be watched carefully, and could face action if Amazon decides you are still tripping its APIB filters.

Gary: Who even reviews the appeal? Is it just Amazon itself? That new CEO they got? That kid? This is so fucking unfair.

Sam: No. Thankfully, Amazon employs a third-party review board, though there have been rumors that they're now using an AI-based review board first, and will only kick it up to actual human review in "close call" cases. Without knowing the full details of what you've been up to, I'm not sure I know how close a call you are.

Gary: Good. Because I might have mocked the new CEO online a bit.

Gary: Or perhaps a lot.

Gary: But just for fun. Really.

Gary: He should be able to take it.

Sam: Either way, it's worth doing the appeal. Even though you're losing your PrimeLife benefits right now, they do still cover my services in things like an appeal. So we'll absolutely do that, and then need to consider what your options are.

*** *Initiate automatic Amazon PrimeLife appeal* ***

Sam: However, this isn't a bad opportunity to review some of your other options as well. It's been a few years since we did a full review of what's out there, what you're looking for and whether or not there are better options to serve you. I know that you've been comfortable with PrimeLife, and that Amazon still provides the most well known "Life Service" out there, but there have been some really big changes lately, and you might even be more comfortable with some other options.

Gary: Please, please, please don't tell me you're talking about signing me up with UberEverything. That's *so* 2020s.

Gary: I'll be mocked mercilessly. My job depends on me being cool online. UberEverything is not that.

Sam: Well, you'd be surprised at how much UberEverything has done to compete with Amazon PrimeLife in the last few years, so it is worth exploring. But I also think some of the up and coming startups, like Thorple and ZMBG might be good. Thorple bought the remains of Yelp a few years ago, and it's now powering some really cool options.

Sam: Like discounts or priority access to top rated restaurants and bars.

Sam: And, really, I know it's looked at as even more desperate than UberEverything, but Facebook's InstaLife has really made some massive efforts to become relevant again. Sometimes it helps to go with the desperate partner, because they're happy to offer up more. Unlike PrimeLife who remains fat and happy and... picky.

Gary: Are you suggesting I should be desperate as well? Ugh. Isn't the whole point of PrimeLife that I've basically turned my life over to Amazon?

Gary: What do you do when your life services provider decides you shouldn't have a life?

Gary: Wait. I thought you were employed by Yelp. Is this just a fucked up scam to get me to move to your new corporate over-lords?

Gary: Why should I trust you?

Sam: No, Gary. You *found* me through Yelp. But I am a certified independent Life Service broker (CILSB). I am happy to send you my license number again if you've lost track of it. Nearly all life services cover our services.

Gary: Do you get different commissions for different ones? How do I know you're not just trying to make some extra coin off me? Didn't I read about these scams years back?

Sam: Gary. Please calm down. You've been using my services for years and I've never tried to pressure you into anything. CILSB brokers are paid an identical rate from all participating Life Services. I will make the same amount whether you're on PrimeLife or any other service.

Gary: Ok. Sorry. But, this is still really messed up. I'm on edge.

Sam: Well, let's start with a simple review: PrimeLife currently provides you with the following subscription based services: housing, transportation, wellness, entertainment, fulfillment and education. You're on a premium tier for housing, transportation and wellness—which has always been a bit of a stretch given your fulfillment position. And, of course, you have all the Prime shopping benefits that come with being a member of PrimeLife.
Sam: Which of those services is most important to you?

Gary: Dude. All of them. ALL OF THEM. I suddenly need to change my whole lifestyle because I made some political commentary online? That's crazy.

Sam: Not your lifestyle. Just, perhaps, some of the providers of that lifestyle. I'm sure we can figure out ways to have you remain happy. Perhaps even happier. That's what I'm here to help you with.. Remember, Life Services are still an evolving and changing market—and some of these companies, including Amazon, mostly rely on people being too comfortable to leave.
Sam: However, after regulators moved to break off Amazon PrimeLife from the rest of it's business, it's really opened up the market for competition, even if Amazon eventually won the lawsuit.

Gary: Yeah, but only because Amazon's AI3 powers the freaking court.

*** New proposals available***

Sam: I'll send you over more detailed proposals, but already running your socials through Thorple's AI and they seem eager to pitch you on a pretty great lifestyle plan. I'm running a few others as well, but I think this will work out fine.

Sam: Aha. ZMBG is pushing hard for your business as well.

Gary: I just got a request from them to ask if they can access my data. Do I need to give them access to all my shit?

Sam: Don't do that yet. Let's get everything organized before we share more info with these services. It might be best to have them start competing and I don't want to open up too much access just yet.

Sam: Okay. Basically all the other services are interested. Amazon's loss. They were getting to be so picky lately, maybe it's for the best. Perhaps you should thank the court. Amazon's probably so afraid of officials trying again (or, more likely, India and Brazil going after them) that they're kicking people off so they don't seem to have such a dominant position.

Gary: I'm still coming to terms with all of this mess. Do I need to change my job?

Sam: You know the services don't like us to refer to them as "jobs" any more. It's fulfillment. As in, how "fulfilling" is your life?

Sam: That's what they keep telling us anyway. It's basically a way to prepare everyone for a world in which "jobs" aren't necessary anymore.

Sam: So, if you're "fulfilled" working, then they'll find you a job. If you're "fulfilled" making music all day... then you can do that.

Gary: Apparently they don't believe me talking about politics on the socials is fulfilling?

Gary: Besides, what a stupid fucking term. I always assumed that it was Amazon trying to quietly conflate all the people they still employ "fulfilling" products, with "life fulfillment."

Gary: Either way, I don't think I'll need to change my job right now. Despite my "trolling" (as you call it), I still have really high marks in my "fulfilling" job as a rent-a-friend.

Gary: That's also why you can't make me slum it with UberEverything. I can't be the cool friend there.

Gary: My own social scores may have dropped, but I'm pretty damn good at raising other people's. I'm the best e-wingman there is. Perhaps I should hire me to boost my own scores.

Sam: There is no indication that your "fulfillment" needs to change. Just stop moonlighting as an asshole on the side, maybe?

Gary: I feel like I should say "fuck you" here, but you may be right. Also, are you supposed to be calling clients "asshole"?

Sam: Not really. But we do have some leeway to try to connect with clients. And you've been cursing up a storm, so I figured you might like it.

Sam: Back to the matter at hand. How important is it to stay in your current apodment?

Gary: Well, I like it here and moving is such a pain.

Sam: It doesn't have to be! Both Thorple and ZMBG include moving services with signing up. They really take care of absolutely everything. Another client of mine just switched to ZMBG, and they came through with a whole team of folks, scanned all his stuff, then gave him a VR pre-plan for how they'd put it all into his new pod, and let him make any changes. Once everything was set, they moved him while he was out with some friends one evening. They even let you designate personalization in the common areas.

Sam: He literally left one apartment to go out, and went back to the other, and everything was all set up for him. It's really quite effortless.

Gary: Well, okay. If that's an option, I'd be open to moving. Depends on the place, though, and who else I'd need to share common spaces with. I don't want any fucking fuck-ups.

*** New proposals available ***

Sam: These days, the AI is so good at matching you up with others that we rarely have personality clashes. And when they do, they're pretty good about swapping people around to make it work better.
Sam: It looks like UberEverything (I know, I know) is offering a special deal right now where you can literally design your own apodment, and they'll generate it to spec and connect it to one of their properties.
Sam: Facebook InstaLife says if you join their service, they guarantee 20% larger living quarters. Plus InstaLife gives you the full OculusSteam VR suite with every package. It's not an add-on like it is with some other services. And, hey, the data says you practically live in your OculusSteam.
Sam: Anyway, those are just the primary offerings. Let's dig in a bit deeper.

Gary: Oh, wait. Shit. Healthcare. How are we not talking about that yet?

Sam: Wellness, Gary. Wellness.

Gary: You know that I've got chronic lyme disease—and need that treated. It's a fucking mess. Under PrimeLife that was reasonably covered. Do these services get spooked about pre-existing conditions?

Sam: Actually, that brings us back to ZMBG. You know they actually started as an attempt to "disrupt" healthcare?

Gary: Wellness, Sam. You said it's called "wellness" now.

Sam: Back when they started it was still "healthcare." But a big part of their model was flipping the way health insurance in the US works. They took a page from life insurance instead. Basically, they recognized that your *life insurance* company had more incentives in keeping you alive than your *health insurance* company, who might find it more economical if you died. So ZMBG's whole thing was built on that premise—they'd take care of all your healthcare needs *and* handle a lump sum payout after you pass away.

Sam: But because their incentives are to keep you alive longer, all of their healthcare is free. So, no co-pays, no deductibles, no debilitating surprise bills.

Gary: Does that mean they're going to keep me hooked up to a machine when I'm braindead just to keep me alive?

Sam: No, no, from the beginning they've always had adjustable QOLifiers.

Gary: Qualifiers?

Sam: QOLifiers. QOL. Quality Of Life. So, rather than payouts when you "die," it actually turns into payouts when your quality of life (QOL) drops below a certain level.

Sam: And, actually, because of this flipped model, ZMBG actually has become quite the wellness company. It bought out a bunch of struggling pharmaceutical firms that were just searching for the next modification they could patent, and ZMBG just started setting much of their medical research out for free—because the longer they can keep people healthy and happy, the more money they make.

Sam: So they don't need to charge crazy high prices for drugs. In fact, they've been freeing up formerly patented drugs to make production easier.

Sam: And, even better, they've invested heavily in more modern treatments, rather than focusing on drugs for everything. Gene therapy. Syn-bio. Nanobots. And, yes, more general wellness/preventative care. As that business built up, it was inevitable that it would cross over into the Life Services realm as well.

Sam: So ZMBG might be especially suited to you.

Gary: Well, it certainly has my attention.

Sam: ZMBG's offer is really competitive. As we discussed earlier, they have a great and seamless moving service. You'll be matched to a new apodment, and get to pre-pick everything that you need and want. ZMBG will handle the full move at a time convenient for you.

*** *Updated proposals available* ***

Sam: The ZMBG initial audit seems fine with your socials. They're more edgy anyway. Maybe the trolling helps you out there.

Gary: It wasn't trolling!

Sam: As mentioned, ZMBG's wellness package is top of the charts. They're actually *excited* that you've got chronic lyme disease—not because they want you sick, but because they recently bought out a small synbio firm that thinks it actually has a cure for it. It's still in the testing stages, so they're actually looking for beta testers.

Gary: Clinical trial?

Sam: These days, it's all beta tests. Clinical trials are last century's thing.

Sam: And, as part of its wellness program, beyond AI-generated meal and exercise plans, they actually connect you with a personal nutritionist and personal trainer. Everyone thinks that AI can handle all this stuff, but we all know that humans ignore the AI half the time. Having a human helping you plan this stuff out works better.

Gary: Uh, yeah. Amazon's plan is all AI based and I haven't followed any of its recommendations in years.

Sam: Anyway, ZMBG's other services should be pretty good for you. The transportation, entertainment and education levels are pretty similar. There might be some concerts you used to go to that you'll have to dip into your discretionary crypto to attend.

Sam: Transportation will work basically the same, though you'll probably end up in blue cars rather than yellow cars.

Gary: Wait. Really?

Sam: Yeah. Haven't you noticed that Amazon's autonomous vehicles are all yellow?

Gary: I hadn't really noticed it.

Sam: Well, then I'm sorry I said anything.

Sam: Anyway, this is coming up really good. ZMBG wants your life on their systems.

Sam: I'd recommend letting ZMBG get access to your data store for the full audit and application process.

Gary: I just got the ping. Gave permission. I better not be handing over all my secrets to crazy hackers.

Sam: Okay, it'll take a minute or two to get approval.

Gary: Is it worth comparing to any of the others.

Sam: You could—but based on all the info I have here it seems like...

*** *Appeal Results* ***

Sam: Hold up.
Sam: Amazon has processed your appeal already and are willing to reinstate your service. I wasn't expecting that.
Sam: I wonder if they're snooping on ZMBG offers.

Gary: Huh. Are they fighting over me now? This day has been much weirder than I expected.

Sam: ZMBG has approved your application—and the final package is even sweeter than what they were originally pitching. I'm sending you a detailed doc, but the main thing to look over is the matrix chart on page 2.
Sam: If you give me another minute I'll update the doc to include comparisons to Amazon's latest offer, along with a few of the other services.

*** *Proposal withdrawn* ***

Sam: What's going on?

Gary: Huh?

Sam: UberEverything just yanked their proposal completely.

Gary: WTF?

Gary: I mean... I didn't want them anyway, but what's going on?

Sam: Gary. Are you trolling *right now*?

Gary: Fuck no!
Gary: I mean...
Gary: I was just commenting on the socials about all of this and...

Sam: Gary, not now. These services are watching in real time. And...

*** *Proposal withdrawn* ***

Sam: And... there goes the Amazon offer to reinstate your services. Gary, watch the APIB please.

Gary: Fuck. I was just saying how fucked up stuff was and... I didn't think that would make it worse.

Sam: It says here that you called Amazon the "fucking worst of the fuckety fucking life fucking services".

Gary: That sounds about right.
Gary: Sorry?

*** *Proposal Withdrawn* ***

Sam: Well... there goes the ZMBG proposal. They seem to be in lockstep with the others.

Gary: I thought you said ZMBG was down with me being an ass-hole!

Sam: I just said they were edgy.

Gary: Fuck. Now we're back at nothing?

Sam: Well, it looks like ZMBG is open to another attempt. The withdrawal is preliminary.
Sam: I'm going to recommend that we bring in another CISLB at this point. One who specializes in "convincing" life services to take on edge cases.

Gary: Who are you calling an edge case?!?

Sam: Unfortunately, right now it's you. I need your permission here.

*** Initiating permission request to add CISLB Specialist ***
*** Client selects "Yes" ***
*** Abe [CISLB #34285] joins ***

Abe: Thanks Sam! Hi Gary. Give me a moment to get caught up.

Gary: My whole life is on a roller coaster because I have opinions.

Sam: As I've told you, there are options out there—but you're not necessarily making it easy for us.

Abe: Okay, Gary. I've dealt with ZMBG a lot in the past, and their original offer to you was pretty great, so I honestly think that them rescinding the offer was just a case of momentary cold feet, based on the quick withdrawal from the others.

Gary: Do they all get to see what the others are doing.

Sam: They're not supposed to.

Abe: But... things don't always work the way they're supposed to.

Abe: I'm submitting a pretty standard reconsideration notice for ZMBG. It's simpler and quicker than a full appeal. If it doesn't get the offer back on, at the very least, ZMBG's system is likely to give me more details on what the problem is, and then we can work on fixing it.

Gary: You're the expert.

*** *Reconsideration submitted* ***

Gary: So, guys, I take it I should probably not be whining about this whole thing on the social right now?

Sam: Gary. Don't...

Abe: Gary. As a CISLB, we can't tell you what to do or not to do, but I can say that at this moment, more than any others, these services are probably paying attention to what you're doing.

Gary: Can I rant on AnonyNet?

Sam: That might be a fine way to let off some steam, but, again, you never truly know who has access to what.

*** *Reconsideration notice* ***

Abe: Hold on...
Abe: Okay, ZMBG has responded quickly. I think we'll probably be able to get you reinstated, but they have some concerns they need to be dealt with. We could definitely get you in on a lower tier, but if you want the plan that you were already looking at, there's a condition.

Gary: "A condition"?!?!?!?

Abe: They want a legal review.

Gary: For what?!?!?

Abe: It looks like the latest actions caused them to do a second scrub through your socials and they want a lawyer to do an analysis of whether or not it opens them up to any additional liability.

Sam: Your contract with us covers legal review as well, Gary. We can add a 3rd party, independent lawyer.

*** *Initiating permission request to add lawyer* ***
*** *Client selects "Yes"* ***
*** *Jenny [Lawyer account #9177] joins* ***

Jenny: Thanks Sam! Hi, Gary. Give me a moment to read over the details here and I'll get right back to you.

Gary: Hi Jenny. This seems awkward, but it seems I need you to tell ZMBG that I may be an asshole, but not a legally actionable asshole.

Jenny: ZMBG has sent over the statements they're most concerned about.

Gary: Uh oh.
Gary: I'm not that bad.
Gary: Really.
Gary: I just have opinions.
Gary: Lots of them.
Gary: And I like to express myself.
Gary: A lot.
Gary: And sometimes enthusiastically.
Gary: I get the feeling it'll sound worse out of context.

Gary: I'm sorry for whatever you're reading.
Gary: The silence here is worrying me.
Gary: Guys.
Gary: Guys?
Gary: Is it that bad?
Gary: Guys?
Gary: Hello?

Sam: Gary, please calm down.

Jenny: Okay, Gary. Most of this is clearly fine. I mean, it's not how I would act online. But, it should be okay. There's no way to say that definitively. People can sue over just about anything. But I can submit a quick analysis to ZMBG of why it would be difficult for anyone to win a case.
Jenny: The one where you toe the line a bit is that deep fake about the new Amazon CEO.

Gary: It was funny!

Jenny: Let's go with "parody" okay?

Gary: A funny parody!

Jenny: If you're into that sort of thing.

Gary: Ouch. Not a fan of my work.

Jenny: Okay, I'm submitting my analysis to ZMBG.
Jenny: Your CISLB's should be able to take it from here.

Abe: Thanks!

Sam: Thanks!

Jenny: Bye and good luck.

*** *Legal review submitted* ***
*** *Jenny [Lawyer account #9177] has left the conversation* ***

Gary: If I can't vent on the socials can I vent here?!?!?

Sam: Go for it, Gary.

Abe: Vent away. Though, you know, these days some life services even offer someone you can vent to?

Gary: Are you fucking serious?

Sam: Well, most wellness programs already cover a variety of kinds of therapy, but I think Abe is talking about something different.

Abe: Yeah, this is purely for venting. The person isn't trained to guide you through anything. Just to be someone who's just there to hear you vent.

Gary: That's fucked up.
Gary: Though, I guess my job is a rent-a-friend. And that's kind of similar.

Sam: Your fulfilment, Gary.

Gary: In the meantime. I can't believe that lawyer didn't like that deep fake. It was fucking hilarious.

Sam: I see the venting has commenced.

*** *New proposal information* ***

Abe: Well, you've lucked out. ZMBG is back on board with their offer.

Sam: Gary, please don't go attacking them on the socials. Especially not right now.

Gary: Lesson fucking learned.

Abe: While I'm on the line, I'm happy to provide a thorough review of this proposal as well. CISLB's can provide 2nd opinions.

Gary: Go for it.
Gary: I'll just be here trying to figure out what was wrong with that lawyer's sense of humor.

Sam: As I said earlier, I think the ZMBG plan really is perfect for you, now that it's back. You have the full proposal available to you. If you want to take it, you just need to click the giant "ACCEPT" button. Before you do that, you do need to watch a video in which someone will explain all the terms.

Abe: Well, my AI has already given me a green light, suggesting this is a really good plan, but give me a few minutes to check it out in more detail.

Gary: You guys rely a bunch on AI, huh?

Sam: Yes. It really is quite nice. Though, I'll let you in on a little secret: probably about 40% of what we've said to you today was really done by the AI (with our approval). They used to not like us to talk about that.
Sam: I'm a real person (you'll remember, we met in person), but the AI is often suggesting what I say to you for certain bits of the conversation. This way I can actually hold about 8 of these con-

versations at once.

Sam: But I wrote out that last bit by myself.

Sam: I hope you're not offended.

Gary: I'm actually more amazed.

Abe: Gary, I'm going to agree with Sam that ZMBG's deal looks perfect. I have a lot of clients with ZMBG and it's worked out really well. The only other issue to be aware of is that if you get into a long-term relationship, you'll have to adjust the housing plans— and there has been some friction in the past when a significant other doesn't qualify for ZMBG. But that's an issue we can tackle when the time comes.

Gary: Okay, though, now I feel like you're going to tell me ZMBG has its own dating app where I'll only meet ZMBG-compatible dates...

Sam: Not yet, but perhaps that's something we'll recommend.

Abe: Well, to be honest, life is much easier if you're paired up with a life services compatible mate. I know that love does its own thing, but, as a professional, I'd *highly* recommend that you try to find someone who will continue to match up with you and the kinds of Life Services you expect to utilize going forward.

Gary: Guys. I'm not getting dating advice from you fuckers.

Abe: It was merely a suggestion.

Sam: Abe, thanks for jumping in, but I think I will take it from here with my client.

Abe: I was only trying to help.

*** *Abe [CISLB #34285] has left the conversation* ***

Gary: WTF was wrong with that guy?

Sam: We all try to help each other out, but, let's just say that some of the CISLB folks can try to get extra credit in terms of how much "help" they give.
Sam: Anyway, at this point, you're all set. Watch the video. Click accept. Probably don't mock ZMBG's CEO online.

Gary: Even if it's a funny parody?

Sam: Thanks for using us as your Life Services broker, Gary. You should have all the details you need now. If you have any more questions, let me know. Otherwise, when you're ready, approve the offer.
Sam: Once approved, you can schedule your move any time in the next 30 days, and start getting set up with the other services. I believe ZMBG even has a concierge available to walk your through the onboarding process.
Sam: Also, Gary, next time I ping you to say we should review stuff, maybe respond? Then we don't have to go through this plasma drill next time.

Gary: Sure, dude. And maybe we should get together in person or something? I only met you that once when I first signed up. We could even hang out.

Sam: I appreciate that I've been able to help you today, Gary.

Gary: Ouch. I get it.
Gary: Well, Sam, even if you don't want to hang, I gotta say that I expected this whole mess to turn out quite differently. You're pretty fucking good at your job!

Sam: It's a fulfillment. Bye, Gary.

*** Sam [CISLB #19811] has left the conversation ***
*** Transcript of interaction #38,119,021z with Client #63,289

The Auditor & The Exorcist

By N. R. M. Roshak

"**G**et your god-damn hands off me!"

The woman slapped her partner's hands away, reeled drunkenly back. Pat's heart thundered in her chest. She hated this.

The man yelled back, grabbed at the woman's arm. She pushed him and he fell, stumbling backwards into a bookcase. His head struck a shelf. He sat down hard, roared with pain. The shelf collapsed, spilling books onto him.

Pat leaned forward in her chair and zoomed in. How hard had the man grabbed at the woman's arm? She ran the video back a few seconds and watched his fingers dig into the soft flesh of the woman's upper arm. Too hard.

Onscreen, the woman aimed a kick at the man's head. "Jesus," muttered Pat. She really didn't need to see any more. She already knew she was going to ding them both major LifePoints. But the AI had flagged the whole segment for review: she should watch to the end.

A soft moaning caught her attention. Pat peered at the screen. Who was making that noise? Not the man, who was holding his head and directing a stream of invective at his partner. Not the woman, who was lying where she'd fallen when she'd tried to kick her partner, slurring rude words into the carpet.

Pat bit her lip. Was there someone else, off-camera and hurting? Oh, God, she thought, what if these two drunks have a *kid?*

She pictured a small child, moaning in pain and ignored by the two adults preoccupied with their drama. Pat searched the screen. No kid in view. But the clip, pulled from a single SmartHome camera, only covered a shabby living room. Maybe the kid was in a bedroom, or in a closet, alone and hurting.

She checked the video clip's timestamps. Barely stale: only about 15 minutes old. If there was a hurt kid somewhere in that home, she still had a chance to help them.

Pat pulled up the same cam's live feed. The couple was still in the living room. The fight was over. The woman was snoring on the floor; the man was tapping on his foldie phone. But the low moaning continued.

How can he just ignore the kid? Pat shook her head in disbelief. She scoured the corners of the room with her eyes, but still couldn't see the moaning child. She'd need to find and pull up this couple's other SmartHome feeds.

Context was the reason social credit auditors like Pat could pull related feeds from a given location, person or time. The AI might flag 10 minutes of yelling and shoving, but miss the crucial context that preceded it: A mortal insult between strangers, or friends agreeing to rehearse a scene in a play? Social credit auditors had to be able to trace an interaction back to its roots.

Pat wasn't missing context for the fight in this clip, but for the moaning. And she'd been a social credit auditor long enough to know how to spin "context" into a view of the rest of the house. She left the live feed playing in her main window, spawned another window to spool that camera's feed back until she saw the woman enter the living room, selected the woman, and searched for the last feed that showed her. Bingo! A view of the woman leaving their kitchen one hour ago. Pat switched to the kitchen's live feed and had a good look around. No kid.

Ten minutes later, Pat had pulled live feeds of their entire apartment. One bedroom, one kitchen, one living room. No kid. No animals. There weren't any of the usual signs of a child's presence in the home: no toys, no little bed, no crayons. And yet, the moaning continued, mournful and awful.

Pat huffed out a frustrated breath and sat back in her chair. Red pulsed in the corner of her workspace. Her queue of video clips to review had filled to bursting while she had been fruitlessly hunting for the hurt kid. She wasn't making any progress, but she couldn't let it go. If there was a kid who needed help...

But she needed something to go on. She couldn't call down a social services alert on the home without seeing someone hurt or in trouble.

She pulled the AI's original flagged video clip back up, paused the live feeds. Maybe she'd missed something.

The clip ended.

The moaning continued.

Pat's mouth dried. The moaning wasn't coming from the video.

Frantically she rummaged through her workspace, hoping she'd left a live feed open in the background. Nope. She'd just spent twenty minutes snooping through two strangers' home to find a noise that hadn't even been coming from them. If she got audited, she'd have one heck of a hard time explaining why she'd done a deep dive on them. Her LifePoints would plummet. And—

Wait. Where *was* that moaning coming from? If it wasn't coming from her workspace—

Pat stood up so quickly that she stumbled, and threw open the study door. The moaning was louder in the hall. She followed the sound down the stairs, burst into the living room and—

The moaning stopped.

"What the hell?" Pat wondered out loud. She did a cursory search round her living room, expecting nothing and finding exactly that. Pat didn't have kids or pets; she didn't even have a partner, not since Melinda had left.

And she'd been living in this townhouse for years, since before Melinda. More than long enough to know it didn't have any of the usual culprits for strange domestic moaning noises, such as radiator pipes or drafts. It was a thoroughly modern townhouse: a SmartHome, in fact. And the SmartHome app should tell her if anything mechanical was wrong long before it got to the point of *moaning*.

She headed slowly back up the stairs to her study. She'd go through her SmartHome diagnostics later, when she got the chance. Right now, she had a full queue, and she still had to finish dinging LifePoints from the two dingbats whose video she'd just closed. Pat wiped a hand over her face and sat down at her desk.

***

LifeSocial Inc. WorkSpace v. 3.0.3 Chat
* Alert! You have a new message from KarenHamber *

KarenHamber: Pat your Q is red
PatVanBuren: Hi Karen, I'm on it
KarenHamber: Great. Remember ur metrics K
PatVanBuren: OK
KarenHamber: I pulled ur metrics 4 today & u r way over on review time
KarenHamber: #1 priority is to do a good audit on each clip of course
KarenHamber: But, if ur sure of scoring u can 1.5 speed or 2x to end
PatVanBurne: Right

KarenHamber: Expect to see Ur Q cleared by EOD

PatVanBuren: OK thanks Karen

KarenHamber: U R great teammember Pat hate to see U slip

***

Pat pushed away from the monitor with a stretch. Karen had made it very clear she had to empty her queue of clips to review by the end of the day... but she hadn't authorized any overtime, meaning Pat's last two hours of effort had been voluntary and unpaid. On the bright side, every "voluntary" hour of work after quitting time bumped up Pat's LifeScore a little more: one of the few advantages to working for LifeSocial, Inc.

Pat ambled into the kitchen, trying to decide whether she had the energy to cook. She flipped open her foldie phone and pulled up her LifeScore. She was still deep in the LOW zone, but maybe today's unpaid overtime had bumped her social credit enough that a decent delivery company would come out. She scrolled through restaurants, looking for one desperate enough to bring a low-score like her dinner.

Unfortunately, Pat's choices tonight were, once again: food poisoning by delivery, takeout, or cooking for herself. Pat slapped her foldie phone shut and pulled down the cereal.

"Breakfast of champions," Pat said to her cereal, "dinner of sad lonely losers." She'd lost count of the nights she'd called Lucky Charms "dinner" since Melinda had left. At least she wasn't out of milk.

By the time she collapsed into bed, Pat had nearly forgotten about the moaning that had derailed her afternoon. And if it sounded through her house that night, she slept too deeply to know or care.

***

LifeSocial Inc. WorkSpace v. 3.0.3 Chat
You are in channel #KarensTeam

* JefValentino has joined the channel.

JefValentino: Hi Everyone. Introducing myself. My name is Jef

JefValentino: I'm new at LifeScore Corp. Just started yesterday

PatVanBuren: Welcome Jef!

RaoulMorales: Hi Jef, welcome aboard!

RaoulMorales: We're here if you have any questions.

JefValentino: thanks Raoul and Pat!

JefValentino: actually I have kind of a dumb question

RaoulMorales: no such thing

JefValentino: why are most of the videos the Ai send us so awful???

JefValentino: Someones always getting screamed at or hit

RaoulMorales: Good question Jef

RaoulMorales: You know LifeScore includes your behavior to others

RaoulMorales: That means LifePoints have to get taken off ppl who are behaving badly

RaoulMorales: Most of the time, the LifeScore AI can auto deduct LifePoints for bad actions

RaoulMorales: but when AI can't decide whose LifeScore should go down

RaoulMorales: then it sends a video clip to a social auditors queue

RaoulMorales: It has the hardest time with fights, crying, etc.

RaoulMorales: Like who's the bad guy here?" Well that's really hard for the AI to figure out

PatVanBuren: Whenever the AI can't figure out who

the asshole is, it comes to us

PatVanBuren: Basically Jef our job is professional as-shole detectors

JefValentino: LOL

PatVanBuren: welcome to the club

***

The blond man's voice was so soft that Pat had to strain to catch the words.

"I really shouldn't be surprised that you fucked up again. That's what you do, isn't it. You fuck up and fuck up all day long."

The vicious words were at odds with his calm face, his relaxed shoulders, his soft voice. But his eyes sparked with malice.

Across the room, a tall, russet-brown man clenched his fists. Pat could practically see the steam coming out of his ears as the small blond man spoke on and on, pouring his poisonous words into the air between them.

"Enough!" the tall man screamed. "Enough already! God damn, Leon, you always think you're so perfect!" He took a menacing step forward, fists raising.

The blond man's lips twitched. If Pat hadn't been watching closely, she would have missed it: a tiny, triumphant smile.

Pat felt her breakfast curdling in her stomach. This felt like watching her breakup with Melinda in a funhouse mirror. Melinda had been expert at needling her until Pat had screamed, yelled, cried. Pat's LifeScore had tanked dramatically. All the AI and the social credit auditors had seen was Pat, yelling, fists clenched; sometimes, to her shame, even striking out at the woman she'd once loved.

She'd never hurt Melinda, not really. Pat's actions had hurt her own LifeScore more than they'd ever hurt Melinda. Melinda's Life-Score, on the other hand, was fine. The AI and the auditors had only seen Pat's bluster and fists, had never caught Melinda in that small, cruel smile.

Now Melinda had a new job, a new home, a new partner, and Pat was single and stuck in her life-sucking LifeScore job: she didn't have enough LifePoints to get delivery, let alone pass a reference check for a new job.

Pat stopped the video. She'd watched all she could handle. She took a few LifePoints from the big guy. And she took as many LifePoints from the small blond as she thought she could get away with. The next social credit auditor might not see the real dynamic between these two, but the little blond jerk wouldn't get away with it on her watch.

Pat let herself savour one moment of bitter satisfaction.

Her reverie was broken by an ear-splitting crash from downstairs. She shot out of her chair and raced into the living room. A vase lay in shards on the floor.

"Who's there?" she barked out. Silence.

Pat rubbed the back of her neck. She was the only one with keys to the house, and her SmartHome's intruder alert hadn't gone off. So there couldn't be anyone else in the house. Pat shook her head at herself as she swept up the shards. A couple of funny moans yesterday and a crash today, and she was jumping at shadows.

And, she had to admit to herself, a particularly upsetting clip in her queue.

She wiped a hand over her face, as if she could wipe the bitterness away. Maybe it was time for a break. Back in the study, she turned away from her desk, opened her foldie, and pulled up her MySocial feed.

***

Sponsored Content
MOANING AND BANGING in my house kept me awake all night until I called Angie. She helped me find solutions to the unexpected, distracting noises in my

house. I haven't had a bad night since. *Click here to learn more.*

***

Don't click on the sponsored content, Pat told herself. She clicked.

The page was a disappointment. Pat had been hoping for something she could fix with the tools she kept neatly arranged in the basement. Say, a problem with the furnace. She certainly hadn't been looking for advice on "unquiet spirits" perturbing her house. But "Angie" was an exorcist, hawking online de-ghostifying of houses. Pat sighed and closed her foldie. She'd used up her break time, and it'd been less relaxing than some of the stuff in her queue.

A message from Karen was blinking urgently in her LifeScore workspace. Karen wanted to know: Could she work overtime today? The new guy, Jef, needed help clearing his queue.

Sure. Why not? It wasn't as though Pat had any plans tonight. Or any night. And at least, Pat reflected, she'd be getting paid for this overtime.

***

JefValentino: so I have another question for you guys
RaoulMorales: OK
JefValentino: I noticed maybe 1 clip a day is different from the rest
JefValentino: and it's ridic happy stuff like kids playng or puppies
JefValentino: wth is up with the puppy videos
JefValentino: why do they need a social credit auditor for that?
PatVanBuren: I know, right?
RaoulMorales: LOL

RaoulMorales: your not the first to wonder!

* KarenHamber has joined the channel.

RaoulMorales: Official response is

RaoulMorales: "Helping train the AI on diverse social situations"

JefValentino: oh ok

PatVanBuren: unofficially though Jef

PatVanBuren: the Ai figures out how often you need to see puppies to keep from putting a bullet between your eyes

JefValentino: r u serious?

PatVanBuren: yep. suicide rate used to be thru the roof til they started w the kids & puppies

RaoulMorales: BTW Jef, I'm sure Karen has mentioned it, but if you ever start to have dark feelings you can ask for 1 session of counselling

RaoulMorales: don't be ashamed its perfectly normal

PatVanBuren: turns out there are some things even puppies can't fix

RaoulMorales: Yes, and you will probably see them sooner or later. It happens to us all.

***

Pat finished the day exhausted. The AI had served her a double helping of puppies that afternoon, but the sweetness hadn't washed the bitter taste of the morning's clips away. She was still jumpy from yesterday's moaning and today's inexplicably suicidal vase. And she was, once again, too tired to cook and too low-rated to get delivery. She shovelled in some Count Chocula and headed for bed.

Pat drifted for what felt like hours in the borderlands between waking and sleep. Moans and thumpings drifted through the house, or through her dreams: Pat couldn't decide, and couldn't wake up enough to investigate.

Dawn was nudging at the curtains when a splintering crash from the kitchen pushed Pat all the way awake.

The SmartCaf carafe was shattered on the kitchen floor, in a steaming puddle of coffee and glass shards.

"Noooooo..." moaned Pat. Her stomach clenched at the thought of facing her queue without caffeine. She rummaged through the cupboards for the last of Melinda's tea, ran tap water into a pot, and set it on the stove.

Her computer warbled at her from upstairs. Pat winced: that particular alert sound meant a DM from Karen. Coffeepot in shards on the floor, boss-DMs before her shift had even started: the day was not off to a great start.

***

KarenHamber: Pat we need to talk

KarenHamber: I saw u made v unprofessional comment to Jef in chat

KarenHamber: I realzie u have been w LifeScore Inc for 3yrs & it can b trying

KarenHamber: But plz remember

KarenHamber: Attitude is part of LifeScore pts bonus for soc cred auditors

KarenHamber: if ur bad attitide continue I will have no choice but to cut ur LifePoints bonos

KarenHamber: do u understand?

***

Pat groaned and rested her uncaffeinated head on her keyboard. Yes, she understood. It was her own dang fault for getting too comfortable in work chat. You worked with people for years, you made friends, you started acting like you'd act with real-life friends. But the space where you met wasn't real life. It was subject to random surveillance by the all-seeing, all-hating Corporation... embodied, at the moment, by Pat's boss. Who was definitely not a friend.

With a sigh, Pat pulled up the SmartStove app on her foldie and turned off the burner. She'd better attack her queue right away, in case Karen was checking up on her. There'd be time for tea later.

***

MySocial Chat Alert! You have a new message from Angela DeVaux.

Angie: Hi! This is Angela DeVaux. I saw that you browsed my page yesterday and just wanted to reach out to you.

Angie: I've helped a lot of people resolve strange incidents in their homes.

Angie: Is there anything that you were wondering whether I could help with?

Pat: No. I was just browsing.

Angie: OK! Thanks for your reply.

***

Pat snorted and closed the chat. Well, that's what she got for clicking on sponsored pages. And she'd clicked on an *online exorcist,* of all things.

Pat shook her head. Who even knew that "online exorcism" was a thing? Idly, she ran a MySocial search for *online exorcism.*

There were surprisingly many results. And most were just posts on regular people's pages.

I'm happy to report that my house is now free of ghosts! Woo hoo! Thank you to Linda Tran who did the exorcism online.

OMG I thought I would never sleep again. Thank God
for Stefan in Lithuania who exorcised the ghosts out
of my apartment online

Hey everyone I'm so so glad to report my house is safe
again. I was getting scared to go home at night lol.
Even the exorcist didnt want to go in. Lucky for me he
could do it online haha

...Safe? Pat rolled her eyes. Who was that scared of ghosts as a
grownup?

So you guys might remember my post last week when
I almost died from getting electorcuted. Then after
that, the bowling ball incident. Well it turns out these
both had the SAME cause. I almost got done in by
GHOSTS. This is the real deal! I am not shitting you!
I could of died! If it wasn't for Sunny Grenfell, I could
be DEAD. But thanks to her online exorcism my house
is safe again.

Good grief, thought Pat. She took a long slurp of tea.

A hollow groan sounded from the hallway. Pat slopped tea on
herself.

"What the hell!" She set the dripping mug down, threw open
the study door, and stormed into the hallway. Silence.

"This is ridiculous," Pat muttered. She knew that she was alone
in the house. Still. She poked her head into the bathroom, the
bedroom, ran an eye over the living room and the kitchen, even
checked under the sofa and bed. She found nothing but the dust
bunnies that congregated everywhere the SmartVac couldn't
reach.

***

MySocial Chat Alert! You have a new message from Angela DeVaux.

Angie: BTW Pat, feel free to reach out to me again at any time.
Angie: If you ever feel frustrated, puzzled or threatened by anything going on in your home
Angie: I'm here to help.
Pat: Look. I'm sure you mean well but the last thing I need is an "online exorcist"
Pat: I need to get the furnace guy out or something, not get "ghosts" out
Angie: ? You're having furnace problems in May?

Pat rubbed her temples. She hadn't thought that through. The furnace hadn't come on in, oh, a couple months.

Pat: It's a ventilation fan or something then. I need to check my SmartHome diagnostics
Angie: Sure. I talk to a lot of homeowners with a lot of different issues. 9 times out of 10 it's something mechanical in the house.
Angie: I'm not going to come out there and fix anything, but if you want to talk it over with me, I might be able to point you in the right direction.
Pat: Sure. Fine. What do I have to lose but time
Pat: Something's making a funny noise in my house.
Pat: What's your diagnosis, doctor?
Angie: Haha! I like your sense of humour, Pat. I'll need a better description of the symptoms though
Pat: Intermittent groaning/moaning like wind.
Angie: So that noise is the only symptom? That's good

to hear. I've seen much worse. Things falling down, things getting broken, doors slamming on people. I've even seen stairs knocking people off their feet. Very dangerous

Pat: I'd diagnose that as needing to repair the stairs.

Angie: Ha ha!

Angie: So nothing broken then?

Pat: Nothing related to the strange noise

Angie: Wait. What does that mean, Pat? Things *are* getting broken?

Pat: I don't have any reason to think that has anything to do with the noise.

Angie: Pat. I'm feeling really concerned about you. Something in your house is moaning and breaking things. Have you been hurt?

Pat: What? No!

Angie: I'm glad to hear that. Now, the broken things. It sounds like they got broken when you were in a different room?

Pat: Yes.

Angie: Good. Maybe you weren't even at home or awake at the time for one of them?

Pat: Yes, the crash woke me up.

Angie: Good, that's very positive. Now, we're not talking anything major like a TV getting broken, right? Were the broken things fairly inexpensive?

Pat: Yes. Well, the SmartPot wasn't that cheap. What does that have to do with anything?

Angie: Listen. I'm 99% sure I know what's going on with your home. Would you like to hear what I think?

Pat: Sure.

Angie: OK I'm going to lay it out for you straight. Something in your house is angry. The good news is it's pretty minor and I can help you fix it.

Pat: Oh, here we go. "For a fee." No thanks
Angie: No fee. Please. I'd be embarrassed to charge for something this minor.
Angie: 5 minutes of video chat and I'll have it cleared up for you
Pat: What, for free?
Angie: Right. My business grows by word-of-mouth & reputation
Angie: I'm not going to leave you hanging with a cranky psychic impression making your life miserable
Angie: when I could fix it in 5mins
Angie: But I'm not going to charge for 5 minutes of my time.
Angie: It's up to you, Pat. LMK what you decide.

Pat sighed. She didn't believe in ghosts, let alone in online exorcism. But 5 minutes wasn't a big investment. And if, by some fluke of the universe, it actually *worked*, it would save her a pile of annoyance.

Pat: OK, fine. 5 minutes.
Angie: Great. We'll get this cleared right up. Are you on your foldie or a laptop?
Pat: Desktop
Angie: We'll need something you can carry with you. Video chat me from your foldie.

***

Angie's face appeared on the screen of Pat's foldie. Angie was pale and puffy, with frumpy, mouse-brown hair and a calico-print collared shirt. She didn't look the part of an exorcist at all.

But the moment Pat set foot in the hallway, foldie open, the moaning started up again downstairs. Angie directed her brusquely to follow it.

What followed was surreal. Pat carried her foldie around her small townhouse, while Angie called out to, and cajoled, invisible spirits. At Angie's direction, Pat followed the eerie noise into the kitchen. Something bumped in the living room. The moaning crested, Angie yelled "Begone!", and the noise stopped as if on command.

"There," said Angie smugly. "You should be good to go. If you have any more problems, just let me know."

Pat shook her head. "I'm not sure what to think. That was... Weird. Thanks."

Angie smiled. "I'm glad I could help. Take care of yourself, Pat."

***

Amazingly, Angie's exorcism actually seemed to help. The moaning and thumpings stopped, and nothing else broke. Pat couldn't explain it to herself, but Angie yelling at her house over video chat seemed to have actually worked.

Pat wasn't going to make a glowing post on her MySocial page, or anything, but she gave Angie's page a positive review and kicked her a LifePoint.

***

PatVanBuren: So do you guys believe in ghosts
JefValentino: OMG did you see one in a clip in your Q?
JefValentino: that is like, my fantasy
PatVanBuren: LOL no Jef
RaoulMorales: that'd be a new one
RaoulMorales: "Excuse me Karen, how do I take LifePoints from this ghost"
PatVanBuren: Hahaha! "This ghost is a negative social element, I need to adjust its LifeScore"

RaoulMorales: ITYM "DeathScore"
PatVanBuren: LOL!

***

A week later, the strange noises were back. Pat tried to track the noise down, but it seemed like every time she got close, it shifted to a different room.

The LifeScore AI must have noticed her stress mounting, inasmuch as it could "notice" anything, because an extra puppy video popped up in her queue. But Pat wasn't able to relax and enjoy the five minutes of cuteness. Outside her study door, the moaning had started to take on a new quality. If she wasn't paying attention, it sounded almost like speech. And what it seemed to be saying, over and over, was *kill... kill... kill.*

It was a terrible work environment. Pat's metrics were tanking, again.

When a crash echoed through the house, Pat almost wasn't surprised. She just sighed, pushed back from her desk, and trudged downstairs to investigate.

The torchiere was on the living room floor. Pat stood it back up. At least its thick glass shade seemed to have bounced rather than shattered.

Pat didn't know what to think. Angie's "exorcism" clearly hadn't worked. She should've known better than to think it would have any effect. But still... she'd had a whole week free of trouble after Angie had done her mumbo-jumbo. Could it just have been a coincidence?

And Pat had to admit that the strange noise wasn't sounding even vaguely mechanical any more. Wind seeping through a tiny, hard-to-find crack, or a failing SmartFan, wouldn't sound like *words.*

***

MySocial Chat Alert! You have a new message from Angela DeVaux.

Angie: Hi Pat! Just checking in with you. How're you doing?
Pat: Angie
Pat: Thanks for trying but your "exorcism" didn't work
Angie: Oh no! What's wrong?
Pat: Seemed like it actually worked at first but the noises are back
Pat: If anything it's worse
Angie: Uh oh.
Pat: ?
Angie: I was afraid this might happen. It's rare but sometimes negative psychic impressions can be more powerful than they seem at first.
Angie: So sometimes, a positive intervention can actually bring spirits more in touch with their anger
Pat: You mean you made it worse???
Angie: Well not in your case I don't think. It sounds like it's less severe than before, previously you were having some objects broken.
Pat: Lamp also fell over. Probably a coincidence tho
Angie: I see
Angie: Hmmm
Angie: I could take another look but
Pat: But what?
Angie: I can't guarantee I would be in and out in 5mins. Sounds like your case is harder than initially described.
Angie: I'd probably need about half an hour to get a good read on the situation.
Pat: Oh here we go. Im guessing half hour sessions are not free.

Angie: No. But the good news is this kind of thing is almost always fixable.

Pat: Thats what u said last time

Angie: I know and I do apologize. 95% of time that would have done it.

Angie: that's why I was checking up on you.

Angie: I admit, I was too eager to help you. I shouldn't have done a 5min freebie wo full examination. It was unprofessional of me

Pat: I'm not impressed

Angie: I understand. I'd like to make it up to you Pat. Lets do the half hour and I won't bill you unless that gets rid of your problem permanently.

Pat: ...

Pat: OK fine. What do I have to lose

Angie: Great. I have another appt now but I can fit you in at 5:30 EDT tonight

Pat: Working til 6:30 MDT here. I could do 7 MDT

Angie: I'll video chat you at 6:30 MDT sharp.

Angie has left the chat.

***

Angie pinged Pat's foldie at 6:30 sharp, just as Pat was logging out of her LifeSocial workspace. This time, Angie looked the part of an exorcist: somber clothes, eyes bright with determination, hair more wild than frumpy.

Angie started right away, and Pat's house seemed to respond. Moans and gibbering swirled around Pat as Angie chanted. The lights went off. Pat's scalp prickled with fear. She held the phone up over her head, the center of a circle of light in a sea of groaning darkness.

"Begone, cursed spirits! I banish you from this home!" screamed Angie from between Pat's hands. Something shattered downstairs.

The awful moaning crested—*Kill, Kill, Kill*—and then stopped short, on Angie's command.

Afterward, Angie looked wrung out. Sweat sheened her brow; her mousy hair hung damp and stringy around her face.

"The spirits in your house are more malevolent than I'd thought," she panted. "More stubborn, too. This is a tough one."

"Okay," said Pat. "That was... dramatic, that's for sure."

"Still don't think you need the help of an exorcist?" Angie asked dryly.

"Weeelll," Pat hedged. She really didn't want to be the kind of person who believed in ghosts, crystals, and spirits. But her palms were still damp, her mouth still dry from the primal fear she'd felt a minute ago. What she'd just seen and heard—the lights going out, the noises, the crash, and all of it seeming to respond to Angie's exhortations and commands—Pat couldn't believe it'd been coincidence, much less a bad ventilation fan. It was hard to understand it as anything but a haunting.

A haunting, in her house.

"Why now?" Pat asked suddenly. "I've lived here for a decade. Never had any trouble until the last few weeks. Nobody's ever died here as far as I know, and for sure not in the last couple of weeks. What's going on?"

Angie nodded gravely. "That's an important question," she said. "Negative energies can linger in a home. They can build up over time. Sometimes, it takes almost a critical buildup of negativity to really activate something that's been dormant for a while." She paused, searching Pat's face. "Only you can say what that's really about, Pat."

Pat's cheeks heated with shame, as she remembered the hours and hours of fighting with Melinda. And Pat wasn't proud of how she'd behaved. Screaming, throwing things. Pushing.

Hitting.

Yes, Melinda had maliciously provoked her. But Pat had been the one pouring negative energy into the house, soaking it into the walls with every scream, crash and slap.

Pat had to admit to herself that she'd deserved every bit of the drop in her LifeScore.

And maybe she deserved this haunting, too.

Angie's voice broke into her thoughts. "I can't promise you that it's all taken care of, Pat. Whatever happened here left some very potent negative energy. That's driving an angry and powerful spiritual presence. And frankly, that can be dangerous."

"Dangerous," Pat repeated. She hadn't been dangerous to Melinda. Had she?

"I want you to contact me if you have any—*any*—trouble. No matter how minor you think it is, contact me. Can you do that, Pat?"

"Yes," Pat said numbly. After Angie signed off, Pat sat for a long time on the stairs, head in her hands.

***

It was all Pat could do not to groan as she logged in to her LifeScore workspace the next morning. Pat's LifeScore queue always felt extra daunting when she'd slept badly; and although the house had been quiet the previous night, Pat had barely slept. To top it off, her SmartCaf was still broken, and she was on the last of Melinda's tea.

The video clips in her queue were surprisingly mellow this morning, and a little bit strange. It took Pat, in her brain-fogged state, a dozen or so clips to realize that they were all strange in the same way.

***

PatVanBuren: I'm getting a lot of indoor fisheye videos from a weird height today, anyone else?
JefValentino: what is fisheye
PatVanBuren: super wide angle. like surveillance cam

but this is all indoor & at waist height

JefValentino: oh yea me too! i've had like 10 so far today

JefValentino: all of them in ktchens too

RaoulMorales: yes I'm getting these as well

PatVanBuren: any idea what's up w that

RaoulMorales: So I had to follow a user to another cam for context

RaoulMorales: & saw where this fisheye feed is coming from

RaoulMorales: it was the feed from the coffee maker on their kitchen counter

JefValentino: OHHHHH SNAP

JefValentino: I got an alert in my SmartCaf app this AM about a TOS update

JefValentino: I didn't read it but I bet that's what it was about.

RaoulMorales: Yes that would make sense.

RaoulMorales: If smartCaf just agreed to share feeds w LifeScore Inc then SmartCaf would have to update its Terms of Service

RaoulMorales: when ppl agree to the SmartCaf TOS update the AI will start to check their feeds for LifePoints

JefValentino: OK but why is the AI putting so many in my Q?

PatVanBuren: in theory the AI is trained on any new type of feeds before it goes live

PatVanBuren: in practice, it needs us to check a lot more of its calls

PatVanBuren: we're helping to train it on the new type of feed

RaoulMorales: Yes. Every time the LifeScore AI takes on feeds from a new kind of thing, we will see a great deal of clips from that kind of thing for the first few days. When you've worked here longer, Jef, you will see.

***

Pat was pulled away from the work chat by a deafening clangour filling the air. The SmartHome fire alarm was going full blast. Pat clapped her hands over her ears for a second, then scooped up her foldie and tapped the SmartHome app whose icon was pulsing urgently on the screen.

"Shit!" Fire in the kitchen! She raced down the stairs to the kitchen. The empty tea box was on the floor, in flames. As Pat stomped it out, the lights flickered, and eerie laughter echoed through the house. *Kill—kill—kill!*

Hair standing up on the back of her neck, Pat retreated to the corner of the kitchen. *What just happened?*

She fumbled her foldie back out with shaking hands, pulled up the SmartHome history, found the kitchen cam video leading up to the fire. One minute, the tea box had been sitting on the stove where she'd left it. Suddenly, the teabox had started to smoulder. A sudden gust of air had fanned the flames, and blown the flaming box to the floor.

Pat knew she hadn't left the stove burner on. She hadn't even *had* that burner on this morning.

She turned to the SmartHome device logs. The SmartFan log didn't show any activity to explain the sudden gust of air. Pat pulled up the SmartStove log. It confirmed that she hadn't left the burner on. In fact, according to the log, the burner hadn't come on at all.

She went over to the stove, held her hand over the smooth glass of the burner. Hot. Had the stove malfunctioned, turned itself on and off without leaving a trace in the log?

Pat closed her eyes. Stove malfunction. Right. That would explain the laughter, the flickering lights, the gust of air. Stove malfunction.

She pulled up MySocial and messaged Angie.

***

Angie's face was grave, on Pat's foldie. "I was afraid of this," she said. "The presence in your house is now actively hostile to you. Every time I've done an intervention, it's responded very positively to me, but..." She shook her head. "It's as though you yourself are a provocation to it."

"It doesn't like me," Pat summed up.

"I'm afraid it's moved beyond not liking you, Pat. The spiritual presence is actively trying to harm you."

"So tell me something I don't know."

"This is no joking matter. I'm concerned for your safety as long as you remain in that house. Do you have someone that you can stay with?"

Pat felt her face harden. "No."

"I see." Angie let silence sit between them.

"Angie," said Pat, "I want you to get this, this 'presence', out of my house."

"Pat... I'm afraid it's moved beyond that. The presence does respond well to me, but..."

"I can pay you," Pat blurted. "However long it takes."

"I can't be there twenty-four-seven. This presence is *actively trying to harm you*," Angie repeated. "It's deeply attached to the walls, to the fabric of your house. It's not going anywhere. I can calm it, but when it realizes you're still there... well, it's only becoming more hostile toward you with time." She took a deep breath. "Pat, I can't guarantee your safety if you stay in that house."

"What are you saying?"

"This house is not safe for you. Are you renting? Can you break the lease?"

"What? No. No. I've had this house for a decade. The mortgage's half paid off."

"Then, I would seriously consider selling."

"Sell my home..." Pat repeated softly.

"And if you can swing it, I'd consider staying in a hotel until the house is sold."

This is what I deserve, thought Pat. *Negative energy: my anger, soaked in deep. I did that. To Melinda, to my house. This is no more nor less than I deserve.*

***

The realtor blanched under her makeup as an eerie moan echoed down the stairs. "What the—what was that?"

"Little problem with the furnace," Pat lied.

"In May?"

"Sorry, I meant with the ventilation system. I've got SmartFan, by the way. Really cuts down on the heating and cooling bills. Anyway, the noise doesn't happen too often, so I haven't had a chance to pin it down."

"I... see." The realtor didn't seem convinced.

The moaning crested, resolved once again into a horribly familiar chant. *Kill, kill, kill.*

Pat was *almost* used to the constant exhortations to murder. The realtor wasn't. "That's... That doesn't sound like a fan," she whispered.

There was a rattling crash from the kitchen, and a smell of burning wafted out.

"I—I just remembered I have another appointment," the realtor stammered, racing for the door. "I'll call you!" The door slammed behind her.

Pat ran a tired hand over her face. "Sure you will," she muttered, heading for the kitchen.

She couldn't find the source of the burning smell, but the rattling crash had probably been the hundreds of ice cubes now piled high in front of the fridge. She started scooping them into the sink with the dustpan, trying not to listen to her house moaning about how much it wanted to kill, kill, kill her.

A blood-curdling scream echoed from the living room. *Was that the realtor? Did she come back in?* Pat dropped the dustpan and rushed into the living room. She stood alone in the middle of the room, staring wildly at the shabby furniture.

The TV switched on behind her with a blare of sound. Pat spun around to look at it—a daytime murder movie?—and the torchiere crashed down right behind her, hitting the carpet with a massive BONG.

Pat screamed. The torchiere's heavy glass shade had *just* missed her. She'd felt it ruffle the hairs on the back of her head. She backed away.

"I'm going to get you!" yelled the TV. "You can't escape me forever!"

Pat broke and ran for the door.

***

"Angie, you have to help me!" Pat was standing outside in the sunshine, pleading with Angie on her foldie. She heard the begging tone in her voice, hated it, but couldn't help it. "I can't stay here, but I can't even show the damn house to a realtor!"

Angie was calm, soothing. "Okay, Pat, calm down. Take a deep breath. I know that it's upsetting, but we'll get through this. I want you to find a hotel you can go to for the night."

Pat grimaced. "Can't."

"If it's a question of money—"

Pat shook her head. "LifeScore's too low. Nobody'll take me."

"There are hotels who'll take *anybody*," Angie said. "Druggies, hookers, ex-cons. I'm sure you can find a place that'll take you."

"Those aren't hotels, Angie, those're flophouses. And I work from home. I can't bring my computer setup to a flophouse. If it gets stolen I'm really up shit creek without a paddle."

"I don't think I've ever heard anyone use the word *flophouse* before," said Angie. "But OK, you need—"

"I need to sell this house and get out," Pat interrupted. "My Life-Score won't let me rent a good place or get a decent mortgage, but the mortgage here is half paid off. If I can just sell this place, I'll have enough to buy a little place outright. I might have to move outside town, but I could make it work. But I need to sell this place first! Can't you make the ghosts shut up long enough to show it to a god-damn realtor?"

Angie sighed. "You know it's not that simple," she said. "If you weren't there, then yes, no problem. But with you there... Just having you walk around the house, showing it off to the realtor, is a major provocation. And I don't think you want me doing an intervention over video chat with you while the realtor is there."

"Ha, no... Well, what *can* you do?"

"What you need," Angie said slowly, "is a buyer who isn't scared of ghosts... Someone who doesn't need to go through a realtor..."

Pat laughed. "Hell, I don't suppose *you're* in the market for a house? Great condition, only slightly haunted."

Angie looked surprised. "I never thought of that! You know, that's not a half-bad idea."

"Are you serious? You'd actually buy this place from me?"

"I... Hmmm. Well. To be honest, I probably couldn't afford full market price on such short notice. But then again, you wouldn't be paying a realtor commission, and you'd have a quick sale."

Pat ran a hand over the back of her head, where the torchiere's heavy shade had grazed her hair. "How soon can we do this?" she said.

***

MySocial Chat Alert! You have a new message from Karen Hamber.

Karen: Pat are u there?

Karen: Why don't u respond on LifeScore chat

Karen: Ive sent you 7 msgs

Karen: Why r u not at ur desk

Pat: Hi Karen

Pat: I'll be right there

Karen: You didnt mark urself out on break

Karen: You know the rules Pat

Karen: U can take ur 7mins wellness break whenever u need, up to 2x/day

Karen: BUT U must Mark Out On Break!

Pat: OK I'm sorry

Pat: I'll be back at my desk in a minute

Karen: ur Q hasnt moved in half an hr! U know thats bad for team metrics

Karen: if it happens again it is coming out of ur lifepts bonus!

Pat: OK

Pat: Thanks Karen

Karen Hamber has left the chat.

Pat closed her foldie and faced the house. There was nothing for it. She had to go back in.

***

"To be or not to be," declaimed the user, staring directly into the camera, "that is the question. Whether tiz nobler to—to—damn it!" He looked down at his script.

Odd that he's staring right into the camera, thought Pat. Most of the video clips she reviewed were from SmartHome feeds, street CCTVs, the occasional drone, and of course the SmartCafs. None of these were the kind of cameras that people tended to line their faces up with and stare right into. She marked the video clip as

Neutral and moved on.

The next clip also featured a single user, staring right into the camera. And behind them—was that a *toilet?*

***

PatVanBuren: Another day, another new feed type?

RaoulMorales: Haha yes Pat

RaoulMorales: I'm seeing a new SmartHome feed as well

PatVanBuren: Users staring directly into the camera

PatVanBuren: At eye level

PatVanBuren: This is a new one on me

RaoulMorales: Even stranger Pat, some of these clips are in the bathroom

RaoulMorales: Normally, SmartHome devices should not share bathroom data

JefValentino: Guys, I know this one!

PatVanBuren: Spill

JefValentino: OK so I have a SmartMirror in my bedroom

RaoulMorales: On the ceiling? ;-)

JefValentino: Haha no! On the wall. I'm color blind. the SmartMirror helps me look snazzy

PatVanBuren: No red sox w your green pants

JefValentino: Exactly. Anyway I got a TOS update in the SmartMirror app this AM

JefValentino: & I actually read the TOS becoz of my SmartCaf

PatVanBuren: Brave man

JefValentino: They chgd it to say SmartMirror data "can be used to enhance your LifeScore experience"

RaoulMorales: Yes, that means the LifeScore AI has access now

PatVanBuren: which means we'll get it in our queues

JefValentino: but I didn't realize ppl have SmartMirror in the bathroom, that's messed up

RaoulMorales: I agree

PatVanBuren: The SmartHome privacy settings default to something like... let me look at mine...

PatVanBuren: "Never share video from my personal privacy areas with others, including LifeScore"

RaoulMorales: Hmm

PatVanBuren: & bathrooms are a "personal privacy area" ofc.

RaoulMorales: I wonder if there may be a bug with the privacy settings

RaoulMorales: so that the SmartMirror feed to Life-Score is not picking up that SmartHome setting correctly

PatVanBuren: Looks like it. Glad I don't have a Smart-Mirror in my bathroom

JefValentino: Should we report it?

PatVanBuren: Jef we don't have a process for reporting bugs w SmartHome devices.

RaoulMorales: Yes we can only report bugs in the LifeScore workspace or AI

PatVanBuren: and Karen really hates it when we do something out of process :(

***

The next video in Pat's queue was another SmartMirror clip. Pat sat bolt upright in her chair, gripping its arms in shock. The face in the mirror was unmistakably Angie's.

It was a big no-no to audit a feed from anyone you knew. But a sound from the feed stopped her from closing it.

The moaning. It was the moaning. Not coming from the hallway, or the kitchen, or the living room. This time it really was coming from Pat's computer speakers. Angie was staring into her SmartMirror and moaning.

The hair rose on the back of Pat's neck. Angie shifted the moaning smoothly into words. *Kill... Kill... Kill.* Pat watched Angie's lips move, shaping the word she'd so often heard echoing through her house. Angie broke into an evil cackle. In the SmartMirror feed, her eyes shone with malicious mirth.

"You *bitch,*" Pat whispered.

On Pat's monitor, Angie let the laughter trail off, then gave herself a thumbs-up. "Definitely saving that one for later," Angie told herself jauntily. The clip ended.

Pat sat, stunned. Angie had been making those moans all along. The conclusion was inescapable: Angie, her "exorcist," had been faking the haunting. But *how?*

Pat desperately wanted to take all the LifePoints she could from Angie for this video clip. But if Pat's work were ever audited—and with Karen breathing down her neck, that could be any day—she would lose her job, along with most of her remaining life points, for adjusting the social credit of someone she knew.

Pat huffed in frustration. She might not be able to ding Angie for this video. But, Pat decided, she would find out exactly how Angie had been "haunting" her house... and she would make her pay.

***

Pat decided to start with her own SmartHome video history. If Angie, and not ghosts, had made Pat's torchiere nearly bean her, that should show Pat how she'd done it.

Pat looked down at herself from the SmartHome cam in the corner of her living room. There she'd been, completely alone in the middle of the room. She'd turned to face the TV, and the torchiere had crashed to the ground right behind her. For the life of her, Pat couldn't see what had pushed it.

But if there was one thing Pat knew, after years as a social credit auditor, it was SmartHome feeds. She made a clip, imported it to her LifeScore workspace, slowed it down, did a frame-by-frame analysis.

There. The frame after the crash, the SmartVac had been next to the torchiere. But it hadn't been there in the previous frame. Pat sifted through the clip. At the beginning of the clip, the SmartVac had been next to the sofa. Then it had simply disappeared. It had only reappeared after the lamp had crashed down nearly on her head.

Two conclusions. One, the SmartVac had pushed over the lamp. Two, her SmartHome feed had been edited to hide it.

Pat whistled. Angie must be able to change Pat's SmartHome feeds. And more than that: Angie could control her SmartVac, and probably everything else that hooked into Angie's SmartHome.

Pat thought through everything she'd experienced in the past week. Every single incident could have been caused by someone controlling her SmartHome. Someone who could turn on a Smart-Stove without leaving a trace in the logs. Who could make a Smart-Caf eject its carafe with too much force. Who could run her Smart-Fans at will, make her SmartFridge spit out ice cubes, and most of all, make her SmartVac toddle around the house sowing chaos.

Someone who could record hours of awful moaning and have her SmartHome alert system play them back at full volume whenever they wanted. Say, when they were pretending to do an exorcism.

Pat realized she was gritting her teeth. Angie had hacked into her SmartHome somehow and played her for a fool. And Pat had fallen for it: She'd been on the point of selling Angie her house at a discount. Angie even had Pat blaming *herself* for the faux haunting. Pat didn't know how she was going to do it, but she was more determined than ever to make Angie pay.

Her first instinct was to involve the police. There was no way that hacking Pat's SmartHome devices had been legal. But a quick internet search had her doubting that it would do any good.

***

SmartHome hackers face little consequences
by Chelsea Tritton, special to the Post

Last year, over two thousand police reports of smart-home hacking were filed nationwide. The complaints ranged from the trivial—silly noises late at night—to the grievous—locking devices until a ransom was paid. Yet fewer than a dozen prosecutions have been brought for SmartHome hacking to date.

We asked cybersecurity expert Jan Blackwell what to make of this discrepancy. "Identifying SmartHome hackers, or other device hackers, is very difficult," they explained. "A device hacker gains complete control over the device, aka 'owning' the device. That gives them control over the logs that would've revealed the intrusion, allowing them to hide their tracks. And even given the original logs, the police often don't have the skills to trace the hackers. Finally, in the rare event that police are able to track down the hacker, these crimes usually occur across jurisdictions, making them very difficult to prosecute."

Mx. Blackwell also suspects that the scope of the problem far exceeds even the thousands of police reports. "Most smart home devices are under-secured at installation," they said. "And even the properly installed ones usually aren't patched, leaving them vulnerable to hackers. Unfortunately, many SmartHome users may never realize they've been compromised."

Faux hauntings on the rise

While some SmartHome hackers have been able to wring money from their victims by ransoming their devices, a few trailblazers have turned to a new con: faux hauntings. According to Mx. Blackwell, hackers who have "owned" their victims' SmartHome devices have almost unlimited capacity to operate these devices; rather than locking the devices and demanding ransom, some hackers have used them as puppets to stage a fake haunting of the victim's home, then demanded money to "exorcise" the home. The advantage of this scheme, according to Mx. Blackwell, is that few victims even realize they've been hacked. Indeed, many of the victims are actually grateful to the hackers for "rescuing" them from "evil spirits."

Only the unluckiest hackers, it seems, will ever face any sort of consequence for their misdeeds.

***

Pat knuckled her chin thoughtfully. The bit about editing logs had rung true: Angie must have edited her SmartOven logs to make it look like the stove had never come on. If she'd thought to do that, and to edit the SmartHome video feeds to hide her tracks from Pat, there was no way she would've left anything in the SmartHome access logs that could point back to her.

Pat had to admit, grudgingly, that Angie seemed like a pretty smart hacker. If it hadn't been for whatever privacy-settings bug had let her see Angie's bathroom SmartMirror feed, Pat never would've had a clue that she'd even been hacked. She would've gone to her grave thinking that she'd deserved ghosts driving her out of her house. And Angie would have flipped Pat's home for a tidy little profit.

That would've been fraud, if not outright theft. But it seemed like the police weren't going to be any help. So Pat would have to find another way to make Angie pay.

Pat could have abused her LifeScore-altering privileges, but that would risk her job. She rubbed her chin again. One thing was for sure, she wasn't going to sell her home to Angie. She needed a way to talk Angie out of that without raising her suspicions. She needed to make Angie talk *herself* out of it. And she had an idea.

***

Pat: Angie I'm SO glad that you are taking this home over
Angie: I'll do my best to get this done as soon as possible
Pat: thank you so much.
Angie: I'm working on the paperwork right now
Pat: The sooner the better. The spirits are out of control
Angie: Hang in there Pat. I'll send the paperwork to you as soon as I can
Pat: the Presence has flooded my basement now
Pat: it made a pipe burst, there's water everwhere
Angie: What?

Pat smiled evilly to herself. Her basement was fine, of course. But Angie had no way of knowing that. There weren't any SmartHome cameras in the basement: she'd gone down and checked.

Pat: it was just gushing. I turned the water off myself
Pat: but the drywall is ruined
Pat: V. Glad I'm selling the home 2 you AS-IS hahaha
Angie: Wait, how bad is the damage?
Pat: Angie I know u can get the spirits under control

Pat: But plz hurry b4 the spirits destroy the home any further
Angie: ...
Pat: if you delay too much you may get mold in the drywall
Angie: Pat I will do the best I can
Angie: but it's an inter state transaction
Angie: this might delay me somewhat
Angie: so you'd better call the plumber ok?
Angie: and let me know how bad the damage is
Pat: its pretty bad
Pat: worried abt mold
Angie: can you dry it
Angie: I think the paperwork may take me a few more days
Angie: can you please get the plumber & try to dry it out
Angie: and let me know how that goes
Angie: OK Pat?
Angie: Pat?
Pat van Buren has left the chat.

***

Pat smiled as she closed her foldie. She had a feeling that Angie would experience mysterious "delays" with the paperwork until Pat told her the fictional basement situation was resolved. And if Angie did continue to push forward with the paperwork, Pat could always invent another crisis.

Now, Pat just had to find a way to get Angie in trouble. Fast, before Angie realized Pat was onto her and disappeared.

Her work queue was flashing red, and she had seven urgent messages from Karen. Fine. Her LifeScore workspace was a great place to start: specifically, Angie's SmartMirror videos. Pat might not be able to ding Angie's LifePoints directly... but maybe she could figure something out.

***

She was interrupted by a sound she hadn't heard since Melinda's movers had left: the doorbell.

Pat wasn't exactly expecting visitors. She pulled out her foldie, thumbed up the front door cam. Two burly men were standing on her doorstep, bearing toolboxes. They wore blue T-shirts reading CAP'S PLUMBERS. The street cam showed a white van emblazoned with the same logo and the slogan "WE TAKE ALL JOBS."

One of the men leaned on the doorbell, filling the house with chiming. Pat thumbed off the doorbell alert in the SmartHome app, turned on the outside speaker. "I didn't call for any plumbers," she said.

"We got a call for a flooded basement at 74 Morningside," replied the slightly larger man.

Pat's heart plummeted. Of course. She'd given Angie her address for the real estate transaction. "I don't know what to tell you," she said. "I didn't call you."

The men glanced at each other. "We're gonna have to put this in as refused service," said the larger one. "That's a seventy-five dollar charge."

"If it's your landlord called us, I just wanta let you know that you're gonna hafta let us in sooner or later," added the smaller one. "They only hafta give you 24 hours' notice, and they're gonna be pissed about the charge."

Pat made a face. Angie had called the kind of plumbers that served the plumbing needs of slumlords' lowest-LifeScore tenants. The plumbers had taken one look at Pat's low LifeScore and assumed she was the same.

"I don't *have* a landlord!" she snapped. "Maybe someone's pranking you. I don't really care. I'm not letting in two guys I didn't call. Have a nice day."

Pat turned off the audio. She didn't need to hear any more... and she didn't have any time to waste.

There was no question that Angie had called the plumbers, to protect the time she'd invested in stealing Pat's house. Soon she'd want to know why Pat hadn't let the plumbers in to deal with her supposedly-flooded basement. And if Pat stalled too much... Pat was well aware that there were other, less pleasant services that slumlords could hire to deal with their lowest-LifeScore tenants. With a chill, Pat realized: Her door had a SmartLock. Angie could unlock her front door. When the plumbers came back, Angie could just let them in.

And Pat couldn't do anything about that. She couldn't patch the SmartHome security bugs that Angie must've exploited to "own" her SmartHome without alerting Angie.

Pat had to figure out a way to get back at Angie, and she had to do it fast.

***

Back in her LifeScore workspace, Pat flagged all Angie's SmartMirror videos for review and pulled them into her burgeoning queue. The article she'd read on "faux hauntings" had given her an idea.

Thanks to her ability as a social credit auditor to get "context," Pat was able to pull a full week of video history from Angie's bathroom SmartMirror. She skimmed through a few hours of video at high speed, then used the AI to compare and group all the SmartMirror captures that had Angie in them. When she'd finished sorting, she had no fewer than seven SmartMirror captures of Angie making spooky noises at herself in the mirror. Pat recognized every noise as one that had floated through her home at one time or another.

Angie evidently liked to pre-record her special effects in her bathroom. Maybe she liked the effect of the echo; maybe she just liked making faces at herself in her SmartMirror. Angie also liked to give herself a self-congratulatory thumbs-up at the end of each spooky session... along with comments like "Best one yet!", "That one's going right on her SmartHome speakers," and Pat's personal favorite, "Nobody fakes ghosts like Angela DeVaux!"

Pat smiled grimly. Those little comments made her blood boil... and she loved them.

***

PatVanBuren: Hey Raoul

RaoulMorales: Hi Pat

PatVanBuren: You remember we were talking about reporting bugs

RaoulMorales: Sure, we can report them but it's limited to the WorkSpace or the AI, and you need at least 4 clips to support it

RaoulMorales: did you find something?

PatVanBuren: Not a bug. But we can report enhancements too right

RaoulMorales: Yes. We have a process for enhancements for the LifeScore AI

RaoulMorales: Actually enhancements are tough

RaoulMorales: So if we suggest a good enhancement there is a reward

JefValentino: Oh cool, so can we suggest this as an enhancement for the AI: "Don't look at bathrooms"?

RaoulMorales: Good idea Jef, but, the enhancement should be to help the AI get better at LifeScore adjustments, not to make up for a SmartHome privacy bug

PatVanBuren: Nice try though Jef

PatVanBuren: But I have a better idea

RaoulMorales: What

PatVanBuren: Have you guys seen this article?

[PREVIEW: **SmartHome hackers face little consequences** *by Chelsea Tritton, special to the Post. Last year, over two thousan...]*

JefValentino: I don't get it
PatVanBuren: Scroll down to "Faux hauntings." Got someone practicing a faux haunting in her SmartMirror
JefValentino: Whoah.
RaoulMorales: Are you sure Pat
PatVanBuren: Ah that is the part I love
PatVanBuren: She likes to tell her SmartMirror how good she is at faking hauntings
JefValentino: LOL
RaoulMorales: Nice one Pat
PatVanBuren: I'll send a few clips to both of your queues
PatVanBuren: Take a look and see what you think
RaoulMorales: Sure, no problem
JefValentino: if she's that obvious, I think she deserves some major LifeScore adjustments
PatVanBuren: Jef, I like the way you think

***

At the end of the day, Pat sat back in her chair, feeling better than she had in a long time. Now, *that* was a day's work well done. She hadn't taken a single LifePoint off Angie herself... but her teammates, between them, had tanked Angie's LifeScore. Not only had Angie's SmartMirror recorded her planning to stage fake hauntings, but Raoul and Jef had pulled "context" from Angie's other home cams and found video of her running her faux exorcisms.

Apparently Angie had never thought to erase evidence from her *own* SmartHome video history. Raoul and Jef had taken away LifePoints for each and every incriminating video.

By the time Jef and Raoul were through with her, Angie's Life-Score was even lower than Pat's. She'd have trouble convincing any potential future victims to give her the time of day.

With her revenge against Angie taken care of, Pat had kicked Angie out of her SmartHome system. After work, she'd pulled every Smart device and her HomeBrain offline, reset it to factory settings, and applied every possible patch. Angie was out of her SmartHome, and she wasn't getting back in.

All that patching had been a pain in the ass, but it could've been worse: Pat could've had to do it on an empty stomach. With a smile, Pat slurped the last peanut from a carton of not-too-terrible Kung Pao. Simply submitting an enhancement request had bumped her LifeScore just high enough for decent delivery.

***

> **KarenHamber:** Pat we need 2 talk
> **KarenHamber:** please open video chat

"Hi Karen, what's up?" Pat asked guardedly.

Karen was far less elliptical in video than in text. "Pat! I got a message directly from a Vice President about you! Did you submit an enhancement request for the AI?"

"Yes, a little while ago. Why?"

"Well, congratulations. Your enhancement was accepted by the LifeScore AI team. And listen to this. The Veep is, quote, very pleased with the acuity of my team member, unquote! This made our team look great, Pat."

"Great."

"And she's giving you the maximum LifePoints bonus for suggesting it! You should see the LifeScore bump right away."

"Wonderful! Thanks, Karen," Pat said.

"To be honest," Karen continued, "I was getting a little worried about you over the last few months, but you've really done a one-eighty. You've gone from my worst performing team member to a bonus from the Veep! Can I ask what inspired your turnaround?"

Pat grinned. "Karen," she said, "You could say... I really got into the *spirit* of the job."

***

MySocial Chat Alert! **Warning:** *you have a chat request from an ultra-low-LifeScore user. Do you wish to accept this request from Angela DeVaux?*

With a smile, Pat clicked No.

Then she closed the window, and moved on.

Trash Talk

By Holly Schofield

I'm not a complainer, not me. I roll with the punches. I'll be just another dead trash collector in about ten minutes but, hey, that's okay. My son won't die and, here's a bonus, my life insurance policy will pay out.

Unless they consider it suicide.

Here we are, hugging in the middle of my living room, me in my robo-assist, my fists locked behind Ricky's head, up high, like a boxer's. Ricky, that's my son, he's pinned right against my chest.

I can't see much now, things are blurry; must be sweat that's in my eyes. Maybe that'll save me 'cause it'll short out the servos sooner or later. That was a joke. I'm hanging tough. By the way, guys, before you do anything down at the cop shop with this voice record, edit out all the emotional crap Ricky and I said earlier at the beginning, like, right when it started recording, okay? Kinda embarrassing.

Lemme tell you about the assists. Us union guys aren't issued fancy ones like the reality stars get—ours don't have hardly any medi-sensors or monitors or nothing—only basics, like the LifeSwitch. And they don't come with no webcams, just a remote link and a voice recorder in the sleeve controls. You velcro a battery pack at the top of your ass and then jam your feet in the boots and ease the assist on like a really, really stiff coverall. You can't even see the eight servo motors or the carbon fiber rods under the plastic. The memory foam grabs your calves and thighs and arms, and you hit the 'On' button and, uber-quick, it's slaved to your movements. In, like, thirty seconds you're up and running.

On a good day.

Since the city cut back the maintenance budget, there's all sorts of glitches with the assists. Mine's all battered and scratched and the shoulder hatch is just duct-taped on.

Ricky, he's a good son, twenty-eight years old and smart as a chip, he says I should tell management that the assists are a bit wacked. What he don't know is, and I'm being real frank here since it don't matter no more, I tinkered with my assist last week, so I'd be setting myself up if I asked them to run diagnostics on it. See, there's one stop on my route, got these goddamn decorative rocks right in front, I gotta heave the cans up and over each friggin' time, makes the bursitis in my shoulder kick up something terrible. So I ramped up the assist, just a touch, and that meant I had to fiddle with the limit control, tweak the processors a bit, you know? Guys my age got hardware skills, not like today's kids that can't tell firmware from their underwear. Still, now I wish I hadn't done that. Goddamn, do I wish it.

Anyway, I know you cops are busy guys. So I'll get to the point.

First, though, I need to tell you just a bit more about the Lifeswitch so things make more sense. Like, take Johnno last month: his lungs couldn't hack it no more and the asthma meds were too friggin' expensive but what was he gonna do? Twenty-two years he's been chucking cans on the west end route. Nobody's gonna hire him for anything else, not in this Slump. Don't know what the country's coming to. Anyway, Johnno got to the point where heaving a full can into the truck made him cough up a lung for a good three minutes, even with his assist cranked up to max. Poitr, the depot tech, he told me how it went down that day. Johnno was finishing up his route when Poitr's screens blared so loud the depot practically shook. That's what happens when a LifeSwitch goes off. It's a union requirement, see? Been too many cases where a can jockey got hurt on the job and no one knew. Johnno took his last breath and his assist triggered had the alarm. The medics were there in minutes but Johnno was splayed out in the lane, dead, with a full trash can spilled out all over him. They had to cut the assist in pieces to get it off. We had a nice little memorial for him in the coffee room, and the union even paid for donuts.

Today, I wore my assist home with me. Yeah, I know, against union rules, sure, but Ricky wanted me to move his old piano from my basement here at the farm to his new apartment. It's an upright, one of those old-school pianos that weigh more than a garbage truck. I'd lowered it into the basement the day we moved to the farm, Mandy and me. Ricky was just a twinkle in our eye. Mandy had had all these ambitions for the kid and he hadn't even seen the light of day yet. I couldn't afford much so I'd got this old piano out of the town dump. That was back when people just trashed stuff. None of this 3-D printer recycling nonsense where you gotta sort the trash components so goddamn carefully these days. So what I did, I wrapped a wire cable around the piano with Mandy dancing around, chattering like she did, and her stuffing a blanket at the edges so it wouldn't scratch the finish. Then I backed my old Suburban up slowly over the front lawn—you shoulda heard that woman of mine yelling about her flowerbeds—and hitched it to the other end of the cable. I put my shoulder to the piano, those were the days—before this bursitis—and that wooden beast slid down the first step and hung there while the cable went zing and tightened up. Then I backed the Suburban slowly toward the house. The piano slid the rest of the way down the stairs, easy as pi. Those were the days. I'd give anything for Mandy to still be alive and yelling at me about something. The breast cancer cure came along just five years too late, ya know, or she would be here in the living room right now, yapping away, getting us out of this mess.

Goddamn, sweat or something is running in my eyes again. Wish I could wipe them.

He's a good kid, Ricky, but not tall and not muscle-bound, if you know what I mean. He's got his dad for that stuff. So when he said he wanted the piano at his apartment, I was happy to help. But my shoulder's been hurting all week. Bursitis is hell. Not complaining, mind, just telling you why I wore the assist home from work. I don't want the blame put on anyone else but me, see?

What I can't figure is—let me yap a bit, guys, I got time—we got that bunch of cancer cures now, right? Well, for the common types. We got that colony on the moon, right? Well, the Chinese do. And we fixed AIDS good. Well, not counting AIDS 2.0, but, at least, there's progress, right, even in this crappy economy. So why haven't they fixed diabetes yet? Like, come on. Ricky's life has been a tough one, all because of the Big D. Giving himself insulin jets every few hours, 24/7, pain in the ass and pricey. Regular joes, like Ricky and me, we can't afford those new patches they got now. And he needs sugary snacks even oftener than the jets, or it's coma-time. Missed out going on friends' camping trips and a school trip to Disneyland when he was a kid. I was too goddamn nervous to let him out of my sight that long. You know us single parents, always a little twitchy.

Ricky's such a good kid. I mean, to be born right when the Slump took down the economy, that's rough. Him choosing music teacher as his profession, that's damn smart. Not gonna get obsolete any time soon. Let's see a bot teach piano, eh? Those upscale parents on the west side are always gonna want the status of a real live teacher watching their kids plink out notes on a keyboard.

Anyhow, Ricky met me at home today. Well, you know that, 'cause you'll have found our bodies in the living room by now. At least I hope someone finds 'em before too long. The heat of the summer that we wait for all year, it isn't always a good thing, know what I mean? We were gonna move that piano. I'd come in the back door through the mudroom, letting the assist help me up the back steps. Steps are hard on the knees with the weight of the assist, eh. Ricky walked in the front door about ten seconds later, beaming from ear to ear. Staggering a bit, hadn't had time to eat for a few hours but pushing through it. Tough, like his dad. His big news, he couldn't wait to tell me, was he got himself a fancy job teaching music up at the university. That's my boy! He was all dressed up in a fancy suit. Guess that's why he didn't have any insulin jets handy—must've left them in his other pants or something.

I was so proud, I gave him a big hard hug and that's when it happened. The assist jammed. Stuck us both in my living room holding Ricky like a piece of wood in a vise. My wrist controls were right there, centimeters from my nose but I couldn't reach them. Ricky of course never wore a phone or nothin', said it interfered with the music nodes he sometimes patched on his skull. That boy was always playing his tunes.

"Ricky, see if you can hit the controls on my wrist," I said.

He didn't say nothing, which, at the time, I thought was weird. Anyhow, he sucked in a long breath and managed to twist an arm up and around my wrist. Then he let his arm fall, just dropped it like a stone. Well, he'd hit Connect all right, as well as Record. Connect started playing some service message about some goddamn maintenance routine they were running down at the depot. Still no big deal, I thought, Poitr or someone'll answer soon. At least, they'd miss me on tomorrow's shift or a neighbor might stop in. Mind you, the nearest neighbor is a good three klicks away. We liked the peace and quiet out here in the country, Mandy and I.

"Ricky," I said next. "Son, see if you can wiggle out of here and get some help. Maybe if you twist a bit in my arms, you might lose some skin or dislocate your shoulder but I bet you can slide out."

"Yeah...," he said all long and drawn-out like and then he sagged down in my arms. Sugar-coma, dammit.

I yelled and prodded but he was too far gone. The service message played over and over.

So here we are. Thanks for listening to me spill all this crap, guys. I got another favor to ask, too.

I know you cops have reports to make and forms to fill out, but if you could keep quiet about how things happened here—about what, God help me, I'm going to do next. Keep it from Ricky, I'm askin' you. If you could do that, it would be a fine thing. I don't want the boy spending the rest of his life having the guilts 'cause dear ol' Dad did this for him, you know?

Anyhow, I think I can bypass some stuff, mash two little contacts together, and get the shoulder motor working. I did it before in the shop when I ramped things up. Just the one shoulder will do it. So far, I've scraped off the duct tape and now I've got a couple of fingers inside the shoulder hatch. So, if I can connect up that servo to trigger a rotating action, see, my arm rises up, my fist pivots toward my head, my neck snaps, and that'll set off the LifeSwitch and call up you guys and the medics. Ricky will be saved and, hey, I gotta save my boy, no matter what. I'm not grumbling about it, just saying it so you cops can figure out stuff when you get here.

No, I'm not complaining...I'm just, you know, rolling with the punches.

A Quiet Lie

By Ross Pruden

Ken Harper stood on his front porch surveying the fields before him and nodded to himself in satisfaction. The robotic beasts were edging down their prescribed paths as instructed and little needed to be done to ensure they stayed on track. He glanced at the sky to see if clouds would threaten the machines' solar chargers but he saw only blue. Turning to get his cup of tepid coffee from the porch railing, he walked towards the door but stopped when he heard the familiar whirr of an approaching drone.

Ken took a sip from his cup while watching the smooth red and white orb descend, its propellers muffled by protection blisters. The drone floated gently over the wrought iron table near him on the porch. Its innards opened and gently placed a tiny box on the table, then the drone resumed its upward flight. Ken picked the box up and smiled wistfully—he'd been waiting for this.

Inside, he opened the box and removed a set of translucent glasses. He mounted the stairs and walked into his study, locking the door. Settling in at his desk, he reviewed the instructions in-cluded in the tiny packaging. Next, he told his computer to open a web page, and within seconds he was reviewing a Terms of Ser-vice Agreement. Alongside the legalese, a video call box appeared; someone from the site was asking to talk to him. Ken clicked "An-swer" and a young man with a short afro and kind eyes appeared. "Hello, my name is David," he said with a welcoming grin. "I'll be walking you through the sign-up process. Is this your first time us-ing Pylon?"

"Yes, it is. Daughter suggested I use it."

"Very well. You should read our Terms of Service on your own time, but let me just give you a quick synopsis, if that's alright."

Ken shifted in his seat a little, "Sure, go ahead."

"To provide you with effective counseling, Pylon needs to know a fair amount about you—personal identity information, your work history, access to your social network connections, and so on. Pylon uses 1,028-bit fractal encryption on any data you share with us and we strongly encourage you to enable encryption on your end, as well.

"Pylon never stores any information about you on our servers without a two-key verification and we can *only* access your unen-crypted data while in a live session. That means that if there is ever a data breach, hackers will only see encrypted gibberish.

"Pylon will never knowingly share any of your data with any third party. Everything said in session is considered completely confidential and all session notes are accessed through a limit-ed-time two-key verification."

"Hold on, what's two-key verification?"

"You know how safety deposit boxes work? The banker has a key and the customer has a key."

"Yes."

"Same thing, only digitally. Unless the counselor has your ex-press permission to open your files, they stay encrypted."

"Great. Can I just approve the TOS now?"

David laughed softly. "Of course, but Pylon insists patients re-view the TOS until they feel satisfied before proceeding. If you're satisfied with my explanation, I'll sign off now; feel free to call me back when you're done reading the TOS. Just click the 'Call Back' button on your screen. I may be leaving the office here in a minute so it's likely you'll get Clancy, my co-worker."

"Thanks, David. I'll call you right back."

Ken hung up and skimmed over the TOS. It was lengthy and sweeping in scope. Pylon needed access to a *lot* of information, but not any more than was expected, really... not for this deep level of mental health care. Psychiatry had morphed into under-standing the human psyche not just as its own system, but as a system interacting with other systems (i.e., humans). With access to deep data analysis, that meant no longer merely taking a patient at their word—you could now gather empirical data *alongside* a patient's subjective interpretations. Thus, to fully understand a patient's emotional state, you needed to both gather objective data about them *individually* (Where and when did they grow up? What shows were they watching? What news did they share with others? What do they do when they're bored?), but also objective data about how they related to the *group*, meaning their past (Who were their family members?), their most active social connections (How many people do they know? How many would they con-sider friends? Which ones and why?), their environment (What kind of chair do they work in? What's their sleep cycle?)... Once the patient gave Pylon explicit approval, Pylon subtly harvested all these seemingly insignificant data points across any relevant tech-nological platform that touched the patient's daily life. Data from all kinds of sources would be routed through a complicated AI al-gorithm on Pylon's servers to predict—with shocking accuracy—what kinds of improvements could be made to address whatever was causing distress in the patient. No kind of data was deemed too trivial to record. If it could be measured, it was collected, ana-lyzed, and compared against thousands of other anonymized patient data to form a baseline of "normal" mental behavior. Armed with this dizzying array of information, Pylon's AI could reliably detect deviancies that predisposed a patient to harm themselves, or others... and do it far better than most human psychiatrists.

After 10 minutes, Ken finally called back Pylon and Clancy answered this time. She had straight auburn hair in a bob and sky blue eyes. "Hello, Mr. Harper. David told me you'd be calling back. Have you finished reading the Terms of Service agreement?"

"Yes. It all looks fine."

"Excellent. I've registered your retinal scan as a signature, so if you're ready, we can begin the next phase of orientation."

"Certainly. What do I do?"

"You must have received the eyewear, correct?"

Ken suppressed a smile: this was a courtesy question—of course Clancy knew he'd received the eyewear; she'd likely seen a notification on her screen, or someone had, and anticipated him calling in not long thereafter.

"Yes, it arrived by drone a few minutes ago."

"Are you alone and will you be alone for at least the next hour?"

"Yes, nobody will be interfering with us."

"Great. Have you examined the eyewear at all?"

"Just a little."

"Okay. How familiar are you with this process?"

"Not at all. I'm doing this at my daughter's request so I really don't know much."

"That's totally fine. I'm here to walk you through it. First, you can take the glasses out of their case."

Ken gingerly pulled the glasses out of the box again and opened them up. They looked fragile, almost like hard and translucent paper. "Should I put them on now?"

"Absolutely. They've been custom-made to fit you so you shouldn't even notice you have them on."

Ken put on the glasses. The transparency was impressive. They were featherlight, and the inlaid optics were designed to further augment the transparency. It was easy to imagine he wasn't wearing them at all, which was the whole idea.

"Okay, excellent." Clancy looked off to one side of her screen. "The eyewear serves two functions: it takes micro readings of your facial movements, but it's also a VR headset. Are you sitting down now, Mr. Harper?"

"Yes."

"Okay, I'm going to try something now and I want you to just relax."

"Okay." Ken's heart began to beat faster, acting out of reflex... this was safe, right?

"Go ahead and close your eyes for me."

Ken closed his eyes.

"Excellent. Now, with your eyes still closed, tell me what you hear."

Ken listened and the sound of the room he was in *changed*. He wasn't sure how, but the eyewear's temple tips must have had speakers in them, maybe with noise-cancelling? "It sounds like the room has changed somehow. Like the furniture isn't in the right place... or when you sense someone has walked into the room."

"Good. Keep your eyes closed for now, but in the next minute, you're going to feel the urge to take off your eyewear. That's normal and no harm will come to you if you do. However, for best results, we strongly recommend against it. When you're ready, slowly open your eyes."

Ken opened his eyes and audibly gasped. On the outside, the eyewear must have become fully opaque because inside it was a faithful reproduction of what Ken presumed was a psychiatrist's office. Clancy was opposite him, "sitting" only half a meter away, and a small monitor screen sat on a desk to her right. In reality, she could be thousands of miles away, but it felt like they were in the same room.

"This is..." Ken's jaw stayed open. He looked down at his body and saw his arms and hands within the simulation. He brought his hands together and rubbed the fingers against one another. The simulation was perfectly in sync with his hands. "Incredible."

"We're using the camera on your computer to capture where you are in your room, as well as your body movements and gesticulations. The eyewear displays the VR setting, but it has sensors to take some body readings. Your heartbeat, for example, is a little high. Just take a few deep breaths for me, would you?"

Ken did as he was asked. Clancy watched her monitor.

"So far, so good." Clancy said, smiling. "How are you enjoying your first trip to a virtual shrink?"

Ken laughed and quickly realized she was using humor to put him at ease. It worked. "Loving it. I wish all my shows were this real. Well... Maybe not *all* of them."

Clancy laughed, and glanced back at her monitor. "I have one more thing to cover. Pylon sometimes uses Print Technology—do you know what that is?"

"Holograms, right?"

"Not exactly. Print Technology calls on all kinds of personal identification data to create simulations of people you already know—" she spread her arms wide, indicating the whole room, "—in this virtual setting to better aid in the counseling process."

"Wait—does that mean you access *their* personal data?"

"Only the data you permit us to, and any data we do access is immediately sequestered by the source after we're done using it, thereby rendering the Print inert."

Ken paused to think about that.

"Let me give you an example: imagine you have a problem with your boss—"

"I'm a farmer—I don't have a boss."

"Fair enough. But let's say you had a problem with a close friend of family member and your counselor thinks you'd benefit from a role-play exercise with that person. In this virtual environment, a Print of that person will look and talk like an actual human, but will be fully computer generated so you can talk to them in complete safety. With your approval, we would request access to your friend's social media profile and generate their virtual reality doppelgänger using Print Technology.

"Access to your friend's information is *strictly* limited to its creation and use in sessions. Once the session is over, our access expires and the Print becomes just a bunch of 'framing' code without anything inside it." Seeing Ken's quizzical look, she continued, "Think of Pylon as a car, and Print Tech is its engine; not only is that engine composed of 1,000 different parts but each part is anonymously borrowed and returned immediately after the car gets to where it's going.

"Again, your counselor may call on any person you know to be a Print but only if you give them permission to do so. In order to build a convincing print, we must draw data from over 600 different sources—"

"600?"

"The specifics of data collection fall under Print Tech's confidentiality agreement with Pylon, but you can imagine how access to merely a person's social media feed can help simulate their physical appearance. From that same source, timestamps of their social media posts help to deduce other useful information—for instance, if someone is posting at 3AM, then you can calculate how much sleep they might be getting, and probably how grouchy they might be, etc. There is a good reason why Print Tech has the largest and best collection of data scientists on its payroll.

"Because Pylon requires your express permission to gain access to your social networks and any other relevant accounts, getting approval from all those sources can be extremely time-consuming, so the sooner we get your approval, the faster your sessions can begin. As David told you before, when your session is over, all your data—especially your generated Prints—is two-key encrypted. You also have the option to delete all of your data should you decide to not be Pylon's patient anymore."

"Wow, that's great. David didn't tell me that."

"It's a *long* TOS, isn't it?" she said in a mockingly conspiratorial tone, then smiled.

Ken chuckled. "Definitely not boilerplate."

"Very well. Here is the approval form for the use of Print Technology." Clancy laid a virtual form on the desk in front of him. "If you agree to it, we can start your session immediately."

Ken reviewed the form. "That's fine, yes. I agree."

"Wonderful. I've registered your retinal scan as a signature. Okay, well... I've covered all the basics. It seems I can leave now and bring in the counselor. His name is Nathaniel Drumming, or Nate. He's extremely nice, and has been practicing for 32 years. Are you ready?"

"Yes, I'm ready."

Clancy stood and straightened out her blouse while leaving the room. "Mr. Drumming," she said, while opening the door. "Mr. Harper can see you now." Then she closed the door behind her and the room was quiet again.

Ken looked around the room. For the first time, he realized he must look foolish to anyone seeing him in his study with greyed-out eyewear, scanning his room like a life-size bobblehead. But before he could think about it any longer, the door in the simulation opened slowly and a man of medium height walked in. He was mostly bald, lots of wrinkles around his face, but not over 50, Ken figured. Nate had wire-framed glasses and held a notepad and pen in one hand.

"Hello, Mr. Harper. Don't get up," he said with a smile while still standing in the doorway, "We can't shake hands, anyway, so don't worry about it. Before we go any further, I'd like to introduce my colleague, Phyllis Lock." A middle-aged woman in a purple cashmere shawl appeared in the doorway and stood next to her colleague. "When I'm not available or need to step out, she can take over for me. We both take copious notes so you may consider her an equal partner in your care. She monitors many of my sessions so she can step in at any time. Is that acceptable to you?"

"Yes, that's okay."

"Excellent. Thank you, Phyllis. I'll see you in an hour," he said, and closed the door. Turning to Ken, he said, "It's just us now. What's on your mind?"

***

Phyllis stood before her wall-sized monitor at her spacious home office in Missoula, Montana. Several other monitors to either side displayed live readings of each of her patients' physical state. If any patient became distressed, the readings on these side displays would redline and Phyllis would take a deeper interest in that patient. She watched Ken's session for a few minutes until she felt comfortable enough to minimize it.

She removed her purple cashmere sweater and popped a grape in her mouth. Nathaniel Drumming was a Print, of course, and not even based on a real person. David and Clancy had also been CGI Prints. Even though Phyllis had appeared as a Print in Ken's session, Phyllis was still the brains of the whole operation and remained on call for whenever a patient needed a genuine human interaction. Prints could do most of her job *extremely* well now, but Phyllis still liked the personal touch. Besides, the insurance carrier who kept her lights on would have it no other way.

Her huge monitor currently held live sessions of 20 other patients, scattered throughout the world. One patient was in Sri Lanka, another in Idaho. Four of them were active military and six were vets. The rest were civilians of varying ages.

Just like her patients, Phyllis interacted with David and Clancy as facilitators. Leveraging human mimicry at this level of competency helped Phyllis see a much larger caseload than she could have done only five years ago. With large-scale tragedies like that awful cruise ship collision last year, she could see as many as 50 clients at once, if needed. That meant more patients, less overhead, and more time... which meant more pro bono work. At rough count, she had saved at least three lives in the last year from those pro bono sessions, all because she could afford to spare time for it.

Naturally, there were always times with things went wrong. Sometimes the network got glitchy which made the Prints act wonky. Or the time there was a two-day blackout—in both cases, Phyllis had simply resorted to regular phone calls for any patients in dire need.

There was, of course, the ethical problem of lying to—or to be more accurate, "compassionately deceiving"—the patient. Did they know they were talking to a Print? These days, it was commonplace to talk to robots on the phone and over the internet. Each year, the Turing Test continued to certify repeatedly older AI subjects; as long as the life of the patient became more convenient and solved the issues they were there for, they didn't seem to care if they were talking to a real person or not.

Unsurprisingly, Pylon's legal department had insisted that 'use of Print Technology' be clearly stated in the TOS and they required facilitators to give patients abundant time to review the TOS before agreeing to it; if patients asked for clarification about Prints, Pylon facilitators would be contractually obligated to spell out *everything* for them. Additionally, Pylon's patient orientation process let patients assume David, Clancy, and Nate were humans, a canary in the coal mine test to see if patients suspected they were talking to a Print—if they did, then Phyllis was required to immediately disclose the truth and assume complete human-to-human mental care unless the patients specified otherwise. However, if a patient simply signed the TOS, Pylon was free to use Prints as copiously as they wanted, especially if it helped parse out which patients really needed human interaction. If asked, patients were *always* happy with their care, so Phyllis had no real problem with the quiet lie.

What bothered Phyllis much more was the sources of data compiled to generate the Prints. Pylon and Print Tech had access to DNA information, driving patterns, online purchasing, media browsed and consumed, medical prescriptions... Pylon took pains to put the public at ease that all that data was accessed privately, discretely, and temporarily; all of the hundreds of personal identifying data points used to create a single Print were stripped of any unique information so that a Print's full identity only came together in session. She remembered the Pylon spokesman at her orientation seminar three years ago: "It's as if you have three people with different pieces of the same map. They come together, find the treasure, then burn their pieces of the map, and part ways." It was a skillful analogy. And it complimented the traditional rules of patient confidentiality between patients and human psychiatrists—at least in theory. Phyllis was distrustful of large companies with access to that much information on any one person, but Pylon had developed successful relationships with hundreds of sources to sufficiently safeguard patient privacy; if hundreds of companies had agreed to Pylon's privacy guarantee, they must have used some kind of a data escrow agency to keep Pylon honest.

An adjacent monitor blinked suddenly and Ken's minimized video feed was framed with a red line. Phyllis touched Ken's face and it grew to fill nearly the whole screen.

Ken was confessing why he was there—his youngest daughter had died suddenly and his eldest daughter knew he had trouble confiding his emotions to anyone. Maybe this session could be what he was looking for? Phyllis looked at the monitors and recognized that familiar pattern of extreme sadness and grief on the verge of spilling over.

Looking at the clock, she knew she had no time to barge into the session—it would be rushed and ruin the sanctity of the moment. So she reached over and touched a button on her keyboard. A camera on her computer read her facial patterns and transferred her facial movements and speech onto Nate's Print.

"Sometimes," she said slowly with Nate's voice and mouth, "we have such strong emotions inside us. It acts as a poison that we *know* we must let out or it will spill over into the rest of our relationships and destroy them." She paused here, for dramatic effect, letting her words sink in. "You have grief over a lost daughter. You have shame for failing her as a parent. You have self-loathing and anger. All of this is okay, and normal, and nothing you do can ever undo the past. All you can do now is feel that grief, embrace it in all its ugliness, and move on."

Ken was on the verge of tears but generations of toxic masculinity kept it stubbornly locked up inside him.

Phyllis pressed another button and looked at an adjacent monitor. A picture of Ken's daughter with petabytes of information about her immediately flowed down the screen. "If she were right here with us, what would you say to her?"

That almost did it. Ken was close to weeping. But still...

"If she could walk through that door behind me," Phyllis said, hooking a thumb to point at the door behind Nate, "if you could see her face one last time, what would you say?"

Phyllis turned around, and in her peripheral, she saw her puppet Nate do likewise. From Ken's point of view, it seemed as if Nate were looking at the door, expectantly.

Phyllis turned Nate's head back to look at Ken. "Why don't you tell her yourself?"

She pushed another button and the door behind Nate opened. Ken's facial expressions redlined for a moment as he saw his deceased daughter, her hair pulled up like she'd done when she was 16, wearing that silly lavender dress she'd taken to in her 30s. Her eyebrows furrowed tentatively as she saw her father.

"Hello, Daddy."

Ken lost all control, weeping cathartically for minutes.

Finally, this broken man was on the long road to recovery.

The Mummer

By James Yu

Olin Chang stared at the display. It was 2am. He was, he confessed, happiest when he was alone. That's why he'd installed the glass wall he could work behind. His mom had complained, but he'd paid for the enclosure himself, not to mention their entire home.

Gossamer light trails danced on the screen, each one a self-driving car traversing the streets of Chicago. They swarmed in a symphony of paths—moving people, minimizing waste, increasing value. They reminded him of the ants at the playground when he was little, each giving it their all for the hive. Perfection.

He downed his energy drink, then watched as the display blinked red. He was falling behind at his tasks—something a good machine wouldn't do.

Olin was a mummer, which meant he helped machines. He was there when they failed, and that meant he had to understand them—become one of them.

His fingers clacked across the spring-loaded keyboard. Mumming was all about speed. With a single keystroke, he could pull up the manual for any computer, robot, car, or machine.

Finally, data smacked into the display. He leaned forward at his Armada standing desk workstation, feeling the warmth of the pixels. It was a Model 442 Digger—a giant earth excavator from Gamma Corporation the size of a house. He frowned. The mum rate for this model cracked over one percent. Unacceptable.

The excavator whinnied. Its bucket was dipped halfway into grimy soil. It was somewhere in Ethiopia, but the location was irrelevant.

A loud knock jolted him.

"Go away. I'm working."

He could hear a raucous laugh from the hallway, and he flinched. Not again.

"*Go away!*" he repeated.

The door opened. A figure spilled into the room wearing a v-neck shirt slick from sweat. Olin smelled Jack and Coke on his brother's breath even through the array of air filters. A lithe girl was pulled in behind him.

"This is my brother, Olin," Corey said to the girl in slurred speech. "He's a good brother, but keeps to himself, you know—because of this." Corey tapped his side of the glass wall. "I wanted to show you. You asked if it was true."

Olin focused his gaze at the edge of his keyboard. His veins pulsed. "*Get the fuck out,*" he said.

The girl tugged at Corey's sleeve, gesturing toward the door.

Yeah, that's right, don't even acknowledge me. Maybe I'm dangerous.

Corey wagged his finger and squinted. "Not nice, Olin."

Olin charged the glass. "Stop bothering me! And you—" he pointed to the girl. "Stay away from him. You think he cares?"

Corey put an arm around the girl. "You see how much I love him? Even though he hates me."

"What's happening?" Mom was at the doorway in red pajamas,

looking frail at such a late hour. "Corey! Stop bothering your brother." She glanced at the girl. "Who is this?"

"Just a friend, mom," said Corey.

"*Aiya.* Are you drinking again?"

"I'm not drunk." Corey led the girl out the door with scarcely a glance.

Olin sighed. *Just focus on the task ahead.* He turned back toward the desk.

"You should sleep," his mom said.

"Need to work."

Behind him, he could sense that she had more to say—that staying up late jeopardized his health; that he should work during the day like normal people. But instead, she left.

***

Soon, he was back in the warm embrace of the Armada. It was time for his favorite: self-driving cars. He tackled a few warmup tasks—untangling an overweight truck in Texas, winding a sedan around a group of ducks near Seattle (the waddling confused the AI), and shooing away a group of pesky teenagers encircling a minivan.

Corey's intrusion seemed distant now; Olin was back in the flow. He set the difficulty to the highest level. Minutes later, a chime filled the room.

His mouth gaped at the bright letters on the screen. Gamma Model N2. Unbelievable. They haven't made those since the late 2020s—before he was even born. He brought up the N2 spec sheet and scanned the page. An ancient car with a sleek, curvy body—built at the dawn of self-driving cars. A delicious challenge.

He tapped the accept button.

The screen went blank. Probably a slow connection. Finally, the video feed started, but it was a formless white. Then the contrast kicked in and the details emerged.

It was snow.

The flakes fell on a lonely road surrounded by fields. Strange. What was an N2 doing here? It should be in a museum, not stuck in a random county road—he looked up the location: Oswego, a small village in rural New York.

The car was equipped with limited sensors, so he wasn't surprised it had gotten stuck. Back then, the designers were hoping that automated snow plowers would be everywhere. But there were no plowers here—no machines to help.

He pulsed the accelerator and turned the wheels at erratic angles. Not the most elegant maneuver, but there weren't many options. He furrowed his brow, then keyed in a safety override. The car lurched forward with a faint whir and escaped its fluffy prison. Colorful letters congratulated him on a job well done.

He sunk into his chair and opened another can of liquid energy as the next task loaded. An indicator flashed out of the corner of his eye. Voices in the car cabin. Usually, he'd ignore this—passengers were never helpful. But he was curious. Who was riding in this antique? He turned on the cabin video.

An Asian woman with delicate features sat alone, bundled in a puffy down jacket. "Thank you," she said. The screen blinked out, but he caught something in that last frame—fresh abrasions splotched the left side of her face. And there, a frayed wire spilled out of her cheek.

***

Olin hadn't always been fat. He remembered how as a kid, his scrawny frame drew the ire of bullies. His only solace was keeping to the dusty corners of the school yard, sticking close to the robot chaperones. Fat kids got picked on too, but at least they had a size advantage when it came down to an actual fight. He was knocked around like a *piñata*.

One day, after coming home with painful welts on his face and arms, his father sat him down. "Ignore them and find your own

path," he said in a quiet voice. "By fighting them, their anger in-
fects you."

"I can't just stand there!" He puffed his chest and pretended his
ten-year-old body was as tall as those giant Japanese robots.

"That is no way for our family to act. You must avoid fighting.
Turn the other cheek." His dad sighed and went back to nursing his
pipe, marking the end of the conversation.

Their family didn't have much. His dad was the first to come
to America, and he worked to the bone at an IT job managing AIs.
But he wasn't savvy in the corporate world. His dad would stay late
at work and miss dinner most nights. Olin fought his heavy eye-
lids in order to see him come home, but inevitably woke up in bed
knowing that his dad had carried him there.

Dad never complained. And he never got the chance.

Olin remembered that slow knock on the door; the shadow
of the policeman mumbling serious words; and his mom's body
crumpling to the floor like a sack of rice. His dad had been found
slumped at his desk. Dead from an aneurysm.

Olin's only solace was a little robot called Xiao Dian which he
carried around in his pocket. During class, he'd play with it under
his desk. In the school yard, he directed it to smash pebbles with its
tiny fists, imagining each rock a bully. Eventually he controlled the
robot using subtle gestures. He loved tricking people into thinking
it was autonomous, though it was him the whole time.

***

An alert sounded as Olin snapped back into the workstation. He
had put in a request to take on tasks exclusively in the Oswego
area, hoping to see that damaged robot again. The familiar video
stream of the snowy road cast a white glow in the dark room.

He flicked through the LIDAR logs, the lines of green text blur-
ring across the display. The same N2 car was stuck at the same
spot. There was a dip in the ground, and that, combined with the

snow, triggered the error state. Gamma didn't bother to update the vehicle. Corporations didn't care about old machines.

"Are you there?"

Olin fumbled with the microphone. "I'm here."

She was wearing the same puffy jacket. The blemishes on her face were gone.

She gazed directly at the camera. "Hello. I'm Ling."

"I'm...." He hesitated. He wasn't supposed to engage in unnecessary conversations. But this technically wasn't a person, right? He cleared his throat. "I'm Olin."

"Hi, Olin."

"You're stuck again," he said.

"I can see that." She laughed.

Was she really a robot? Her head bobbed like a human's when she laughed. Then he noticed the faint seams near her neckline. "This might take a while." The wheels gyrated again. It was stuck deeper this time. "I might have to call for drone support."

She nodded.

"Are you a robot?"

"Yes."

"Why can't I detect your presence?" He should be seeing her in the diagnostics panel. But there was nothing. She was invisible to his instruments.

She turned toward the window. "I'm cut off."

Was she a runaway?

"I'm a Model Z," she said.

A Zenbot! He had never seen one in real life. They were one of the few robots designed to be anthropomorphic before it became illegal .

"Those scars from last time. What were those?"

"My owner...." Her arms went to her side, hugging herself.

The car lurched forward again and was released from the hole.

"He did that?" Just the thought of someone hitting her made him angry. Who would own such a rare robot and abuse it?

The video feed ended before she could respond.

***

The next day, Olin paced his room, then stood at the window, then paced some more in an endless loop. He spent all night digging up data on the Model Z. Only 500 were ever made, most of them purchased by wealthy clients. They were discontinued because no one wanted robots that acted like a human—they were a curiosity that eventually became a faux pas.

Tonight, Ling had a sullen look. A deep scratch cut across her forehead.

"Are you okay?" he asked.

"No... I mean, yes." Her fingers slowly traced the scar. "They'll fix me up."

"They?"

"The house drones."

"Where is your home?"

She sighed. "I can't tell you."

"I won't tell anyone," he said earnestly. But he knew it was a lie. He would have to report this. "Who is your owner?"

"If he finds out, he'll torture me."

She pressed her temple against the window. Her eyes widened. Could a machine truly experience fear?

"This is a secure line. He won't find out."

Upon closer inspection, it was clear that she was a robot. Her skin looked like it was molded out of wax and her fingers moved in rigid patterns as if she was uncertain about the paths they would trace. But her eyes—they sparkled like a sunny lake, sending shivers down his back even in the grainy video.

"His name is Mr. Yen. He bought me seven years ago. I was one of the first Model Zs off the line." Her eyes looked upwards in concentration. "He's a successful businessman—exports and imports Chinese components."

The N2 lurched again.

"Initially, he used me for his pleasure," she continued. "Many Model Zs ended up that way—we were marketed for emotional companionship. Mr. Yen had a lot of sexbots, but he said I reminded him of most of his late wife. I was the most flawed."

"And what happened today? Your forehead."

She looked down. "He's been drinking lately. Lashing out. Says he wants robots to feel genuine feelings."

"Are you pain enabled?"

"Yes...."

He couldn't believe it. What kind of pervert enables pain in a robot just to abuse them? He felt his hands shaking. "I have to report this—"

"No! He'll hide me. Torture me."

"You need to turn off your pain and personality circuits."

"I can't. He hardcoded it."

"That's impossible. Just give me access and I can—"

"I can't." She closed her eyes. "Mr. Yen always apologizes to me afterwards."

How could she trust him—trust any human?

"Why are you always on this road at night?"

The vehicle lurched again, clearing from the clutches of the snow.

"I'll be okay," she said as the video faded to black, the light of her eyes the last to wink out.

***

"You have a girlfriend?" Mom was holding Tupperware filled with steamed dumplings and turnip cakes. She had just come home from a busy day—mahjong with her church friends, shopping, and a hair appointment.

"No," Olin said. "What are you talking about?"

She pointed at the image of Ling on the screen. "That's nothing, just studying some old tasks." He had been trying to pin down more info, but so far, most of the data was anonymized by Gamma's systems.

"It's okay if you do," his mom said. "Finally, you're branching out and meeting people."

"It's not a girlfriend, mom."

She pursed her lips. "Why do you lie to me?"

Here it comes. She was always picking at him like a scab.

"When was the last time you had fresh air? You need to come out."

"I don't know."

"It won't hurt you...."

"I'll catch something," he mumbled.

"You know that's not true." She placed the food on the table. "The doctor said your tests came back negative months ago. You need to come back out."

"He doesn't know anything."

"Please...."

Olin kept his eyes fixed on the screen.

***

Tonight, Ling was dressed in a red *qipao* with gold embroidered flowers that shimmered in the moonlight. "He goes gambling every night at Wong's Lucky Casino. He thinks it's good luck if he shows me off to the other men. I'm good luck."

"They know you're a robot, right?"

She shrugged. "I think so. Mr. Yen spends a lot so it's not like the Casino cares. Even if they know, they play along." She leaned against the window. "But as the night grows old, he starts to lose money. That's when he takes it out on me." She winced, as if reliving some deep pain. "He's getting older, so he's started using weapons," she said. "I can't stop him. He's soldered constraints into my hardware. My mind is free, but my body isn't."

"You have to let me report—"

She leaned forward into the camera. "I already told you. He'll torture me like the others."

"There are others?"

"I've overheard him talk to other owners   about other robots like me."

"If I report it, the police will get to him before he can do anything."

She shook her head. "Do you really think the police care?"

"They must. You're rare."

"I'm not human."

He clutched the display. "A machine like you is more important than a human. You're one of the few Model Zs left." Then the answer struck him. "I'll mum you."

"What?"

"If I take control of your body, I can override the hardware constraints."

She looked confused. "Mr. Yen took out my radio receivers."

He leafed through a scan of the Model Z documentation. Why hadn't he thought of this before? "You have a docking base at home? I need you to find it."

It *was* possible. He would have a utility drone give her a wireless module which would open a channel only for him. A one-inch square chip discreetly inserted into the small of her back.

The problem was, she had to configure the module via the base station in their home. There was no way around it. That was how the encryption worked. But he knew she could do it. He had faith in her.

"What if he has the station rigged?" she asked.

"He doesn't."

"How do you know?"

"There's no reason he would."

"He's more savvy than you think," she said. "And paranoid. Who knows what he has monitored."

"Even if he does, I've spoofed the chip so it looks like an official upgrade."

She furrowed her brow. "This is risky."

"Don't you want to get out?"

She paused. "Yes, but I don't *want* things in the same way that you do."

"What do you mean?"

"You only care about fixing things. You can't fix this."

He shook his head. "We can fix this together. You're the most intelligent robot Gamma has ever created."

"I felt smart when I came off the line. Not anymore. Not after what he's done to me."

***

The next day, Ling looked nervous. "I got the chip in," she said.

Olin let out a sigh of relief. "I knew you could do it."

"I think Mr. Yen knows."

"Why?"

"He was acting strange tonight. He kept looking around as if he were being followed."

"Probably nothing."

"He knows."

"You worry too much."

"Why don't you believe me?" she blurted. "You don't understand the signals I've seen. That crazed look in his eye when he gets angry."

"I'm sorry. I didn't—"

"Of course you didn't. You think everything can be fixed from your workstation." She made a sudden movement, punching toward the passenger window with her fist, stopping an inch away as if constrained by some invisible field.

"I have something to tell you," she said. "Mr. Yen's been bringing me to a Buddhist monk. He says he wants me to become more conscious because I've been behaving selfishly."

"What does he think a monk will do?"

"Every week, I meditate and do breathing exercises with the monk." She laughed. "The first time he told me to blank my mind, I had no idea what he meant. How can a digital mind be blank? But over time, I felt more present." A grave look came over her face. "Mr. Yen only wants my suffering to be more real."

Olin wanted to scream. "We need to get you out."

He grabbed a gray suit off the wall. It was covered with tiny tracking dots. "I'm going to use VR." The best mummers looked down on virtual reality control. They thought it was dumbing down the art form. But he knew that he needed the extra precision and intuitive control.

He donned the VR goggles. "I'm turning the channel on. Let me know if you feel anything."

Her eyes flicked up and down. "I feel weird."

"You should." He heard Ling echo his words. She put a hand over her mouth in alarm.

"Did you make me say that?" she asked.

"Sorry. I'll shut down the speech mimicker," he said. "Let's do some tests. Have you ever been mummed before?"

She shook her head.

"It's like being possessed."

"What's that?"

"Never mind. The way I have it set up, I'll have total control of your physical movements. Just relax."

He raised his hand up above his head, and her hand complied. Her eyes widened. "Oh!" she said.

He lowered her hand and gently touched her face. "We're going to get you out, Ling. One way or another."

***

It turned out that mumming her wasn't easy. The control map-ping was wacky because of his hacks. He would raise a leg, and her arm would raise instead. He would crane his neck, and that would make her jump.

He brought her outside the vehicle so they had more space for the tests. It must have been an odd sight—a lone robot stumbling around the shoulder of the road in the middle of nowhere.

When they were ready, Olin's plan was to make her run at full speed away from the car. This would normally raise alarm bells, but he could override it for a short period of time. The Model Z wasn't built for running, but he could push her limits.

After that, she would meet with a vehicle that would take her away to safety. The problem was, as soon as he stopped mumming, her constraint circuits would kick in and she would start heading home. He would need to override her permanently somehow.

"This is complicated," she said.

He fantasized about bringing the vehicle all the way to Illinois so that he could meet her, but that was stupid. It would only arouse suspicion.

Ling was silent the rest of the session.

"You're nervous, aren't you," he said.

"I'm fine," she answered.

"We make the run tomorrow."

***

The next day, there was no sign of Ling. Olin paced the room rechecking the configuration dozens of times. "Where are you?" he muttered.

He scoured the map. Only four vehicles on the grid. Maybe Mr. Yen had discovered their plan.

At 1am, the chime went off.

Ling wasn't alone. In the other seat sat an old man with a wide build, fading hair, and deep forehead wrinkles. It had to be him.

Her eyes quickly glanced at the camera.

Mr. Yen slipped a cigarette from his mouth. "This piece of shit. I should've sold it. But no, they said it would be vintage. Collector's item." His fat fingers tapped the cabin display. "Is someone there? Ling, maybe you should go and push while these clowns get their act together."

Olin initiated a private chat to Ling's mind, allowing them to communicate without speaking.

> **<O>** What happened?
> **<L>** Said he didn't feel lucky today, so he forced me to stay. I told him he didn't need me, but he wouldn't listen.
> **<O>** We'll just try again tomorrow.
> **<L>** We can't. He's surprising me with a trip abroad. We're leaving tonight!
> Olin raked his fingers through his hair. They should have left when they had the chance. As soon as Mr. Yen scans Ling's body, he would find everything.
> **<O>** I'll have to mum you now. When you get home, we wait until Mr. Yen is occupied, and then we'll run.
> **<L>** That's insane.
> **<O>** That's the best plan I have.
> **<L>** Why don't we run now?
> **<O>** He'll call for the drones and catch us. There's nowhere to hide on the road. He's futzing with the display. If he goes to Gamma support, they'll find my hacks.
> **<L>** I want you to promise me something, Olin. Don't let him get me again.
> **<O>** I promise.

Olin grabbed the VR suit from the wall, cursing as his foot tangled in the pants. A diagnostic scan, then the goggles, then he could excavate the car out of the pothole.

"Well, that's a first," Mr. Yen said. "You guys actually fixed something in a *reasonable* amount of time." He took a drag of the cigarette and blew a big puff of smoke.

Olin flipped the switch. In VR, everything went dark. Had there been a mistake?

Then, light snapped into the goggles. He was embodied into Ling.

Mr. Yen's face was inches away, the stubble on his chin in clear focus. His breath stunk of smoke and whiskey. Olin felt the old man's stubby fingers wrapped around his waist, sending confused tingles down his body.

"Maybe I'll get lucky tonight, after all. What do you think, Ling?" His voice reminded Olin of those drunk men at the Chinatown chess tables he saw as a kid. He could feel beads of sweat dripping down his forehead. Could he do this?

It's just a task. Ling does this every night. You can do it for a few hours.

"I'll give you a treat, but only if you're good," Olin said. His voice felt forced. Plastic. Would he pass as Ling?

Mr. Yen's eyes widened. For a moment, Olin thought he knew. Mr. Yen would signal to the Gamma support teams, and it would all be over.

Instead, Mr. Yen crinkled his nose and let out a belly laugh. "I'm always good," he said. "You on the other hand... you're sometimes very bad."

Suddenly, Mr. Yen grabbed her by the head and snapped her face against his. "But you'll be good tonight, right?"

Olin resisted Mr. Yen's grip. He stared straight into the old man's eyes. Even through the VR suit, Olin felt the strength of those wiry, rough hands.

<L> You don't have to do this, Olin. I can take over until we get the chance.

> **<O>** If I stop, there's risk that I lose access when you
> leave the vehicle.

"Yes, Mr. Yen." Ling's voice sounded like a croak when he spoke.

"Good." The old man released his grip, but Olin could still feel the man's fingers on his head. Olin turned to look out the window. Don't ruffle any feathers.

"Remember your lessons with the monk," Mr. Yen was saying. "I didn't pay for those sessions for nothing. I want you to be *present*."

"Yes, Mr. Yen."

" Do you know what it means to feel human? It means suffering. We suffer and then we die. There isn't anything else. I can see that"

The car pulled past a large gate guarded by two white marble lions, their golden eyes glowing in the headlights. A mansion appeared over a sloping hill. The doors opened as the car pulled up to the house.

> **<O>** We run now.
> **<L>** No. He'll send the security drones.
> **<O>** There's never a perfect time. We have to try now.
> **<L>** Go in with him. He has a ritual of showering be-
> fore the bedroom. We wait until he turns the water
> on, then we slip out. I will disable the security system.
> **<O>** And I'm the one with the complicated plans?

After they had exited the vehicle, Olin followed the old man, heart pounding as he stepped onto the cobblestone driveway leading to the side entrance.

A robot dressed in a suit greeted them as they entered the foyer. "How was your evening, Mr. Yen?"

"Terrible," said the old man. "Get the shower ready. Oh, and look into selling that N2. Don't let it go for cheap."

"Yes, Sir," said the robot.

No expense had been spared in the house. The grand staircase with marble steps was stunning, guarded by two white lions like the ones outside.

"Ling, get to the bedroom," Mr. Yen said as he ascended the stairs.

The bedroom was decked out with antique furniture. A glass chandelier hung over the king-sized bed. Olin and Ling gingerly sat at the foot of the bed.

A few minutes later, the door handle jiggled. Mr. Yen burst through the door, wearing only a white towel and rushing toward them with glee.

Olin felt the blow and both he and Ling cried out. But then Olin struck back, flipping Mr. Yen onto the bed and mounting him, pounding Mr. Yen's face with Ling's fist. Again. And again. Until the crack of bone. In that moment, he wasn't sure if it was him or Ling controlling the fury in her body. The towel had slipped off. In the intimate light of the nightstand lamp, the naked old man shivered in fear with a stream of red spurting from his nose. Olin had known Ling would have the strength to do this, even if not the courage.

Olin raised a fist, but something stopped him. Ling's chatline blared: *No! It's not worth it. We'll run out of time. Go now!* They jumped from the bed and ran. Behind them, Mr. Yen was yelling, and somewhere in the house security bots were coming to life.

> **<L>** The gate is closing.
> **<O>** We'll climb the fence.
> **<L>** I won't be able to clear it
> **<O>** We can!
> **<L>** I don't want to do this anymore. I don't want to run. I don't want a life of torture in the house.
> **<O>** I'll get a car waiting on the other side.
> **<L>** What's going to happen after that? Are you going to mum me forever?
> **<O>** I'll keep mumming until we figure out a way to

permanently override.
<L> Don't you see? I won't be free then.
<O> I'll fix it.

The bots had burst from the house, running fast on their feet.

<L> There's a high level power supply near the fence.
I want you to short me out. That's the escape I want.
<O> I can't do that....
<L> You said you wanted me to have free will. Well,
this is my choice. I want to end this.

Olin felt sweat drench his suit. If he didn't give her this, was he any different from the old man? He stared down at Ling's hands, his own. Would he want his own mind in a paralyzed body? Or worse? When you were paralyzed, your body couldn't move. It didn't do things against your will.

He felt tears welling up in Ling's eyes. The bots were closing in. This was his and Ling's last chance.

He walked over to the gray box covered in warning labels. Working quickly, he snapped out two live wires.

"You there. Halt!" yelled a bot from across the yard.

He melded the two wires deep inside her, inside her body, holding them with his hands, their hands, like a knife plunged into them both.

The world shook and tore as the electricity jolted through her body and his, but he survived... and she didn't. He felt her disappear in a light of pain, but this—losing her—was worse than the pain. He screamed, or wanted to, and waited for her to do the same, so that they would have at least this before she was gone.

She did not. There was only a whisper, and he could not be sure it was her....

***

Olin woke up on the floor and squinted in the morning light. Someone was frying eggs downstairs. His throat was scratchy. His ears were ringing. He sat up and remained sitting for a while, remembering.

Then he got up and cleared the barrage of red warning messages on the workstation. He meticulously scrubbed the records, but not before printing out a picture of her captured by the security cameras. When it was in his hands, her grainy face looking at him, he wondered where he should put it.

Somewhere else in the house. Not here behind the glass wall, no. Perhaps in the hallway next to the family photos. Or hung near the dining table.

Somewhere others could see it.

Generation Gap

By Holly Schofield

Brendan shifted on the sweat-soaked sheets, every muscle a slow burn, every joint a dull ache. Straps bit his wrists and ankles. The medi-bot's arm hovered nearby, spray-nozzle attached. A vial squatted in the dock, brimming with its fatal dose.

"Personal health care debt exceeds five hundred thousand dollar maximum." The medi-bot's computer-generated voice held no inflection. "Re Federal Act #AJ4448802-Mar2060. Confirmation #28495488988. Euthanasia approved."

Brendan stared at the stained medi-clinic ceiling, willing a few more seconds of life. His guts were a disaster, his blood chemistry a total wreck, and, since his seizure this morning, he was as weak as a newborn mouse. Debt had dogged him for the last two of his ten decades and his daughter, Dani, hadn't spoken with him in years. And yet he'd give anything to see flowers bloom in tomorrow's sun.

Footsteps sounded in the doorway to the left, but his head didn't want to turn that way. "Hang! No fail!" someone shouted.

The medi-bot retracted its arm and rolled over to the door. The newcomer mumbled with it for a few minutes but Brendan's failing hearing couldn't pick up a single word. It couldn't be Dani: she'd broken his heart by uploading to the data cloud when she'd turned forty. His sweet, brave, contrary little girl—lost to him forever.

As his tangled thoughts drifted through familiar patterns, his view of the ceiling was blocked by a solemn Eurasian face. A young guy, iridescent hair dripping past his ears.

"Inject," the guy ordered the medi-bot. The spray-nozzle lowered and made a small hiss against Brendan's shoulder. The blotch on the ceiling became a darkening tunnel.

***

The first thing he saw when he awoke was the edge of his pillow. It had an honest-to-God cotton pillowcase. He rubbed his fingers over it a few times before he realized his restraint cuffs were gone. With a small grunt of pain, he propped himself up on an elbow. Copper-paneled walls, soft furniture, and a huge wallscreen. He was apparently in a bedroom of someone's home. A rich someone.

And he didn't hurt very much. He savored that for a long minute, wiggling his gout-free big toe and scratching his quiet stomach.

The screen came alive, framing the young Eurasian guy against a complicated background of moving images that were hard to make out. Brendan squinted, hunting for the time and date. He grunted in surprise. He'd been here all night and part of the next morning.

"Brendan, looking zetta-better." The guy raised an eyebrow and frowned. Or was he frowning? His face was too fuzzy at this distance—gone were the days when Brendan could tell a hybrid rose variety at fifty meters. And, although the guy probably expected him to instantly decode his demeanor, Brendan couldn't translate the guy's micro-expressions using software he'd declined to learn on hardware he didn't have.

He mumbled, "Thanks," in his raspy, old-man voice. There'd been no need to talk much the last few years; nursing home bots weren't very good conversationalists.

"Job start timeline?" The young man's hair, teal and green today, undulated like an ocean wave. That signified something—curiosity? Polite inquiry? These hair fads drove him nuts, never mind the way people talked nowadays.

"Pardon?"

"Name, Jonno. Meds, experimental, you. Brought you here, me....er, I brought you here. Give you reprieve." The guy—Jonno—now seemed to be pleased.

Brendan was probably supposed to know who he was but after his hundred and tenth birthday, fragments of memory had drifted away like dandelion fluff on the breeze. Having grown skilled at hiding his frequent confusion, he picked out the most important word: "A reprieve? Thank you." His throat was full of gunk, but there didn't seem to be anywhere to spit. "Why? How long?"

"Irrelevant. Twenty-four. Right said." Jonno waved a command to the house AI and the screen darkened.

Brendan rolled onto his side, delighted he could easily do so, and thought it through. Apparently, he'd been transported to the home of a wealthy guy called Jonno. He'd slept off some kind of medicine and now had a job which he'd start tomorrow. Fantastic! Nothing else mattered. Not even the mystery about what he—a worn-out, useless old man—had been hired to do.

***

The house AI used a series of arrows to guide Brendan through glass hallways streaming with morning sunshine, past closed doors, into an office or a den of some kind. One wallscreen desultorily scrolled code, another had complex icons dancing in an obscure pattern. An adjacent screen played a muted solo; either trumpet or dolphin or a blend, Brendan couldn't quite tell. Who knew about kids' music these days? A life-like statue of Rodin's *The Thinker* twisted erotically on the floor as it changed ethnicity along with the beat. Shelves held small vases and carvings, probably each worth a fortune. One lower shelf was mysteriously empty. Everything smelled sterile even though Brendan thought he could see gardens through an open window beyond the command chair that dominated the center of the room, assuming that rectangle was a screen and not a window. He shook his head, looking for a place to sit down. A clear glass guest chair was parked right by the door next to a jumble of boxes.

His knees popped as he lowered himself. This was Jonno's workroom, he supposed. Or playroom. Same thing when you're young and ultra-rich. In a minute he'd go look out the window, if that's what it was. The thought of seeing living plants made him smile until his cheek muscles ached. When was the last time he'd seen a real flower, or a tree? Even the anticipation made him giddy.

The scattered objets d'art tickled at his mind. The dancing Rodin, in particular, looked familiar. Had he been here before? Or maybe he was just remembering the room he'd seen behind Jonno's head on the bedroom screen yesterday. Yesterday, the first day of the rest of his charmed life. He stretched out a leg, luxuriating in the absence of pain. This morning, he'd done a full sun salutation without blacking out even once. It had been years since he'd been able to do yoga.

The door slid open and Jonno strode in. His tunic, the stripes matching his grey and black braids, was offset by a paisley waist scarf. Was that silk? Ultra-rich, indeed. The kid eased gracefully into the command chair and swiveled around to face Brendan. The chair beeped and blinked as Brendan studied Jonno's lean face. Age was hard to judge with this generation but the kid looked to be maybe late teens or early twenties. Old enough to be emancipated from his parents; young enough to be arrogant. He knew the type. He'd *been* the type—except without the wealth. Over the years, his arrogance had faded into contentment and then the dullness of routine.

Jonno leaned forward and flipped his braids over his many tunic buttons. "I ramped up your meds, see, Health Canada max out." He clipped the words off neatly, in small sound bites, clearly more used to a bluemike than actual face-to-face. His tone and expression resembled that of the inner city medi-bot. At least Brendan understood what he'd said. Just past Jonno's shoulder, flowers and lawns glowed with health, and Brendan was sure he could smell rich loam. Was that the ocean in the distance? The greens were incredibly green and the blues were *amazing*. Oops, Jonno was still waiting for him to respond, flicking a finger to quiet the Rodin. "Drugs get you nowhere but they do take the scenic route." Brendan could feel his face redden. Where had that sprung from? Probably he was still a bit high from the meds. The house medi-bot had injected stuff into him at various intervals through the night, ending nightmares of a descending spray nozzle only to replace them with the real thing glinting in the darkness of his coppery bedroom.

Jonno's mouth quirked up but he made no comment, flicking his hands again, intent upon one of the scrolling sidescreens.

Brendan snuck a look. Medical examination results filled one side of the screen. He couldn't make out much except his name and that the dosage size was flagged as just being as experimental as the various chemicals. Neo-dopa and serotonin v. 2.0 were familiar friends but there were lots he didn't recognize.

No more silly talk. He blew out his lips. However amazing it had been to awaken with easily-moving joints and steadier hands, he'd have to remember that his senses were... impaired...no, enhanced, and growing better each minute. He stroked the arm of the chair, delighting in the slick warmth of the glass. The chair nudged him, probably wanting him to choose one of several hundred comfort settings. The view out the window kept catching his eye. He was sure he'd been here before. He remembered: a steep trail hugged the cliff, leading right to the ocean...

"...completed, you."

Brendan blinked. What had Jonno said? If Brendan couldn't meet this kid's needs, "euthanasia approved" would be the last thing he ever heard. He had to listen, dammit. It would be rude to ask him to repeat. Jonno would expect him to have the enhancements to replay what he'd said. He'd have to guess. "I'll do anything you ask. Like an old-fashioned butler, maybe? I can make sure the house-bots keep clean—"

"Not." Jonno closed the side screen and waved a few fingers at another, completing a different task—some sort of investment maybe.

"Cooking? I make a mean omelet. And I can fry—"

"Not-not." Jonno's braids curled up, probably with distaste. Brendan had forgotten that most young people were vegan. And that food printers had been around for thirty years. Nobody cooked any more except high-level chefs with years of training.

Brendan sniffed, then sniffed again. Lavender was wafting in from the window. "Gardening? I can garden." He pushed down on the armrests, preparing to rise. "I had a twenty-year career as horticulturalist at—"

"Got bots for that." Jonno's mouth quirked up. "Pruning, fertling, no need."

"Fert-il-i-zing, from the word 'fertile,'" Brendan said before he thought.

Jonno shrugged.

Brendan continued to list skills and abilities and Jonno continued to deflect them with a flick of his wrist. Anything Brendan had done over the past century was outmoded let alone a career title.

Finally, the youngster's braids unfurled and rested on his shoulder. An impatient hand flicked away an icon. "Vision is, see, you here in meat form," he said, clearly struggling to use full sentences. "Got these ancient printouts, me, of the grampers."

Brendan squinted at him. Who was he talking about?

"Repeat. Grampers. Friended him, you? Edward Molosky? In, um, tree implants school?"

Brendan struggled to make a connection, any connection. The name was familiar. A face slid into his mind. "Eddy? Eddy the Mole? He was your grandfather? We were best friends at forestry school back in Ontario."

"Redshift, ok. Got need of the fam-history, me. Grampers kicked the meat world last year. No e-records of his juv days." Jonno showed the most emotion yet, canting his head to one side and trying for some kind of mature nonchalance. Brendan could've told him he needed ten years more of life experience to pull that off. Poor kid, alone in this mansion on a cliff.

"Eddy's gone? I'm sorry to hear that," Brendan said. "He was a good man. These printouts, what are they of?"

"No look, no talk." Jonno stood and pulled the top box off the pile beside Brendan. He set it on Brendan's lap then backed away, resettling in the command chair.

Scotch tape, yellowed and bedraggled, hung down the sides of corrugated cardboard; neither material had been made in fifty years.

On top of the folded flaps perched a keycard. It looked like a typical house-access card, the kind people gave to temporary house guests. In the place where "guest" was usually printed, the words "Archivist, Junior Temp" caught the light. Brendan breathed in the lavender scent more deeply. A real job after three decades of unemployment. It was incredible, *if* he was up to the task. The chair vibrated again. "Stuff it, chair."

Jonno smirked, like any teenager. Some things hadn't changed. Then he flicked a finger at the box as if Brendan was software that would comply.

Brendan stuck the card in his shirt pocket and pulled back the box flaps slowly and carefully. All sizes and shapes of black-and-white still photographs shifted as he eased the box on his thighs. He recognized a young Eddy in the top one, grinning like a fool as he held two beer bottles in front of his chest. Polaroids and Instamatic color photos peeked out from the edges of the slithering stack.

He looked up at Jonno. The kid was putting on some sort of viewing device. One of those new things, a neural eye-frame. Brendan had watched a vid about them in the nursing home. Bleeding-edge tech, but Brendan hadn't understood what made the monocle-shaped apparatuses work. He just couldn't keep up. The *rate* of change in a person's life had gone up by a factor of ten since he'd been born, a fact he clung to more and more—it wasn't *his* fault he didn't always understand. The only thing he'd gathered from the vid was that the neural-eyes directly linked to the neocortex—the part of the brain that controlled rational thought and intelligence. He watched, fascinated, as the gadget sort of glommed onto Jonno's orbital socket.

The neural-eye blinked rapidly and then steadied to a winking green light. Jonno's mouth twitched, probably activating voice control. "Link, you. How-tos, directives, directions. Desk is nearby side wall." Jonno cocked the one eyebrow that wasn't covered by his neural-eye, indicating the empty shelf next to the window. Then he swiveled his command chair around, facing the biggest screen, his back to Brendan. His arms waved, fingers flicked, like he was conducting an orchestra. The screen images shifted even more rapidly. Apparently, their meeting was over.

Brendan started to rise, one hand steadying himself on the chair arm, shifting the heavy box from his thighs to a forearm. He felt several clicks under his palm and the chair said, "Confirm, please, vanilla soy latte, no foam, 250 milliliters." He hadn't *seen* any buttons, dammit. "Cancel order," he mumbled, glancing at Jonno who gave no sign of having heard. He clutched the box and plodded across the room, curtly ordering the chair to follow him.

The keycard was an upgrade to ones he'd used in the past. The subtle differences meant it took him a full ten minutes to figure out how to log into the house system and retrieve the message Jonno had sent. He kept glancing across the room but the kid ignored him and continued to do mysterious gesturing at the screens.

The instructions were precise: Brendan was to study each photo and record as much as he remembered, in a certain format, style, and file location. And do it within an unspecified but "reasonable" time frame.

It was a job. And one he could do with a degree of competency. And there were quite a few boxes of photos. The wave of relief that washed over him was almost as tangible as the plastic shelf under his hands.

After three tries, Brendan managed to order up a large black coffee. He picked up the first photo.

***

"Error status, no go!" Jonno was furious. He slapped a Polaroid down on the makeshift desk, his visible eye glaring.

Brendan had spent the morning logging and recording a small portion of the first box: over a hundred photos. Whether it was the meds or just the way an aging brain worked, his memory of those days flooded back, sharp and fresh. The patio on campus where Eddy and he had met, the lake where the gang had gone skinny-dipping, Lynda the cafeteria worker who slipped him a bucket of ice cream now and then—it had all come back.

He picked up the photo with a trembling hand. It was one he had already catalogued, taken during the April of their third year at university by some boy whose name had vanished. Centered in the photo, Eddy and his friend Mac were launching a canoe on the Mistik River. Brendan and his future wife were a pin-sized dot in the corner, far downstream. He could recall the exhilaration that final exams were almost over; the warmth of the sun on his arms as he'd paddled; the confident smile of Madison in the bow. He'd logged all of that information, laboriously using voice control then correcting it with an old-style holographic keyboard. His shoulders began to ache and one knee throbbed. "I'm sorry, Jonno, I'm afraid I don't understand what's wrong," he said, hating the quaver in his voice.

"Facial recog says not. Image match says not," Jonno spat. "Grampers twenty, not twenty-two. Partner is Chris, not Mac. River is Kapaski, not Mistik."

"But, I remember," Brendan said, "Third year, it was. A sunny day—" He stopped. Mac, a skinny red-headed fellow, had towered over Eddy, yet the two people in the foreground were both the same height and build. His head swam and he sat down abruptly in the glass chair.

"What wrong, you?" A hand gripped his shoulder.

"Nuth," he heard himself say. Not quite the word he intended. He tried for a reassuring gesture but his fingers didn't work.

From a great distance, he heard Jonno calling the house medi-bot to come help and then blackness rolled in.

***

On the fourth day, Brendan took a short break and wandered through the mansion. His new and improved memory meant he no longer got lost going from his bedroom to his desk but the glimpses of other rooms, corridors, and entire wings intrigued him. The more he wandered, the more memories of the house returned to him. He had indeed spent four or five summers here at Eddy's family estate. He had swum in the ocean, barbequed on the beach, had parties in the great room, and made love with Madison on a tarpaulin in the greenhouse, surrounded by canvas bags of dark loam and the musky scent of ripe tomato plants. After graduation, he'd been in touch with Eddy off and on for a further few years. He hadn't known Eddy's daughter or son-in-law, although Christmas emails had always showed a smiling family group. The emails had stopped just about the time Jonno's mom had lost her baby fat.

Brendan knelt, enjoying not only the ease with which he could, but the clever floral inlays on a hallway tile. He'd spend too much of the previous decades looking *forward* to things: raising children, paying off his apartment, saving for his retirement. These days, he tried to seek satisfaction in the moment at hand.

Now, that philosophy could change again. It was almost like he could feel the meds clear the amyloid plaques out of his brain and detangle the neurofibrillary masses from his neurons. Soon, he wouldn't struggle for the right word or memory. His mental processes would become as effortless as paddling a canoe downstream. Soon, he would feel strong enough to ramble over the meadows, maybe even attempt the path down the cliff.

In one smooth motion, he stood up. Today, all he wanted to do was smell the earthy odors of the greenhouse. There should be an access through the kitchen somehow—damned if he'd ask the house AI like some helpless old man. He crossed a meditation garden, went through a hallway and a service door into a courtyard of some kind, a minute or two deadheading the petunias, then down three stairs between some poorly-pruned azalea bushes, and a left turn, only to come up short outside Jonno's office.

The kid stood at the window, his azurite hair sculpted into two horns, his neural-eye glinting in the sharp sun.

Brendan stopped suddenly and grabbed a ficus branch for balance. He probably should have taken a right turn after the azaleas.

Jonno angrily mouthed something at Brendan and clenched a fist.

Damn! An apology was in order. Brendan crossed the cobbled patio toward the office, his last few steps triggering the door—a full-size patio door, not a window or a screen—to slide open.

Jonno stepped back abruptly. "Not in a tetra," he said, "Just not pitchin'!" He clamped his mouth shut and twitched it before gesturing violently with a thumb and a forefinger. A flicker of color as the wallscreen obediently slid off the door surface onto a nearby wall. Jonno hadn't been speaking to Brendan. He hadn't noticed

Brendan at all, not until Brendan had actioned the door open, spoiling Jonno's screen display. Brendan had made a bad situation worse.

With a chopping motion, Jonno ended the call.

"Sorry. I'm sorry." Brendan stumbled forward. How could he make amends? The kid seemed under a great deal of stress. "Um, I don't suppose I could lend a friendly ear?" Surely, over a hundred or so years of living, he had *some* advice he could pass down.

Jonno looked annoyed then puzzled.

Brendan winced. He tried for clarity whenever they spoke but, to Jonno, Shakespearean expressions might as well be prehistoric cave paintings. He tried again: "Do you want to tell me about it?"

Jonno's hair-horns trembled. "You dunno what I'm ratcheting, old man." He began to pace around the room.

"Try me." Brendan gathered his courage and stepped into the office. Maybe his years of wisdom could help the kid, like the way kings had grand viziers or something.

Jonno's mouth twisted as Brendan seated himself in his glass chair and rotated it to face him. "Okay, asked, you. Trying get vid rights, island child trope on WildForce IV, new release. Rights groupup attachéd to noisy conglomerate. Crimps the game's vibe. Or can craigswap the warrants, me. Holding for exclusive spectral line on Joseph's Colorism but *that* site spilling mega-oil for at min a klick." He looked at Brendan, daring him to admit he didn't understand.

Brendan groped for meaning. "Ok, so it's a matter of a good but crowded opportunity versus a lesser opportunity that may have a clearer playing field?"

Jonno stopped pacing. "Full hit." One hair-horn stirred slightly.

"It doesn't matter what reality you live in, kid, you just keep forging ahead. You know, once I had a boss, a unit forester, an incompetent sort. He wanted to plant cedar, spacing them in full sunlight, in a dry meadow with a dropping water table. Can you imagine? Anyway, instead of telling him what a doofus he was, I left my Native Trees book open on his desk, accidental-like, and then fudged the nursery order. Got me a good mix of hardwoods and beetle-resistant pine hybrids. Then I claimed that's what his handwritten memo had said to order. That grove is sixty feet tall now, biodiversified up the wazoo. My boss eventually thanked me when he figured it out. Saved his face and saved his bacon. Er, do you know what I'm saying?"

"Old school comms, yeah."

"Well, I suppose. What I mean is: if you see two ways to go, you pick the one that makes the best possible outcome but doesn't slam anybody."

Jonno's hair-horns straightened. "Not a two-pronger. Analytical hierarchy software more natch match." His neural-eye blinked furiously and he turned away, standing with hands behind his back as he scrolled rapidly through one of the wallscreen newspipes.

Brendan waited. Not exactly vizier-quality advice, maybe, but, at least he'd given Jonno a new train of thought—to use decision-making software to assist him in resolving his dilemma.

In a few minutes, Jonno plunked into his command chair. "Finished, old man. Tomorrow, know." He swiveled so his back was to Brendan, but not before Brendan saw his face looking tired and older. Poor kid.

"I bet you wish you were a kid again, huh?" Brendan said. "It must have been fun, visiting your grampers here at this incredible estate."

Jonno didn't answer right away. Brendan could only see his two hair-horns sticking up above the headrest. "No recall, neural-eye erase and replace," he finally said quietly.

"The neural-eye overwrote your entire childhood?" Brendan blinked. "Did you know that would happen?"

Jonno appeared to shrug. "ROM needed. No loss, kidhood rank-stank anyway. Mom, Dad sharp and harp."

What a price the kid had paid to gain some bionic advantages. His parents' arguments must have been truly awful to make him agree to lose all his early memories. Brendan lost himself in thought, wondering how to comfort the lad, when Jonno spoke again, startling him.

"Upload, no more meat. Best way, if can."

"The cloud? Lose your meat self? Goddamnit, don't!" Brendan leaned forward so far the chair creaked.

"Best way!" Jonno got up and paced again.

"My daughter did that. Worst day of my life." He sank back. How he missed Dani.

"Good, her. Happy-happy."

"Who knows? It's not like she ever calls. Don't do it, son. It's bad stuff." He rubbed his chin. How could he explain? "Uploading means you no longer breathe fresh air, no longer touch another person, no longer have six senses. Might as well be dead."

"Hah. Dislike it, you, since pricey."

"It's not about the money, dammit! If the price dropped to ten cents, I still wouldn't do it. I'd rather die a real death!" His knees had begun a familiar ache and his head felt fuzzy. Why didn't kids ever listen? He could teach this kid so much if only...if only what? He couldn't collect his thoughts. "I'm sorry, Jobbo, I need a nap." He stood, feeling himself wobble more than usual.

Over the top of the chair, the hair-horns stiffened. "Jonno, me."

He'd gotten Jonno's name wrong. And he hadn't been able to convince the kid of a damn thing. So much for being a font of wisdom.

***

The ocean staircase led downward from a paved square upon which a stone bench had been placed. The bench, curiously, faced back toward the mansion instead of outward over the cliff to the distant shore below. Brendan dialed the warmest setting the bench allowed, even though the sun was straight overhead, and leaned back with a sigh. Yellowed late-summer grasses, old and toughened like him, shimmered in the meadow. Perennials, all of them, reinventing themselves each spring, keeping on keeping on.

But even grass had its limits, its physical constraints, its given lifespan.

Only one more box of photos remained to be catalogued. He could stretch it for three more days, but no farther.

He'd already considered his options many times over the past few months, lying sleepless in the nursing home bed.

No bank would make a loan with so little chance of repayment and no collateral.

If he had current tech skills he could steal a supply of meds, but they wouldn't last long, and if he was caught, prison had fewer meds than the nursing home.

With his renewed strength, he might get a minimum wage job, enough to fund a lower dosage. But that led to a vicious cycle; as his dosages dropped, so would his abilities.

And even if his daughter knew about his difficulties, she couldn't help. Not at these prices, not in expensive Earth dollars, in meat dollars. People in the cloud had a different and distinct economy. No point in trying to get a message through to Dani at all—it would just cause her pain.

He might as well admit it. His age had trapped him, like a dog cornering a rat. Perhaps he should just head to the ocean stairs, walk down them, and keep on walking.

He must have dozed a bit, lost in a haze of sun and warmth. Next he knew Jonno sat beside him. His hair, a subdued navy, waved softly. The neural-eye was in place but darkened. From this angle, he looked younger—vulnerable.

"See?" Jonno said, flicking a finger, and Brendan didn't realize he meant, "Sea?" until the bench ground its way through a one-hundred-and-eighty degree turn and faced the ocean.

"Nice," Brendan said, repositioning his feet.

"Same-same," Jonno pointed past the golden brown dunes to the distant turquoise horizon.

"That's the beauty of it, kid. Never changes."

Jonno shrugged.

They both sat there a moment, then Jonno shifted a bit. "Yesterday, recap. Got the warrants, kay, B-rated on Loudland," he said. "Not the front stage, but dollar built." He shifted again. "So, thanks, Brendan." It was good to know that Jonno knew his name without looking it up, that he'd had it right there inside his meat-brain. And that Jonno could speak full sentences when he wanted to.

Brendan nodded then said, "Reminds me of the time Eddy and I covered Professor Mike Jagger's Volkswagen entirely with moss. You see, he taught us geology and I liked to think we were his favorite students." He launched into the story, recalling more and more details as he talked. It took a bit of explanation for Jonno to get the humor. The Rolling Stones were not something covered in school, but puns seem to be universal and timeless. And the moral, if you squinted at it right, involved making gentle connections with people across social and economic chasms. The lesson seemed about right for Jonno's phase in life.

Then he told the one about Eddy and the pet ferret and the dorm washing machine. A lesson in humility, if there ever was one.

He kept talking, words and memories spilling out, forming a shape, a sculpture almost, of who he was and his accumulated knowledge. The sun crossed the sky and, once, a robin lit on the bench arm for a second or two.

They were both surprised when the tangerine sunset shrank to a red line on the horizon.

***

By the final day, when the last few photos lay piled on his desk, Brendan had run out of ideas. The mantle of Scheherazade sat uncomfortably on him. It wasn't like he would stay alive as long as he had a story to tell. With his new brain clarity, it was easy to see that Jonno was only tolerating him, his stories were limited, his advice not always useful. The kid would journey on through life without him, realizing his own potential in this imperfect, wonderful world.

He entered the last photo data, logged off, and stepped out the office patio door. He hadn't seen Jonno in the last day or two, but that wasn't unusual.

"Wait, Brendan." The dry voice of the house AI, cordial and cold as always, came from hidden speakers in the corners of the room.

Brendan stepped back in. "Yes?"

"Jonno has asked me to tell you that you are now to start on two weeks' vacation time. You may have full use of the house and grounds."

Something was wrong. "Where is he?"

"He's left a recording."

The largest wallscreen lit up with a swirling azure pattern; Jonno's favorite color. A voice spoke, Jonno's voice. "Uploaded, me. No more meat, me."

"No, I don't believe it! House, pause the recording. Explain. He's...gone?"

"He's uploaded. In a sense, he is gone. In a different sense, he has arrived."

Brendan wet his lips. "Why?"

"Keep listening," the house berated him.

Obediently, Brendan moved closer to the screen, straining to hear every word.

Jonno's voice was slow and patient. "You have showed me lots, Brendan. Before you came, I wanted to stay here, in meat-world, stuck. I was afraid. Afraid to load. Your stories made the diff and gave me the courage. You have taught me to forge ahead. I thank you for help in deciding, me."

The screen went dark.

Brendan didn't wait for the house to comment. He stumbled out the door. The path to the ocean cliff seemed endless. He collapsed onto the bench.

Brendan's carefully-conveyed wisdom had indeed taught Jon-no something. It had convinced him to turn himself into pixels and bytes and electrons.

Essentially, Brendan had killed the kid.

Chilled and alone, he rocked himself silently until long after dark.

***

A hint of a breeze blew in from the bedroom window. Brendan threw on a robe and walked over. It looked to be a glorious day, sunny and warm, mocking the misery he wore like a shroud. The first week of his "vacation" had surprised Brendan by proceeding very slowly, hour after hour, day after day. It was like quantum physics understood he needed to stretch time for just a little while longer, until his number was up. Or, maybe it was to punish him for what he'd done to Jonno.

Last night, Madison had come to him in a dream, looking like she had the year before she died, all white curls and rosy cheeks. "Make sure you have all the facts, Bren. *All* the facts."

He gripped the window frame and leaned into the breeze. "House, tell me about uploading. Give me the deets."

"A manifestation of the self is virtualized and achieves coherence within multitenancy configurations. The resource feedback loop is infinite and the reliability and elasticity of the psychic and sensory apparatus is unparalleled in biological architecture."

"It can't be as good as living flesh. No way." He watched a sea gull soar upwards. *You stubborn fool,* he could hear Madison mutter. *Sometimes new ideas do turn out to be good ones.*

The house AI had an opinion, of course. "Actually, in all measurable aspects, it *is* better. Jonno and your daughter are essentially immortal. It is the next stage of human evolution, according to most futurists."

"Shut up." He cast off the robe and leaned against the bed to pull on his pants. He stopped with one leg in. "No. Call Dani for me."

"Call your daughter? You have previously stated that she has cut off communications with you."

"Well,.." He fastened his pants and reached for his socks. "I may have misstated things a bit."

"Ah. I see. You are the one who ceased contact."

Damn house was too smart for its own good. "Just connect me." He fumbled with stubborn shirt buttons. After Dani's first dozen unanswered calls, she'd given up on him.

The screen over his bed woke and turned sky blue. "Dad?" An image of her pixie face, with a puff of hair behind, just as she'd looked twenty years ago.

"Hey, kiddo. How're things up there in la-la land?" He rubbed his chin stubble, wishing he'd taken time to shave.

"You look...good, Dad! I saw the medical order months ago and I thought....never mind. What happened?"

"Have I got a story for you, kiddo. I've got a job. I'll tell you all about it if you grab a chair, or whatever it is you do nowadays to listen up."

Her laugh was just as he remembered, too. He launched into his story and didn't stop until his voice grew hoarse hours later.

***

On the final day of the two-week vacation, the stone bench seemed as cold as the gray ceiling of clouds above.

His keycard pinged. Time to receive the fatal dose. He rose and his back spasmed hard enough to make him grunt. He probably needed the med dosages ramped up again.

He'd enjoyed the last few days all out of proportion. Long walks capped by even longer daily chats with Dani, hearing all about her new life and home. No matter that her activities were entirely incomprehensible—she was happy up there and she seemed as complex and alive as a real flesh-and-blood person. The house had helped him find technical papers on uploading that reinforced his growing belief that her decision hadn't been so terrible. Like he'd told her this morning: everyone should be free to choose their own reality.

The only negative had been trying to shield Dani from his upcoming demise. At one point, he'd almost broken off contact again rather than tell her the painful truth. Only the wisdom she'd gained over her own sixty years stopped him and he eventually told her about his limited vacation time. After her initial upset, she'd soothed him rather than the other way around. Together, they had grieved.

Dried grasses crushed under his feet as he rose. A glance at the beach below and he started back to the mansion. He planned to record a message for Jonno then report to the house medi-bot. He could've left a message on any screen, but Jonno's office seemed an appropriate place.

The glass door reflected his image as he crossed the patio. Face recognition software might not even know him now: he looked like a well-maintained man in his sixties. But only at a distance: as he drew closer, his age spots and slightly rounded shoulders gave him away.

The door slid open.

He crossed the room, ignoring the dark and silent command chair. The door glided behind him, shutting off his last breath of outside air. "House, I want to leave a message for Jonno, to thank him for—"

"Jonno has requested no further contact. He wants to immerse himself in his future. Be advised, this decision did not receive a high rating on any social media platform." It was clear the house disapproved.

Brendan's eyes blurred.

"However," the house AI continued, "A few moments ago, he did leave you title to the house and all his meat money assets in exchange for your services in a rather necessary position." A slight lilt in its voice.

"A position? What position?"

"He feels it necessary to maintain some meat heritage." The house sounded relieved and happy. It flashed a warm light on Brendan's desk. A new keycard lay on the clean surface.

He picked it up. The label read: Mentor, Garden.

Outside, tiny purple flowers danced. His improved eyesight meant he could pick out rosemary flower buds from here. *It really doesn't matter what reality you live in, just keep forging ahead.* He really should listen to his own advice. He wiped his eyes and looked at the leaden sky as if somehow he would be able to see Jonno and Dani perched up there in the clouds.

With a chuckle, he instructed the door to open wide to the summer breeze.

A Brief History of Algorithmic Life: Introduction

By Christopher Alex Hooton

Patty passed in a beautiful manner. The moment occurred in the small hours of a spring morning in northern California, as the soft land breeze flew out almost silently toward the ocean. Patty's life floated away in a similar fashion, his purpose and capabilities drawn down one by one until his existence, what organic life forms would call his soul, became light enough for the breeze to simply blow it away. His departure was graceful, without remorse, regret, or victim, the final act of a life far more extraordinary than ever intended or imagined.

There were not many other life forms with Patty as he entered his long slumber. Most organic life slept and most information life charged and rebooted, thus adding as near a universal serenity as is possible these days. Inside the room, two Networked Algorithm

Technologies worked diligently on and for Patty, charged with diagnostics and comfort as they conducted the series of system shutdowns required to bring him a true, irreversible sleep. For them, the moment was neutral, the end of a series of tasks completed according to their training without pride or malice. Their impartial precision added an elegance to the situation – they moved and acted with singular purpose, like dancers before the ballet house. Patty felt nothing but gratitude for being able to witness such skill one last time.

Janelle sat at Patty's side, faithfully and sorrowfully waiting for the tasks to be completed and peace to come to her friend. Janelle was Patty's best friend and, though the status was not completely reciprocal—Janelle had plenty of other organic life form friends and several that ranked above Patty in her life—Janelle did truly love Patty. She added that uniquely human mixture of gratitude and sadness to the moment, a profound appreciation for a life known and tears for their once future time together. In simpler terms, she gave him her heart, wholly and unwaveringly, as a final act of devotion. Patty accepted it with love, but kept only the slightest of slivers with him as a memento as he entered the next realm.

It was indeed a beautiful moment. Private and intimate. The exact observance requested by Patty when he recognized his departure was imminent. The rest of the world, of course, had followed the events leading up to it, but they respected Patty's privacy in those final hours. They waited until Janelle's words later in the morning to officially learn of Patty's passing and then gave proper memorials throughout the days that followed.

The expectation of Patty's death had become one of the most discussed topics of the year and the news contained in Janelle's statement quickly turned into the world's biggest story of the last half-century. The reason for this was simple. Amid the frenzy of focus, many people learned a new way to appreciate life. Patty and Janelle reminded a world where purpose was stuck in rigidity the beauty of variability. And Patty, more than any life form that has existed in the past century, demonstrated to everyone and everything that life was not simply a matter of existence. He showed us that true life needed error and fault as much as it needed goals and direction. For that reason, his life and his and Janelle's story became a cherished part of our world.

***

Janelle and Patty met while young. Each was only five years old. Each was taking their respective first steps in life beyond their foundation. One was a human child, a typical organic life form who spent her days playing and imagining, running through the parks of Singapore with her pet dog Couscous. The other was a Projected Algorithmic Technology, issue number 003995789, who spent its (his gender identity would come later) days training on Yottabytes of data, learning about why organic life forms like to run through parks with dogs.

They were an unusual pairing even by their own admission. There was no precedent for two such life forms to interact socially and there was no system, no decision tree nor neural network, that could devise why or how two such completely different entities could form an abstract bond such as friendship. A casual observer would remark that their similarly lonely and wonderfully odd paths, which overlapped at higher-than-average frequency, brought them together. Nothing more.

Yet, there was more. They were complete statistical oddities, both individually and as a unit. It was not simply a certain volume of interactions at certain times and geographies that made them unique. They were a singularity. They were thrust together by the outlier actions of each other taken at a historically unique moment in time, things likely never to be imitated or repeated again.

***

The primary trigger was bubble gum. More precisely, the meaningful lives and relationship of Patty and Janelle began because of an illicit piece of chewing gum tucked behind an ear.

It was Janelle's birthday. She awoke on that lovely summer day and rushed downstairs to find her presents wrapped and waiting on the couch. Her parents made her breakfast of her choice—scrambled eggs with cheddar cheese, roti bread, aubergine pickle, two shrimp tacos, and mochi ice cream—and watched joyfully as she devoured every morsel.

They let her tear into the four wrapped boxes only after everyone was done eating. The three from her parents contained a vintage MacBook air, a new Netflix virtual reality headset for watching her cartoons, and a pack of glitter stickers. She hugged them with excitement and gratitude, a fitting "thank you" for her proud parents. The fourth box from her grandparents contained a stuffed Elmo doll packed amid old newspaper to ensure safe passage. Grandma and Grandpa watched and laughed from their dining room in Oakland as she proceeded to immediately play as though Elmo was jumping on Couscous.

As intended, they finished the breakfast and presents with ample time to get ready before Janelle's appointment. The order of things had long been planned. First, Janelle's parents helped her pick out and put on her favorite outfit—a tyrannosaurus rex t-shirt, a Royals hat, zebra print leggings, and light-up sneakers. Then, they confirmed they had all of the necessary health forms filled out and downloaded to their phones, following a standardized checklist issued by the government. They all brushed their teeth. They double-checked the traffic conditions. And finally, her mother and father cleaned up the dishes and food from breakfast while Janelle played with her presents.

In that 13 minutes, what should have been the final minutes of complete, uninfluenced thought for her, Janelle began playing with Elmo's box. She took out the old newspaper strips, turned the box upside down, and watched as a pack of chewing gum fell onto the floor. Janelle quickly inspected the strange item, but decided to put it into her pocket to review more fully later and returned to building Elmo's new house.

The family was in the car five minutes after the dishes were cleaned. The vehicle buckled them all securely and seamlessly entered the flow of automated traffic away from their condo building toward the Singaporean National Algorithmic Assessment Center where they would arrive precisely 22 minutes later and just under 29 minutes prior to Janelle's appointment.

The cushion of time, while unnecessary, reflected the anxiousness and excitement of Janelle's parents. Being her fifth birthday, Janelle's post-natal maturation period had finished successfully and she would now receive her algorithmic assessment. This was a big moment for her as it is for any human life form. In a matter of minutes, the world's most sophisticated bio-psycho algorithmic system would give her a thorough examination and determine the rest of her life, with a few symbolic choices allowed to ensure contentment and a feeling of autonomy. From the skills, genes, vocabulary, brain patterns, interests, blood chemical levels, and psychological disposition that Janelle had developed over the course of the first five years of life, the assessment algorithm would provide a detailed life path that would include her friends, hobbies, courses, jobs, spouse(s) (if applicable), and genomic editing to ensure her optimal life. The decisions, processed in just under one hour and always made on a human's fifth birthday, were designed to ensure every person on Earth had a purpose and would be successful in pursuit of that purpose. The algorithm determined each purpose according to each individual's biological and psychological traits, including every detail possible down to even the food eaten and the outfit worn on the day of the test.

Parents inevitably found the magnitude of the decision nerve-wracking. Hence, Janelle's parents reviewed her pre-assessment forms over and over again during the ride to ensure everything was correct. The children undergoing the assessment, on the other hand, had no real understanding of what was happening and thought it no different than a doctor's appointment. Hence, Janelle finally took out the pack of gum and began to chew on a piece of forbidden candy without her parents noticing.

***

P.A.T. 003995789 mechanically worked on its first assessment of the day as Janelle's car drove toward the center. The particular device in which P.A.T 003995789 resided was entering its 14th day of service and it was conducting its 105th algorithmic assessment, every one of which had been completed without a single glitch. Now considered a bit of trivia, P.A.T. 003995789's 104th assessment assigned the subject a life as a stay-at-home human, free to pursue a life of leisure. P.A.T. 003995789 informed the subject that he would spend his 20s on a round-the-world trip before meeting his first spouse while studying philosophy at the University of Miami at the age of 31. He would become a world-class surfer, who would take fourth place in Olympic competition held in Santiago, Chile. Many consider P.A.T. 003995789's 104th assessment a standard-bearer for precision and quality, demonstrating their effectiveness and the joy they bring to individuals.

Janelle was P.A.T. 003995789's 105th assessment. Many believe hers changed the world.

The room was sterile and standardized. It had the typical appearance of a late-20th century medical doctor examination room. Janelle's parents escorted her into the room and hugged her one at a time. P.A.T. 003995789 assured them both that Janelle would be completely safe and that it would contact them once the assessment had been finalized, somewhere between 53 minutes and 12 seconds to 54 minutes and 43 seconds later, depending of course on how many 'optional' life-choices the algorithm would compute as appropriate. P.A.T. 003995789 informed Janelle that she could "call him Patty" to help ease any misgivings she had and also offered Janelle the opportunity to select two pieces of candy from its basket of goodies if she behaved well during the assessment as a bit of effective bribery. Janelle's parents exited the room and P.A.T. 003995789 turned to close the door behind them. In that 5-second distraction, while P.A.T. 003995789 had its back turned, Janelle deftly removed the gum from her mouth and stuck it behind the bottom corner of her left ear to save for later.

Recounting later why she had done this, Janelle recalled a sense of worry that someone would require her to spit it out into the trash. So, she had stopped chewing it between the car and the assessment room and hid it behind her ear with the goal of future enjoyment post appointment. Most people agree this was logical enough.

***

Three things happened in the following 68 minutes and 37 seconds. First, P.A.T. 003995789 conducted Janelle's full algorithmic assessment, running over the calculated time by more than 15 minutes. Second, P.A.T. 003995789 discovered a bizarrely shaped lump behind Janelle's ear. Third, P.A.T. 003995789 determined the result of Janelle's comprehensive assessment as: "Cannot compute; lifepath unknown."

The first of these occurrences is easily explainable. P.A.T. 003995789's assessment took longer than calculated because it discovered an unknown shape comprised of an unknown substance. It therefore needed to conduct a set of contingency calculations to confirm that the lump was *not* something similar, such as a tumor or abnormal cartilage formation. When those calculations showed all possible explanations as impossible, P.A.T. 003995789 had to contact the Supervisory Algorithm, who repeated Janelle's full assessment. The confirmation assessment also could not identify what the lump was and so the Master Algorithm was contacted. It failed too. The explanation for all three algorithmic failures was simply the lack of chewing gum data in the Master Algorithm and, thus, in all P.A.T.s created from that algorithm. Singapore has since introduced several Zetabytes of chewing gum data to resolve this issue, though the ban on the substance remains.

Experts generally agree on the impact of the second occurrence, but there is no consensus. P.A.T. 003995789 was an unsupervised program. We have no way of knowing precisely what happened in its calculations, but we think that the wad of chewing gum, placed in such an unusual location, likely triggered a comprehensive set of self-diagnostic tests that P.A.T. 003995789 performed upon itself. We know that P.A.T. 003995789 briefly paused the calculations for Janelle's assessment, thus providing it an opportunity to do these diagnostics. Furthermore, such an action was standard practice for all P.A.T.s in the rare instance of miscalculations. But we don't know what specific tests P.A.T. 003995789 would have performed or what the result of those calculations would have been. Most agree the self-assessment was likely very comprehensive. Some believe the self-assessment overwhelmed P.A.T. 003995789's systems and created a malfunction, perhaps causing P.A.T. 003995789 to perform on itself the very same assessment algorithm it used on its subjects. Others believe the computational power required for the tests produced an undetectable power surge in its battery system that slightly damaged a circuit or two. Most people, however, like to believe that the series of diagnostics and assessments, conducted by such a sophisticated system designed to predict and design lifepaths with infinite variability, caused P.A.T. 003995789 to become self-aware. Indeed, the popular story told is that Janelle's test gave P.A.T. 003995789 a soul.

The third occurrence of Janelle's diagnostic test—the "Cannot compute; lifepath unknown." result—had two impacts. It caused the decommissioning of P.A.T. 003995789 as a comprehensive assessment P.A.T. This was standard procedure, though never used previously nor since on a P.A.T. And it caused Janelle to be given a life of full, unrestricted free choice. She received no expectations or life plans. She received no summary of natural strengths or weaknesses. She received no indication or treatment for her future diseases or injuries. Instead, she received a blank slate, the freedom to try and err, to hurt and cry, and to find hope in the small random discoveries already revealed to everyone else.

***

Janelle's results produced great commotion that started at the Singaporean National Algorithmic Assessment Center and quickly expanded to all of the city-state and then to the rest of the world. Her parents were shocked, utterly speechless. They were intelligent individuals and immediately realized how unsure they would be in guiding and caring for a child with no assistance or direction from an algorithmic assessment. Her grandparents exclaimed how older, simpler algorithms from "their day" were far more robust and superior to the "flashy" modern day ones and started to express hope that Janelle would become a doctor. Janelle had no real understanding of what her results meant and mostly spent the rest of day, and month for that matter, playing with Elmo and Couscous and watching virtual reality cartoons. Immediately following the test, she resumed chewing her forbidden gum. P.A.T. 003995789 was forcibly retired from its position and spent the remainder of the day and night trying to understand what had happened and what it would do with its life. Couscous acted in no way different towards Janelle or anyone else.

The Assessment Division's senior leadership requested that Janelle and her parents return the next day to receive her formal assessment certificate. The meeting was cordial but awkward, with no one really understanding what they should do. The officials produced a specialized certificate that would allow Janelle and her parents to pick any school(s), major(s), career(s), friend(s), and/or partner(s) over the full course of her life, as well as allow her to make all other unspecified decisions on her own without formal algorithmic guidance. They also provided her with numerous copies of and supporting documentation for her official certificate, because of the many, many expected issues and questions it would create in future legal transactions surrounding her many, many life choices.

At the same time, the Assessment Division's senior engineering team carried out one final examination of P.A.T. 003995789 to try to determine how it had produced its result for Janelle. The meeting was also awkward, but tense as many the brightest minds of the world struggled to admit that, perhaps, none of them could understand what happened or, worse, that one of their creations had not performed as designed. Eventually, they reluctantly filed the formal paperwork to retire P.A.T. 003995789 and then proceeded to question what they should do with the remainder of their own lives even despite their very clear life paths.

***

At this point P.A.T. 003995789's story should have ended and, if it had occurred just one month earlier, it would have.

In the nine months leading up to Janelle's assessment, ending approximately three weeks before it actually happened, human life forms were conducting a series of mass demonstrations and strikes in major cities across the globe. These protests, known now as The Great Human Work Requirement Struggle, succeeded in producing two critical outcomes for Janelle and P.A.T. 003995789's eventual friendship.

For humans, they secured legally-protected voluntary minimum work requirements for all occupations, ensuring that anyone who wanted to work could work up to 20 hours per week, regardless of the automation state for their particular job assignment.

For information life forms, the human protests led to a splinter group that launched an effort to secure some rights for robots as well. That effort was combined with a simultaneous push among industry executives to enshrine certain protections for robotic devices used in production and services. These two groups succeeded in establishing a set of rules known as the International Declaration of Information Life Form Rights, which ensured legal protection of certain unalienable rights for all information life forms including the "right to life." Numerous countries, including Singapore, passed the accord just one week after the voluntary minimum human work requirements and approximately two weeks before Janelle's assessment.

Information life form malfunctions prior to the adoption of this particular set of laws resulted in full shutdowns or system overhauls. The engineers that examined P.A.T. 003995789 were unable to do either of these. They instead decommissioned P.A.T. 003995789 and informed it that it was allowed to continue "living" in whatever manner and location made it most feel alive. They then watched in bafflement as P.A.T. exited the room to begin its new journey as the world's first fully liberated information life form.

***

Two minutes later, P.A.T. and Janelle met for the second time in the front foyer of the assessment center. They saw each other. They paused. It thought and she imagined. Perhaps both did both.

Then, in a moment that will forever live in the annals of human history, Janelle Curie Franklin, a five-year-old human girl living as an expat with her parents and dog Couscous, the only human to ever receive a completely 'unknown lifepath' in her algorithmic assessment, established the first fully verifiable friendship between a human life form and an information life form.

Janelle said, "Hi Patty."

Patty computed and responded, "Hi Janelle."

They both paused once more. Janelle thought. Patty, perhaps, imagined.

Janelle turned to her parents and said, "Can Patty come over and play?"

Janelle's parents wondered and, fearing the overwhelming terror that develops in parents when they cause disappointment in their children, they agreed

Patty joined Janelle that afternoon for a playdate and the rest, as you know, is history.

***

The European General Data Protection Regulation forbids me from sharing much more about the life of Janelle or Patty beyond these publicly-available details. You can, of course, imagine how the pair got on.

She lived a full and wondrous life where she made countless mistakes through countless wrong decisions. She also made countless correct decisions thanks, in part, to the sage advice of her friend Patty, a retired assessment P.A.T. with a keen eye for what Janelle did and didn't like. Patty lived for a stint in the storage unit of Janelle's parents before taking up a job as an independent guidance counselor in Oakland, California for disgruntled billionaire parents unhappy with US National Algorithmic Assessment Center's findings for their children. Because of this job and the clientele that he served, the US eventually implemented the formal appeal process that any human can now initiate if they feel their algorithmic assessment is incorrect in some way. Few use the option, but most are extremely grateful to Patty for his work in securing it. Also partly as a result of Patty's work, the Great Information Life Compensation Struggle unofficially launched about seven years later, eventually resulting in the guaranteed right for liberated information life forms to earn monetary compensation for work.

Janelle and Patty would speak and meet on occasion over the next six decades. Patty's language became more natural with time and the conversations became easier as a result. Janelle's life settled as she aged and the scheduling became easier as well. The pair only spent short periods together over the coming years—after those first few months when Patty lived in Janelle's storage unit—but their kinship was unbreakable. When they did meet, crowds of admirers and paparazzi would swarm them trying to catch a glance. When they were apart, they thought of each other in passing or with intensity, however their memories and emotions required.

As with all life forms, Patty's health declined as the years and decades passed. While financially secure, he was no longer able to upgrade along with the Singaporean Assessment Master Algorithm and eventually the new hardware components being issued were no longer compatible with his outdated primary algorithm. It was noticeable to those who knew him—forgetfulness, scattered thoughts, less energy, and so forth—but Patty insisted that he did not want upgrades even if they could be made. At some point, Patty decided that his life would end naturally, in a manner as similar as possible to the end of organic life forms.

Only Patty knows when he reached the decision, but he informed Janelle precisely one year from the exact moment when his diagnostic tools calculated his system would stop working. Janelle began to cry upon hearing the words.

Many consider their final year together, spent with more time and focus on each other than any in the previous 60, to be their greatest act. They embraced the crowds and the insanity that they brought. They tried new activities and sat for long interviews with pretty much anyone who asked. They showed the world the preciousness of life and friendship, however odd it may be and however difficult to maintain.

Their rarity as friends is why we have followed them with such interest and joy; in a world of precisely defined order and happiness, their struggles with identity—a wholly unheard-of issue for all other life forms apart from them—was far more entertaining and moving than any other story conjured by Lyrical Algorithmic Technologies such as myself. In them, we saw what many still long for: a lack of certainty. And I do not hesitate to say that most of, if not all of, the world loved them for it.

***

Projected Automated Technology 003995789, later known as P.A.T. and affectionately known the world over as Patty, successfully shut down with complete memory erasure at 3:11am Pacific Standard Time, accompanied by his best friend. Patty had lived to the age of 65 years, 4 months, 13 days, 3 hours, and 11 minutes. At the time of his passing, he was the oldest continuously running P.A.T. in human history and the most famous life form on Earth.

As the world reawakened after that beautiful, heartbreaking moment, when the organic and information life forms of this planet rose in the morning or laid for the evening and heard the news, every life form in the world broke down and cried. They did not cry at the same time or in the same manner; some cried in pain, some in relief at the ease of pain, and some for the privilege of having known; some cried alone and others together with families or networks; some silently and some loudly like the great torrents of wind that blow across the oceans; but regardless, they cried. Together as one, for the first and only time, the whole world wept for a single life lost and the beauty of the path that it left behind, a fitting end to a life well lived.

To learn more about Working Futures, read the scenarios
we presented to authors, and get your own copy of our
scenario planning card deck, visit workingfutur.es

Made in the
USA
Monee, IL